REA

DO NOT REMOVE
CARDS FROM POCKET

10-28-94

HALF
NELSON

Books by Jerome Doolittle

Body Scissors
Strangle Hold
Bear Hug
Head Lock
Half Nelson

Published by POCKET BOOKS

HALF
NELSON

JEROME
DOOLITTLE

POCKET BOOKS

New York   London   Toronto   Sydney   Tokyo   Singapore

This book is a work of fiction. Names, characters, places, and incidents are products of the author's imagination or are used fictitiously. Any resemblance to actual events or locales or persons, living or dead, is entirely coincidental.

POCKET BOOKS, a division of Simon & Schuster Inc.
1230 Avenue of the Americas, New York, NY 10020

Doolittle, Jerome.
     Half Nelson / Jerome Doolittle.
        p.   cm.
     ISBN 0-671-50289-1
     I. Title.
PS3554.0584H3   1994
813'.54—dc20   94-16733
                                                               CIP

First Pocket Books hardcover printing November 1994

10   9   8   7   6   5   4   3   2   1

POCKET and colophon are registered trademarks of Simon & Schuster Inc.

Printed in the U.S.A.

To Mike

HALF
NELSON

LIKE ANY OTHER UNIVERSITY, HARVARD SUCKS.
What makes it a great university is that it
sucks harder than most.

1

Back in the 1980s, a Harvard fund-raiser
told the newspapers how he planned to meet his five-
billion-dollar goal. "You can't get this kind of money from
alumni mailings," he said. "You have to concentrate on a
couple of hundred individuals, most of them in the
greater New York area." The giant sucking noise coming
out of Cambridge was about to get deafening, down there
in the greater New York area.

By comparison what Washington hears from Harvard's
John F. Kennedy School of Government sounds more like
a long, gentle kiss. Or usually it does, except sometimes
the kiss gets all wet and slobbery. For instance when the
school gave a public service medal to Reagan's unindicted
consigliere, Ed Meese.

Mostly, though, the JFK School's courtship is more dig-
nified. The school provides a sheltered environment for
politicians temporarily sidelined by the voters. It helps
out promising young wonks and pols who might someday reach the level where they could swing a government

1

grant this way or that. It cycles professors in and out of
Washington. It sponsors books and reports and studies
and seminars and symposiums and forums.

And sometimes the speakers at the forums are
interesting.

So sometimes I go to hear them.

Most times I go alone, but this particular night I had a
handsome woman next to me. She was Hope Edwards,
my longtime and long-distance lover since the days when
both of us were working to keep Reagan out of the White
House by keeping Carter in it.

Ever since that nasty and disastrous 1980 campaign,
Hope and I had helped each other through the nights and
the days as often as we could. This meant whenever she
was able to get up to Cambridge or I was able to get
down to Washington, where she lived with her lawyer
husband and their three kids.

This time Hope had come up to Cambridge with one
of the speakers at tonight's forum, Robert Rackleff. He
was on the speakers' platform, a tall man all long bones
and angles who looked to be in his thirties until you
looked a little closer. Gray had started to mix in with the
fine blond hair that drifted down over his forehead, and
the beginnings of lines showed around his mouth and
eyes.

"What kind of guy is he?" I asked Hope.

"Hard to talk about Robert without sounding like some
airhead groupie," Hope said. "What the hell, though. I
still think he's sort of a saint."

"Pretty strong language."

"You'll see for yourself, after," Hope said. After the
show we were going out to eat a late dinner with Rackleff,
so he could tell me about a nasty problem he had.

The crowd quieted down as a JFK School professor took

2

the mike and set to work introducing and introducing and introducing the panelists. By the time the professor was done, we were ready for anything except more of him.

The first of the panelists to do his five-minute opener was a guy named Don Frith, who was the director of public affairs for an industry lobby called the Council on Forest Rehabilitation. He seemed to be saying that the road to responsible rehabilitation begins with cutting down all the trees. Made sense, the way he told it.

Frith was diffident, decent, politely accommodating or pleasantly firm as required, modestly self-assured, well informed, responsible, rational, reasonable, intelligent, plausible, sincere, serious, and yet with just a touch of self-deprecating humor. The kind of smooth and soothing man who does most of the real damage in Washington.

He was doing as well as any card-carrying clear-cutter could, considering that his audience was mostly eco-freaks, grad students with backpacks, undergrads with book bags, young mothers with long, straight hair and babies in slings, and professors in khakis or corduroy. They spluttered and muttered softly as he talked, and scribbled angry questions for the Q and A period.

The JFK School puts on its forums in a space that holds cafeteria tables during the day. There's only room on the ground floor for a hundred or so folding chairs, which means that the rest of the crowd has to settle for the peanut galleries overhead. The latest arrivals of all are stuck with a view of the speakers' heads from the rear, looking down from staircases and balconies on the second and third floors. Normally I would have been up there in the back myself. But I was with Hope, who was with one of the speakers, and so we had big-shot reserved seats over to one side of the low platform where the panel sat.

Mr. Frith finished with fifteen seconds of his five min-

3

utes to spare. I amuse myself by timing these things, a holdover from my days on political campaigns.

"Guy's pretty good," I whispered when the lobbyist sat down to applause that ran from polite to nonexistent.

"Unfortunately he is," Hope said. "Those are the nut-cutters I have to put up with all the time in Washington."

"I bet they speak just as highly about you."

Hope ran the Washington office of the American Civil Liberties Union, which at the moment was involved in protecting the First Amendment rights of six members of Rackleff's environmental movement, Earth Everlasting. The ACLU's argument was that ringing a threatened redwood tree with handcuffed greenies was an exercise in free speech. The rehabilitators of the forest figured it was criminal trespass.

Hope was up in Cambridge partly because Robert Rackleff's group was a client but mostly, in fact, to visit me. Her husband, Martin, was a late-blooming homosexual who had fathered three children before coming to grips with his nature. After the birth of the youngest he finally told Hope his secret, but otherwise he stayed in the closet for the sake of the kids.

For the same reason, Hope and I stayed in our own version of the closet. Until recently we had pretended to Martin that Hope and I were just friends. In those days Hope wouldn't have come up to Cambridge on what was essentially a personal trip, since she wasn't directly involved in the tree-hugging case. She would have waited for a legitimate office reason, and stayed at the Charles Hotel on the expense account.

She still could have stayed at the Charles, since she approved her own expense accounts. John Sununu would have done it in a shot. Not being Sununu, she was paying her own way. And not being in the closet anymore, so to

4

speak, she was staying with me. There were turning out
to be advantages in the three of us coming clean with one
another. We should have done it long ago.

"... whom I am sure will be as refreshingly outspoken
with us as he was before the president's timber commis-
sion," the moderator was saying. "Let us welcome the
chairman and chief executive officer of the Dixie-Cascade
Corporation, Hap Overholser."

Overholser grabbed the mike firmly by the neck. His
hand was heavy and thick and square, a meat hammer
covered with reddish fur. Overholser had been a defensive lineman for Tulane back in the 1970s. Now *Forbes*
magazine listed his personal wealth at between $500 and
$750 million. He had got his hands on all that—the word
earned seems wrong—by floating junk bonds to take over
the company. To pay off the bonds he was currently taking his best shot at scalping the states of Washington,
Oregon, and Idaho.

Overholser waited for the polite applause that no doubt
came after he was introduced at things like stockholder
meetings. But it had just barely come for the forest rehabilitation guy, and it didn't come for Overholser at all. It
kept on not coming for an embarrassing length of time.
This was Cambridge, where the most popular disk jockey
is still Robert J. Lurtsema and the municipal bird is the
spotted owl.

Hap Overholser wasn't bothered a bit. It wasn't the first
time he had faced a hostile line. He let the embarrassment
grow while he smiled and settled his grip tighter on the
microphone, as if he were squeezing the whole scruffy
bunch of us into submission

"You want to know what this entire so-called contro-
versy is all about?" he said at last into the mike, so close
and loud that feedback distorted his words. "The spotted

owl, like they want you to think? Why hail no! This whole thing is purely and simply about the federal government trampling all over the rights of the private individual."

"Give me a break," I whispered to Hope.

"Shut up and listen, Bethany. Guys like him built America."

Overholser wore one of those Italian suits that look like a hundred dollars even though they actually cost twenty times that much. Sticking out from the sharp Italian trousers were Wellington boots made of some kind of snakeskin. Possibly python. Nice-looking boots, if you're an asshole.

His five-minute opener ran nearly ten minutes. It was rambling stuff, complaining and boastful by turns, about how Big Government and its faithful sidekick, Big Media, were keeping he-men like himself from solving America's problems. A microphone in the locker room of any restricted country club in America would have picked up the same mixture of snarls and whines. I tuned out.

"John Wayne used to wear cowboy boots everywhere," I whispered to Hope.

She nodded and I went on. "He was six foot four but he wore four-inch lifts anyway."

"What is this obsession with John Wayne's boots?" Hope whispered back.

"This Overholser is built a lot like him," I said. "Wears boots, too. Did you know there's a John Wayne International Airport in Orange County, California?"

"Everybody knows that."

"Yeah, but don't you find it amazing?"

"In Orange County? No."

"I guess it isn't, come to think of it. Did you know John Wayne got a draft deferment in World War Two when

he was thirty-four? Did you know his maiden name was
Marion Morrison?"

"Go pester somebody else, Bethany. Leave me alone
with my dreams."

I checked the other shoes under the panel's table. The
moderator wore those clunky Rockports with the thick
rubber soles. The brown leather uppers were unpolished
but cared-for. Probably dressed with the brand of waterproof dubbing rated best-buy in *Consumer Reports*. The
smooth lobbyist wore black, gleaming loafers. Rackleff
wore sneakers that were just a little off-white, the color
they call natural in the catalogs.

Rackleff's total fashion statement was hard to make out.
Sixties hippy? Don Johnson? His thick wool hiking socks
were the color of oatmeal. His loose canvas pants looked
like the fabric that artists paint on. His shirt was Guatema-
lan, those heavy, nubby cotton things that look so comfortable but always turn out to be too short or too narrow
through the shoulders or both. Rackleff wore it buttoned
to the neck with no tie, which used to be the sign of the
dork but is now high fashion if you can believe the ads.
On the other hand the guys in the ads all seem to be
dorks, so maybe nothing has changed.

Over the shirt Rackleff wore what Brooks Brothers calls
a sack coat. Doctors wear practically the same type of
cotton jacket and so do supermarket clerks, although the
clerk version comes in blue or green or red. Rackleff's
jacket was a light tan, only a few shades darker than
white. The shirt and pants weren't quite the same color,
but came close. The effect of his outfit wasn't blinding
like Michael Jackson or ice-cream-colored like Gatsby or
dove gray like Adolphe Menjou, but just a general
paleness.

"I should point out," the moderator said, "that this

evening's forum was not planned as a two-on-one drill, but our other representative from the environmental movement unfortunately will not be present. I have just received word that Harrison Deets of the Nature Conservancy has been unavoidably delayed in St. Louis by nature, in the form of an apparently impenetrable line of thunderstorms.''

He paused for the imitation of laughter that professors extort from their classes. He got it. This was an audience trained in its duty by decades of academic wit.

"I'm sure our last panelist is up to the challenge, however. And so let me present without further ado one of the most unusual and charismatic leaders of the environmental movement, Robert Rackleff of Earth Everlasting.''

What followed was not the polite application of palms to one another that the lobbyist had drawn and Overholser had not. It was immediate, spontaneous, and enthusiastic. A few people even got to their feet briefly, before figuring it was uncool and sitting down again. Till recently I had been only vaguely aware of Rackleff's existence, but plainly he was a major hero to the Birkenstock crowd.

Rackleff waited until the applause was over. In the silence that followed, he let his eyes wander over the audience in front of him, and up to the balconies. He looked over his shoulder, first one way and then the other, at the latecomers stacked up behind him. The only expression on his face was a vague pleasantness, just short of a smile. Then he turned back to the mike.

"Up to the challenge," he said. He seemed to be talking to himself. "Funny word, isn't it, *challenge?* Climbing Everest. First on the moon. Acing a test. Always an idea of dominance, isn't there? Climbing over things. Pushing things out of your way. Or people, I guess. Things or people. Both, maybe.

"It's not a comfortable word for me. I'm more comfortable with words like *flow* or *sway. Harmony. Cycle, rhythm,* words like that. Easy words to get along with, those are the words I like.

"Well. Challenge. Does a rock challenge the stream, do you suppose? Does the stream feel challenged? How about the rock? The stream changes course a little for the rock, doesn't it? Runs over it or around it. The rock just sits there, but it changes shape over time. Gets round, smooth. Does it mind? Who won? Who lost? Was there even a game? The stream is still there. That's the important thing, the stream. That's the challenge. I imagine we all agree on that."

Rackleff looked over at the smooth man, and said, "You agree, don't you, Mr. Frith?"

"Please," the lobbyist said. "Call me Don. Sure I agree. We may differ on means, but the challenge is certainly preserving that stream."

"You'd agree, too, I imagine," Rackleff said to the Dixie-Cascade man, and then paused for a second. "Wouldn't you, Mr. Overholser?"

Mr. Overholser didn't say call me Hap. He didn't say anything. He just stood there, chin up and out, with his jaw muscles locked.

Rackleff rippled right on, like that stream over the rock. "You'd agree with us that the real challenge is the whole ecosystem, wouldn't you, Mr. Overholser?"

"Don't think I'm going to help you," Mr. Overholser said. His face had turned red, as if his head was about to blow up. "Give your own speech."

Rackleff smiled mildly, and did so.

It was a curious speech, all about being gentle. Gentle

9

with the land, gentle with the plants and creatures on it, gentle with one another. From just about anybody else, it would have made me want to throw up, and not so gently. From this tall, pale man, it was moving.

Rackleff seemed to be transparent, so that you could watch his thoughts start in his heart and come out as words. A man like that couldn't lie. He would find the whole idea of a lie puzzling. Why would a person want to say a thing which wasn't so? Wasn't the purpose of words to search out the truth? And so you had to believe him, or at least believe in him.

The discussion followed Rackleff's talk. It went along the same lines as the opening statements. Frith was persuasive in a linear, lawyerly way. Rackleff hardly bothered to answer his arguments. He just went around and beyond them, as if they didn't exist. The world he called up wasn't made of logic and right angles and straight lines; it was tumbles of clouds, swirls of light and colors, fluid and not fixed. His arguments were more theological than scientific—founded on love and faith, not skepticism and experiment. In Congress, Frith would have won. In Cambridge, it was Rackleff hands down.

The clear loser was Overholser, not that he seemed to care. Plainly he figured he could hire and fire the whole crowd, bag and backpack. If they were so smart, why weren't they rich? He kept saying things like, "A lot of you are going to be looking for jobs pretty soon, and just where do you think they're going to be coming from? You think you're all going to work for the Sierra Club?"

Overholser just didn't get it. To this crowd, the Sierra Club was a bunch of opportunists who had sold out to the polluters long ago.

To most of the crowd, anyway. The person who had been waiting longest at the nearest microphone to the

platform looked like any other student, but he turned out
to be a Harvard Business School android in grad student
drag. "My name is Vernon Cogswell, and I'm a second-
year student at the business school," he enunciated
clearly, for the benefit of anyone out there who might
want to hire him after graduation. "My question is directed at Mr. Overholser. Sir, we have heard a good deal
about gentleness from Mr. Rackleff. Would you tell us,
from your experience as a successful businessman,
whether it is possible in today's internationally competi-
tive marketplace to create jobs and meet a payroll by
being gentle?"

"I'd be out of business in six months," Overholser said.
"Then ten thousand jobs would go right down the tubes.
Maybe he knows how to do it. I'd give a lot to know
where he gets the money to meet his own payroll, matter
of fact. Why don't you ask him?"

"Mr. Rackleff?" asked the business school guy.

"Let me think how to answer . . . ," Rackleff said. "I
guess the short answer is that I don't really have to meet
much of a payroll. It's harder for Mr. Overholser, I guess.
Mr. Overholser's problem is to get people to do something
every day that they don't really want to do. Most of my
people are volunteers.

"To answer this gentleman's question, though, I don't
really know whether you could be gentle and meet a large
payroll. There's something kind of nongentle in the whole
idea of payrolls, isn't there? Isn't money a form of force,
in a way? Aren't you using it, really, to make people do
something for you that they wouldn't do otherwise? I
don't know. It's a tough question."

"You damned straight it's tough," Overholser said, facing the B-school student. "That's why he can't answer it.

Why don't you ask him how he pays the rent on his office, son?''

"Mr. Rackleff?" said young Vernon Cogswell, all crisp and challenging. Vernon Cogswell was just loving it, running macho messages for a real *Fortune* 500 CEO.

"We don't really have much of an office," Rackleff said. "Just an answering service and a bunch of those plastic milk crates in the back of my truck, to keep papers and records in. Now and then I sleep in the truck, too, but mostly I stay with supporters. If they don't have an extra bed, I have a folding cot I use. So we don't have much of a budget, really. Some, but not much. We have a few people who work full-time out of their homes for minimum wages, because you need to have some kind of an institutional memory besides just me. But you can do an amazing amount without much money. People are wonderful, they really are."

Go for it, Vernon Cogswell, I thought. I waited for him to translate the question for his idol. Something like: "Well, Mr. Overholser, what do you say to that one? In your experience as a hard-driving, successful executive, are people really wonderful?"

Instead the moderator regained control by calling on someone at one of the other mikes. The rest of the forum was in standard form, with the panelists answering their questioners directly. The smooth guy was smooth, and the tough guy was tough, and the gentle guy was gentle.

At the end it was Rackleff once again who got the greatest ovation, this time a standing ovation.

"Hard to imagine the type of mind you'd have to have to want to kill a man like that, isn't it?" Hope said when the applause had died down.

That was what I was there for. Rackleff had been getting death threats in the mail and I was supposed to ad-

vise him on what to do about them. I was supposed to
know about death threats because during the early pri-
maries in 1980 I had been the occasional pilot and the
full-time body man for Teddy Kennedy.

In politics, the body man is the rememberer who stays
next to the candidate at all times, whispering into the
man's ear everything he needs to know. Names of local
politicians and journalists, details about the area's history
or problems, scheduling information, whatever. The body
man knows where the nearest men's room is, so the candidate can download his last three cups of coffee or change
to a fresh shirt. He checks for spinach caught in the candidate's teeth, a necktie off-center, shirttails out, problem
hair, whatever will look bad on camera. He makes signals
to the candidate when the speech is running too long. He
writes down the names of voters the candidate talks to,
or promises something to, so they can get a personal note
later and of course go on the mailing list.

I was a body man in another sense, too. I wasn't a real
bodyguard, but I was sort of an unofficial one. After years
of working toward it I had finally won myself a spot on
the 1980 Olympic wrestling squad, and damned if Carter
hadn't boycotted the games. Carter's idea was to punish
Brezhnev for being as stupid in Afghanistan as we had
been in Vietnam. My idea was to punish Carter for flushing my years of effort down the toilet, in a useless PR
gesture. Since I had already been training at the Hawkeye
Wrestling Club in Iowa City, I signed on to help Teddy
in the Iowa caucuses.

Later in the campaign I hung around a little with the
Secret Service guys, which was touchy at first because
they're as jealous of their turf as any other bureaucrat.
But the wrestling thing helped. Those guys go through a
few hours of half-assed hand-to-hand combat instruction,

but it isn't much and it gets rusty fast. They were impressed by the Olympics thing, and they were glad to learn a few new control holds.

Another reason we got along was that most of the Secret Service agents didn't like Carter a whole lot more than I did at the time. Apparently Ford had been a much nicer guy to work for. So one way and another the agents and I wound up getting along pretty well. They learned a few things from me and I learned a few things from them.

One thing I learned is that anybody can kill anybody in public life, even a president, if the killer doesn't mind getting caught. No one, for example, had screened tonight's crowd at the JFK School in any way. You showed up early enough, you got in. If you wanted to kill a major environmental villain or a major environmental hero, there they both were, defenseless in the crowd.

"They're practically mobbing your guy," I said to Hope. "Maybe he *is* a saint."

"Some of them seem to think so, don't they? Look at the way that girl is gazing up at him."

"Or maybe he isn't a total saint. That business about the volunteers was pretty cute. So was that 'Mister Frith' and 'Mister Overholser' stuff."

"Cute how? Overholser just stepped into it."

"Sure, but Rackleff put it there for him to step into. I've been to a lot of these forums. Unless the other guy has a title like judge or senator, you always call him by his first name. It's a way of showing he doesn't outrank you."

"I don't follow you," Hope said. "Rackleff just asked first, to be polite. How is that one-upmanship?"

"He could have gone ahead and called the other guys by their first names without asking, which is what most panelists do. But instead he carried the game one step further. Frith was smart enough to duck, but Overholser wasn't."

"Duck what?"

"Duck looking like an asshole, the way Overholser did when he didn't say, 'Call me Hap.' From then on, Rackleff stuck it to him. Called him Mr. Overholser every chance he got."

"Or maybe Robert never gave it a thought and was just being polite. Saints aren't as devious as you, Bethany."

"I doubt it. I bet there's nobody as devious as a saint."

BY THE TIME THE FORUM WAS OVER MOST RES- *2*
taurants were closed or getting ready to
close, so I steered Hope and Robert Rackleff
to Charlie's Kitchen. It's more bar than
kitchen, but the kitchen stays open late so the drinkers
can line their stomachs with grease.

I don't drink enough these days to need the protective
coating, but I ordered a cheeseburger and fries anyway.
I'd work the calories off in the Harvard wrestling room,
where I help out as a volunteer coach in return for access
to both the gym and workout partners.

Hope had them bring her spaghetti with just olive oil
on it, and a shaker of Parmesan. She didn't need to watch
her weight any more than I did, because she was an oars-
woman who worked out hard on the Potomac nearly every
morning. But she ate very little meat, on the theory that
meat made you feel slow and heavy. Maybe it did. Something must have been making her fast and light, because
she came in second in her division last year in the Head
of the Charles, behind a two-time national champion.

Robert Rackleff had pizza with mushrooms and pep-
pers. Did this make him a vegan or a vegetarian, and

what was the difference, anyway? Maybe it just meant he had toured a pepperoni factory once. I knew a guy at college who had a summer job at a sausage company, and it marked him for life. He'd never eat a piece of meat unless he could see a bone in it.

For a briefcase, Rackleff carried one of those plastic folder things with a zipper on the top edge. It was green, and had EARTH DAY REGIONAL PLANNING CONFERENCE, SEATTLE stamped on it. He unzipped it once the waitress had our order.

"Maybe you could look over some of this nonsense while we're waiting," he said, handing me a thin sheaf of letters held together with a paper clip.

"Where are the envelopes?" I asked.

"They were just drugstore envelopes with nothing but the address on them. I didn't save them. Should I have? Fingerprints?"

"Probably doesn't matter. If the guy was dumb enough to leave fingerprints on the envelope, he'd leave them on the letter, too. And fingerprints aren't much use, anyway, unless you have a good idea who did it and you want to match them up."

I had seen plenty of nut mail before. The assassinations and the Chappaquiddick business made Teddy Kennedy into a kind of giant alnico magnet for the psychiatrically challenged. One of my Secret Service buddies used to show me samples from the flood. Nut letters can generally be spotted by format as well as content. Handwriting tends to be tiny, with the letters cramped up together. Whether handwritten or typed, the words fill practically every inch of space from margin to margin. Typing tends to be single-spaced on both sides of the sheet. The sheets can be odd-size scraps. Often the paper is thin, practically tracing paper, as if the writer figured that the thinner the paper, the more of his thoughts would fit in a given space. This can make it hard to read if both sides are used, but legibility doesn't matter. Neatness doesn't count, either. The authors aren't much for retyping; they prefer to let strikeovers stand. Lots of words are capitalized, often for no apparent reason. There's lots of underlining. If the typewriter has a two-color ribbon, the red gets a heavy workout. So does the key with the exclamation point on it.

"Thousands of these Looney Tunes, all over the country," I remember the Secret Service guy saying. "How come they all had the same typing teacher?"

Because the medium was the message, probably. A typography of confusion, incoherence, pain, and rage. Of pressure building up inside the brain until it has to squirt all over the page or explode.

"Know what's frightening about nut letters?" the agent had said. "Whenever you're on the job, you can bet your ass there's one or two of those guys out there if the crowd is any size at all. And you haven't got the slightest idea which ones they are."

I scanned Rackleff's letters quickly. There were four of them, no two alike but all of them along the same lines. The first was a fair specimen:

To the Top mongrel alias Rackleff: The wicked shall know no Refuge! Soon JUSTICE will Sear you with eternal fire like a Crippled Rat that must die like the quarter-Jew Franklin D. Rosengelt. Rackleff must suffer the Vengeance of the everlasting Flame so others will Cringe with Fear and Horror at the Terrible SCOURGE of the Lord. All Who would come to the forest and worship trees like gilded Idols must be Warned so they will see the Fate that awaits them. God gave America to CHRISTians for an Aryan promised Land and gave MAN Dominion over beast and Fowl And Forest. Justice will strike from the Shadows!!! The Top mongrel will be the first to pay the final price with super Pain and no exemptions made. Christ spared some X-Killers from his Ovens but their lesson was UnLearned!! They made common cause with the People of Mud. Therefore the Aryan Hammer must strike against the Kike Anvil despite all the gold of Jewry!!!

The typed signature was the same on all of them: The Brotherbund.

"Is this an organization anybody's ever heard of?" I asked Rackleff.

"It's one of our local skinhead groups," he said.

"Who are the People of Mud?"

"Afro-Americans."

"Where does this scourge of the Lord stuff come from? Are these skinheads Jesus freaks?"

"I don't really know. Although I imagine it's all pretty much one package, isn't it? White supremacy, Protocols of Zion, Christian nation."

"Why pick on environmentalists, though?" I asked. "What did spotted owls ever do to the skinheads?"

"What did the Jews ever do to them, for that matter?"

"Good point."

"My sense is that the skinhead groups are just fishing in any troubled waters they come across," Rackleff went on. "The timber companies do their best to stir up the loggers against the environmentalists, and the skinheads tag along behind. The neo-Nazis see a lot of fear and anger out there, and they try to channel it their way. They've been showing up at rallies and demonstrations all over the state, looking for recruits."

"Have they had any run-ins with your group specifically? Any assaults on your people? Charges brought on
either side?"

"Not really."

"Anything at all? Letters to the editor? Speeches? Van-
dalism? Shouting matches?"

"Just these letters."

"What do the police say about the letters?"

"I haven't taken them to the police. The truth is, I don't
feel that the police are on our side."

"How about the FBI?"

"We know the federal agencies aren't on our side."

"How do you know?"

"For years now they've been harassing us, both the FBI
and the Forest Service. They've searched our people's
houses, forced them to give fingerprints and hair samples.
Handwriting and printing samples, too."

"You need a warrant for that stuff. What did the war-
rants say they were looking for?"

"Initially they were investigating the death of a worker
in Dixie-Cascade's mill in Cobb's Bay. Or the mill used
to be in Cobb's Bay. Overholser shut it down two years
ago when he moved all his milling operations to Mexico."

"How were you supposed to be involved in the death?"

"The man was killed when a saw hit a spike in a tree
and exploded."

"Your spike?"

Some eco-terrorists will drive heavy, headless nails or
ceramic rods into timber that's headed for the mills. Saw-
mill workers come and go, but those huge circular saw
blades cost money.

"It wasn't our spike unless somebody did the spiking
on his own," Rackleff said. "We abandoned all potentially
dangerous forms of ecotage well before the accident."

"Abandoned. Does that mean you once did stuff like spiking?"

"Once we did, yes. We would always warn the timber companies that a stand had been spiked, of course. The object was to prevent the cut, not to injure innocent people."

"Were any of your people arrested for the death?"

"Nobody arrested, nobody indicted. Although one young woman was held in jail for three months for contempt when she refused to answer questions before a grand jury. Apart from that, it's just been incessant harassment.

"They've seized notebooks from environmental students who worked with us, and they still have them. In one case, two years of work on a doctoral thesis. Also personal belongings, textbooks, computers, address books, articles of clothing. It's been very tough on those kids."

"This is supposed to be a new day," I said. "New president. Al Gore. Bruce Babbitt."

"Well, that's true, and it has made some difference. There's a new U.S. attorney now, and of course that's a blessing after the Reagan people. The new man seems to feel he's there to enforce the law, which is a big change right there. But the same people are still running the FBI office in Portland."

"Have you complained to the new U.S. attorney about the harassment?"

"I mentioned it once, yes. The FBI told him there wasn't any harassment on their part, so they couldn't very well call it off. They said they couldn't answer for other law enforcement agencies."

"Did the harassment stop after that, though?"

"It's hard to tell. Once you're in that paranoid mind-set, every noise on the line sounds like a bug. Just last

21

week in Portland police towed my van when I was sure I was legally parked. Was it harassment? Maybe just a cop meeting his quota. Who knows?"

"What did they say when you complained?"

"Nobody wins that kind of argument with the police. It cost me a hundred and forty dollars, with the towing and the lot charges."

"Like you say, though, it happens to lots of folks."

"I know it does. I only bring these things up to explain why I don't expect the authorities to show much interest in anonymous threats in the mail."

"I think you should make copies of the letters and take the originals to the FBI anyway. Just to get the whole business on the record."

"Probably you're right. I will."

"Apart from that, I don't know what to say. There's no way to tell whether these letters are serious threats or not. Most nut letters aren't, but you can't tell which ones are. Or at least I can't. I doubt if the FBI can either."

And so that was all the help I could come up with. None.

The food came, and we ate it. Afterward, we walked out Mt. Auburn Street to the new hotel Harvard has built where the old Gulf station used to stand, on the triangle of land between Mass. Ave. and Harvard Street. I had never been inside the new hotel and had no plans to, not that Harvard cared. I liked the old Gulf station better. It had a funky blue cupola on it. The hotel had fake windows on the ground floor and they were kind of funky, too. But not like that cupola.

"Let me ask you something, Robert," I said outside the hotel, where the JFK School was putting him up. "When you're on a panel, do you always start out by calling the other guys mister?"

"Oh, sure. Mostly they're smart enough to insist on first names, but once in a while you get lucky the way I did with Overholser."

Hope and I said our good-byes to him and headed toward my apartment on Ware Street. It was only a block or so away, but still I wasn't able to hold out for the whole distance. "Nice night out," I said, before we had even got as far as the old Baptist church.

"Oh, shut up, Bethany," she said. "I don't want to hear it."

I ran my finger down the thin bridge of Hope's nose, down and over her lips and chin, along the soft skin under the jaw and then down the neck, into and out of the hollow made by her collarbones, down between her breasts and onto the smooth firmness of her stomach. Her skin was wet with her sweat and mine. I stopped with my finger socketed in her belly button. We were resting, friendly.

"I like it that you're staying here in my place," I said.

"I like it, too," she said. "I like being here a lot." She kissed my shoulder, which was handy. "Of course, I miss the little chocolates they used to put on my bed."

"At the Charles? Those little chocolates at the Charles?"

"Those are the little chocolates which I am referring to, yes."

"Look in the drawer there."

She looked.

"I believe I could learn to love such a person as you," Hope said.

"I believe I could learn to do the same," I said. "But not just yet."

So we ate chocolates and waited for me to regroup.

"What did you think of those letters?" Hope asked after a while.

"Some pretty odd things about them."

"Even for nut letters, you mean?"

"Particularly for nut letters. Nuts don't sign death threats, not as a rule."

"Maybe they would if they wanted to put the blame on somebody else."

"Maybe. Probably not. Nuts is nuts."

I told her what the Secret Service's nut letters tended to look like.

"There's no hard-and-fast rules," I said at the end. "But here you've got none of the elements at all except the actual content. Regular-size margins, regular paper, double-spaced, no strikeovers, no misspellings. It's like a nonnut was writing a nut letter."

"The content sounded genuine, though, didn't it?"

"Yeah," I said. "There is that."

Hope put a chocolate in her mouth, and gave me the last one. "This place gives you more chocolates than the old one did," she said. "I think I like it better all around. Does it bother you that I'm here?"

"Bother me? How would it bother me?"

"This is your secret tree house. Girls aren't supposed to go in secret tree houses."

On the apartment's mailbox it said Tom Carpenter, who paid his rent and his phone bill with postal money orders. The neighbors knew me as a consultant who was vague about what he consulted on, and kept to himself. A few friends knew where I lived, but you couldn't find me through the phone book or state or city records. I didn't want to make it too easy for any of my many nonfriends to come and visit.

"You can come to my tree house anytime you want.

You can be an honorary member, even though you're a girl."

"You can't come to mine, though," Hope said. "I don't have one."

"Girls aren't supposed to have secret tree houses."

"What do you know? Boys are so dumb."

"You got that right. Where are we going with all this tree house stuff, anyway?"

"I was just thinking. I've never washed your underwear. Not even so much as a handkerchief. You've never seen me in the second day of a really bad cold. When you were talking about the handwriting on hate mail, it occurred to me that I've never seen your handwriting."

This was probably true, although I had never thought about it. We always used the telephone.

"I don't think I've ever seen yours, either," I said. "Are these things that are bothering you?"

"The handwriting, a little. The underwear and the colds don't bother me at all. It seems like a good trade to me. That's what I was thinking about. That we've got a pretty good deal for ourselves, in our odd way."

"Seems to me, too."

"Do you think we'd spoil it if we spent longer than a couple days together?" Hope asked.

"I doubt it. Why?"

"Because we've never really had to . . ."

"What are we talking about here?"

"Well, now that it's all out in the open with Martin . . ." Martin was her husband. ". . . Anyway, now there wouldn't be any reason why we couldn't go off together for a few days sometime. If we wanted to."

"But we wouldn't have to unless we wanted to?" I said.

"No, of course not."

"You're too much," I said in her direction. "Do you

25

know that?" During all this, she had been looking out the window into the dark.

"You're not afraid we'll get too used to each other?" she said.

"I'll take a chance."

"Okay," she said, and turned to face me. "Where do you want to go?"

"I haven't thought about it. Give me some ideas."

"Vancouver or Nova Scotia, maybe. Maybe that place you liked in Maine."

"Islesboro."

"Or maybe a place neither of us has been," she said. "Anyway, think about it. You're sure you want to do this?"

"I've thought of it lots of times," I said.

"Why didn't you say something?"

"You're the one with responsibilities, not me. I figured you ought to be the one to bring it up."

"Bullshit, Bethany. You were scared, weren't you?"

"Actually, yeah."

We didn't have to explain to each other what we were scared of. If it ain't broke, don't fix it. Better not load down the system with head colds and dirty underwear. One of us might not be able to stand up under the strain, and that one was me.

Next morning we woke up slowly, and after that I made us corned beef hash and poached eggs with Tabasco sauce for breakfast. We didn't head out for Logan International until rush hour was over and you stood a chance of not being caught in the Callahan Tunnel and gassed to death.

At the boarding gate, Hope said, "How about Mackinac Island?"

"Sounds good. Where is it?"

"Way up near Canada in Lake Huron. I saw pictures of it in the *National Geographic* once. They have great porches up there."

"Porches sound good, too."

"Anyway, think about it. I can get off pretty much any-time in June and July. Our first real trip."

And it would be. A couple of times I had hung around, more or less incognito, when she was attending out-of-town conferences. Making myself scarce during the day, and ordering our meals from room service. But this would be different, the days together as well as the nights.

A couple of days later was Harvard's commencement. Years ago I went to one to look at all the pretty clothes, but that was enough. Nowadays the closest I come to commencement is bucking my way through the dressed-up crowds till I make it to The Tasty, where I eat my breakfast just like any other day.

"You know something, Joey?" I said to the counterman, Joey Neary.

"No, I don't know nothing. That's why I'm behind this fucking counter instead of across the street getting my diploma."

"Learn something, then. One of those Branch Davidians down there in Waco was a Harvard lawyer. Clinton burned him up right along with Koresh and all those lit-tle kids."

"That so?"

"Would I lie to you, Joey?"

"Not about stupid little shit like that, no. Stupid little shit like that, I got no doubts you're telling the truth. In fact you probably got a newspaper clipping right in your pocket, ready to rub my nose in it."

And in fact I did, so now I couldn't use it.

2 7

The pay phone on the wall rang. "Catch that, will you, Al," Joey said to the new kid who was helping him. "Me and Bethany are having a salon."

"A salon, Joey? A fucking salon?"

"Hey, I'm not stupid, all right? I heard it on Joan Rivers."

"Define it for me, Joey. Tell me what these salons are."

"It's for a Tom Bellamy," the kid hollered. "Something like that."

"Bethany," Joey said. "That's this guy. He takes his calls here. He got no home."

And I didn't really. The closest I had to home was on the other end of the phone. It was Hope. She wanted to know if there was anything about Robert Rackleff in the *Globe*.

"Not that I saw," I told her. "What happened?"

"They shot at his house night before last. Not his house, but where he sometimes stays when he's in Portland. Not Portland, really. Lake Oswego. It's some kind of a suburb I think. What's the matter with me? Who cares if it's a suburb? I'm kind of upset, that's all."

"This was in the papers down there?"

"In the *Post*, but they didn't say much. A couple of paragraphs. He just called. It's six out there. He couldn't sleep, but he didn't want to call before business hours here. What the hell's the matter with me? I'm babbling."

"Go on and babble. What did he say?"

"They fired five shots."

"Three in the morning, how do they know how many shots? Were they up with the baby?"

"I don't know. This is just what Robert said. You could ask him."

"He wants me to call him?"

"He didn't specifically say so. He may have been calling

because he hoped I'd suggest it, but I didn't want to give
him your unlisted number before I talked to you."

"He didn't mention my name over the phone?"

"One of us might have said 'Tom.' You think his line
is tapped?"

"He seemed to think it might be. You want me to call
him?"

"Maybe it wouldn't be a good idea. I should have remembered about the tap."

"I can't get around that. But I don't know how much
use it'll be calling him. Even if I was there, I couldn't be
much help to him. Even the police can't, if somebody
really wants to kill him. Which maybe they don't. Shooting at the house would just be to scare him."

"Still, maybe next time it won't be to scare."

"Maybe."

"Robert is really important to a lot of people, Tom."

"I saw that at the forum."

"He's one of the really good guys."

"I'll do what I can. Where can I reach him?"

After Hope and I had visited a while on the phone, I
called the number she had given me.

"Mr. Honig?" asked the man who picked up. He
sounded like Rackleff.

"Listen, Robert," I said. "This is going to sound weird,
but can you just answer a question yes or no?"

"Who is this?"

"I don't want to say. Or you to say either. Do you
remember Charlie's Kitchen?"

"Yes."

"In Charlie's Kitchen, we talked about phones being
bugged, okay?"

"I remember."

"So you know who I am, and nobody else needs to. You remember my voice?"

"Now that I make the connection, I do."

"Okay, great. Do you think we should sit down and talk things over?"

"You've got a long way to come. I don't know how much we could afford in consultant's fees."

"That's all taken care of."

"By our friend from Charlie's?"

"We'll talk about it later. I'll be giving you a call in a day or two. Are you going to be at this number?"

"Either me or somebody who can take a message."

"I'll try till I catch you home. If I have to leave a message, I'll tell them Charlie called."

"Fine. I understand."

"I'm sorry for all this cops and robbers bullshit, but I'll explain it all to you later. Who's Mr. Honig?"

"Paul Honig. He runs the FBI office here. What they call the SAC. Special agent in charge. We were talking just before you phoned, and he had to take another call. He said he'd get right back to me."

"They being helpful on this?"

"Yes, very helpful."

"You never happened to mention me to them, did you? Or our friend from Charlie's Kitchen?"

"No, it never came up."

"Good enough. See you soon."

I hung up the phone but stood by it, thinking for a moment. My privacy is especially important to me when the FBI is involved, which was why I hadn't wanted to give my name over the phone. I'd need a name for Rackleff to call me by once I got to Portland.

That name came to me while I was on my way home, threading through the crowd of people headed for the commencement exercises. A guy with a class of '68 button was pointing out Bartley's Burgers and telling his family about how he used to pig out there when he was young and wild.

So that was it. I spent the rest of the morning fooling with my Macintosh, until I had a full set of ID ready to be laminated, all in the name of Bartley T. Berger. The *T* was for Thomas, or could be if I wanted it to. Mr. Berger was an industrial security consultant from Passaic, New Jersey.

PORTLAND INTERNATIONAL AIRPORT LOOKED just like all the rest of them. But Portland itself was new to me, and different. I had paid jacked-up airport prices for a city map because I feel better knowing where I am. The route to Lake Oswego, where Rackleff was still staying in spite of the shooting, took my cab through a good deal of the city.

"Is the weather always like this?" I asked the cabbie.

"In June it is, pretty much. Some days it rains harder."

The wipers were on the interval setting, but he had to turn them on full whenever we got behind someone. The sky wasn't threatening at all, but it was gray and not much light got through. There had to be a sun up there somewhere, because you could see. But the light seemed to have no source. The fields, the lawns, the trees and shrubs, everything was green. Not the bright, amazing green of Southeast Asia, though, but soft green like England in the *National Geographic*.

The trees were a better grade all around than the trees back home. There was much more variety, scores and for all I knew maybe hundreds of species. And many more of them were specimen trees. Back East you'd only see trees that size in parks or campuses or old country places. Out here, bungalows came equipped with oaks that would have towered over a manor house. Shrubs grew the size of trees. Hedges hid houses completely from view.

When we crossed the Willamette River into downtown Portland, the trees thinned out. But it was still green and parklike compared to Boston or Cambridge. The sky had lightened a little, although the light still seemed to be coming from nowhere. The air was damp and cool and windless, as if the whole city were an unheated greenhouse.

The cabbie had turned off his wipers entirely, only flicking them on again for a couple of wipes when a car passed us. "Nice neighborhood you're heading for," he said. "Got friends there?"

"I know a guy staying there, yeah."

He shut up, since he had made his point. It was a minute till I got it, though. I must be going to the Heights to visit somebody, since I obviously wasn't a rich guy myself. So much for my rich guy clothes, which I mostly buy secondhand at Keezer's in Cambridge, it's true. But if I had been the previous owner of these same clothes, still wearing them, somehow the cabbie would have known I belonged in the Heights. You can take the boy out of the poor, but you can't take the poor out of the boy.

As it turned out, the heights above Lake Oswego Heights weren't nearly as upscale as Shaker Heights or Sewickley Heights or most of the other suburban high grounds of the really rich. The houses were moderately big, but they were crammed together practically as tight as condos. And they had the little bit of rawness about them that comes of fairly recent construction. They managed to look expensive without looking attractive.

I had used my map to pick a spot for the cabdriver to let me off that was three blocks away from the house where Rackleff was staying. Probably this was unnecessary, but cabbies keep manifests and airlines keep passenger lists. It was at least possible that the FBI or the local cops had somebody keeping an eye on a house that somebody had recently taken five shots at. Nobody needed to know that the person about to show up at that house had just come from the airport, and had therefore landed at a time that could be easily estimated. And from a city that could therefore be guessed.

When I turned into the dead end where the house was, I saw a truck parked on the concrete apron in front of the three-car garage. Rackleff had said at the JFK School that his office was in his truck, but I had pictured a pickup with one of those detachable tops that they call a cap. This was a real truck, though—a small one but tall enough not to fit inside the garage. It was the kind of vehicle you see mostly in the cities, blocking the side streets while the driver makes deliveries. I don't know much more about delivery vans than I do about trees, but this one was about the size of the smallest Avis and Hertz rental trucks. There would be plenty of room in the back for a person to sleep comfortably, and maybe have a chair and a little table, too, and still have room left over for the office files Rackleff had said he carried around.

Rackleff came to the door, wearing what looked like the same clothes he had on at Harvard. "Good to see you again, Tom," he said. "Oh, I'm sorry. Should I be calling you that?"

"Sure, it's okay. Here's my new card. The *T* can be for Tom." I handed him one of my Bartley T. Berger cards.

"Not bad," he said. "All the times I walked past Bartley's Burgers, and I never would have thought of making a name of it."

"Did you go to Harvard?"

"Not really. I started at the Divinity School but dropped out after a semester."

He seemed too young to have had one of those pre-foxhole conversions that used to overcome people like David Stockman when the Vietnam draft got too close. So he must have had another reason to drop out.

"What went wrong?" I asked.

"Nothing very original. I just had the usual trouble reconciling the existence of pain and evil with the existence of God. It seemed to me then that the whole structure of Christian theology really amounted to nothing more than a rickety attempt to rationalize that coexistence."

"How does it seem to you now?"

"The same way," he said, with a smile that, damn it, you could only describe as sweet. "It started out as a religion for slaves and subjects, and there are still plenty of those around. It might be better for them to have false hopes than none at all."

"Of course you can't eat pie in the sky," I said.

"Maybe in a way you can, if you believe it exists. It's like the placebo effect, isn't it? Maybe those pills are only sugar, but they can still make you feel better if you think they can. If there's a shortage of penicillin, maybe that's the next best thing."

Rackleff took my suit bag from me and headed toward the stairs. "Come on," he said. "I'll show you where you're staying."

Once I had hung up the suit bag and unpacked the big nylon equipment bag that held everything else, I headed downstairs and found Rackleff going through a pile of newspapers. "I try to read as many local weeklies as I can," he said when I asked what they were for. "Often they'll have stories about timber company activities that the big dailies don't carry. Some of our best leads have come from little items like that."

"Makes sense," I said. Leads to what, I should have asked, and would sooner or later. But I had been wondering about something else while I unpacked.

"You think somebody can be a saint even if they don't believe in penicillin, so to speak?" I asked. "An agnostic saint? An atheist saint?"

"Why not?" Rackleff said. "I can't imagine a God so petty that he would care if we believed in him, or in some false god, or in none at all."

"Maybe Hope is right, then," I said. "Her theory is you might be some kind of a saint."

Rackleff smiled.

"Tell her what Orwell said about sainthood," he said. " 'Saints should always be judged guilty until they're proved innocent.' "

"Innocent of what?" I said, stupidly. Fortunately Rackleff was caught up in his own thoughts.

"Fashions change. Even god changes," he said. "Mine has."

"To what?"

"From a spiritual god to a physical one. I think that's happening a lot. I wonder if the Apollo mission didn't do it. That picture of Earth from the moon. That beautiful blue marble. We already knew it had to look like that, but we only knew it theoretically. Then all at once we knew it in a completely different way. We really knew it, all the way down inside us. That was our blue marble in the photo. It was the only blue marble we had, and the only one we'd ever get.

"It changed us all forever, that picture. And the

younger you are, the more it changed you. The children understand the best. A hundred years ago if you asked children what was the most important thing to them, they would have answered something to do with God, Jesus, salvation. Next they would have said the flag, meaning just about the same thing. Now they say the environment, by which they mean that blue marble.

"They don't think about heaven so much nowadays, because heaven is the blue marble and we've become its guardian angels. God is the blue marble, too. We're alone on our blue marble in all that blackness, and we'd better take good care of it. That's what the kids see."

"And that's what you see, too?"

"That's what I see, too."

The first time I saw that picture of Earth from the moon was in Vientiane, where I was a Spec/4 assigned to the office of the army attaché in Laos. Later the U.S. Information Service put moon rocks on display out at the That Luang fair. They looked just like any other rocks, which didn't surprise the Lao. Most of them figured the whole exhibit was fake, anyway. They knew that the moon was carried on the back of a giant frog that bit bigger and bigger chunks out of it every night until it was all gone, and then slowly puked it back up again. Or that's what we thought the Lao believed, although what we thought we knew about the Lao was mostly wrong.

I might have had my own doubts about Apollo, since I was just then doping out that Kennedy and Johnson had been lying to me nonstop for most of my young life. But I knew they hadn't faked that picture. They were only schemers, not dreamers, and they could never have imagined the blue marble.

The blue marble really was our planet, all right. Before Apollo, the Earth had looked big and indestructible to microbes like us. Now we could see that it was all alone and friendless out there in the black nothing, and not so big after all. It was as if a few cancer cells had gone off on a rocket and brought back a photo of the patient for all the other cancer cells to look at. Most of us would probably keep right on multiplying and killing our host, but a few of us, anyway, might get the idea.

"You ever think that maybe we're all cancer cells?" I asked Rackleff.

"Oh, absolutely. The only way to understand the space race is as metastasis."

So much for original metaphor, and back to business.

"Fill me in on this shooting," I said to Rackleff. "Did you hear the shots?"

"No, we all slept through them."

"All meaning who else?"

"Bill and JoEllyn Belter. It's their house. None of us knew anything had happened till the police came and woke us up."

"Who called them?"

"A woman down the street who was up with her baby."

"Did this woman see anything?"

"The car was gone by the time she thought it was safe to look out. She didn't really know what had happened till she spotted the broken window."

"Let's go upstairs and look at it," I said.

There was nothing much to see. The windowpane on the second-floor landing had been replaced. The bullet hole in the wallboard on the opposite wall had been patched with Spackle but not yet painted. "The police said they were forty-four caliber," Rackleff said. "Does that tell you anything?"

"Not much. I'm kind of dumb about guns." As a kid I

had hunted, like practically every other kid in Port Henry, New York. Rats at the dump, rabbits, woodchucks, eventually deer. Then more guns during basic training at Fort Dix, ready on the right, ready on the left, ready on the firing line. A couple of times in Laos I borrowed a revolver to wear while I poked around in the jungle. But soon I figured out that the gun was a whole lot more likely to get me killed than to save me, if I ever did stumble across a Pathet Lao patrol. Without it they might buy the truth, which was that I was looking for orchids. With it I'd just be another CIA cowboy.

The other thing I had about carrying a gun was that it makes you feel like an asshole at first. Then once you've worn the thing long enough to get used to it, you don't feel like an asshole anymore. You are one.

"I guess I just assumed you would carry a gun," Rackleff said.

"No, I've already got a dick."

Rackleff looked surprised and I looked stupid, if I looked the way I felt.

"Sorry," I said. "Force of habit. It's just something I used to say in the war, whenever some red-hot would ask how come I didn't wear a side arm in the field."

"I thought everybody in Vietnam had to."

"Not in the rear echelon. And actually I was in Laos, anyway."

"With the CIA?"

"Army attaché's office at first. Then I took my discharge over there and went to work for Air America."

"Wasn't that the CIA?"

"Our paycheck came out of their budget, but we just flew the planes. You call, we haul—that was the arrangement. I didn't think of it as working for the CIA exactly, but I suppose it was."

We went outside to look at the holes in the wall, which hadn't been fixed yet. They were scattered, as if there had been no particular target except the house itself. If the window hadn't been broken and the mother next door hadn't been awake, nobody might have noticed the holes.

We went back inside. I hunted up some tea in the kitchen and put water on to boil. Rackleff got himself a glass of orange juice.

"I think we ought to operate on the assumption that somebody seriously intends to kill you," I said.

"Why not just kill me, then?" Rackleff asked. "Why send letters and shoot at the house?"

"They're warning you to stop something."

"What? The letters don't mention anything specific."

"Maybe everything you do. Earth Everlasting, all of it. Would you stop all that?"

"Of course not."

"That's why you should take the letters and the drive-by shooting seriously. The Klan sends warnings, too. But that doesn't mean they won't string you up if you keep on whistling at white girls."

"I do take it seriously."

"I mean the way a president takes the danger of assassination seriously. Would you wear a flak jacket?"

"I don't think I could, really. I'd feel too foolish."

I couldn't argue with that. Plenty of people would rather die than feel foolish. In fact, it's a major reason for dying.

"Well, there are other things we can do," I said.

"Tell me about them."

At the end we agreed on a package of measures, most of them aimed at making it difficult to locate Rackleff.

"It's going to be a pain in the ass," I said, "but we know they know about this house, and we've got to assume that the phone lines you mostly use are bugged by somebody or other. Probably the cops, as you say. Some two-bit red squad, or whatever they've got."

"But that's a separate problem from the threats," Rackleff said. "Don't you think so?"

"Sure, but the point is that we don't know who the local red squad might share their stuff with. A while back they arrested a San Francisco cop for selling counterintelligence files to the South Africans and the Anti-Defamation League."

Rackleff agreed to move out the next morning. We would hopscotch around to the houses of various supporters, a couple days here and a couple days there, making the arrangements face-to-face or from pay phones. The closest Earth Everlasting had to an office was a handful of paid part-timers who worked in a donated carriage house on a Dunthorpe estate. All of them would be instructed not to discuss his movements or his schedule over the phone.

"Will that really do any good?" Rackleff asked. "You read about surveillance teams and tracking devices and helicopters."

"Those things cost money and they don't always work. We're trying to make it even harder for them. Once surveillance loses sight of you, it's really tough to pick you up again. That's why we need that second vehicle."

I had explained to him earlier that I wouldn't do much good riding around in the small delivery van with him, especially since I didn't carry a gun. Instead, I'd stay behind him or in front of him in an old green pickup that somebody had donated to Earth Everlasting. That way, I stood a good chance of spotting anybody tailing Rackleff's fairly distinctive truck without being spotted myself. It seldom occurs to people following somebody that they might be followed themselves.

"Once we know there's nobody behind you, we can relax a little," I said. "At least until they have another chance to pick us up."

"What sort of chance?"

"If you're giving a speech, for instance. Anything where people know you have to be a certain place at a certain time."

"I see. How long does all of this go on?"

"Until we figure out who's behind it."

"So it might be more or less indefinitely."

"I don't think so. I met a guy in Laos once, one of the CIA contract employees who ran around playing soldier with Vang Pao's troops. Back in the fifties he was a union organizer and one day they send him down to Greenville, Mississippi, to sign up the electrical workers in a plant there. One night somebody sets fire to his rental car and pisses him off.

"So he rents a new car and goes around town throwing dynamite on two or three lawns and after that they left him strictly alone. Harry, I say to him once, how did you know who torched your car? Harry says I didn't have to know who torched my car, all I had to know was who sent them."

"How do we find out who sent them?" Rackleff asked.

"Well, let's work on it. Who might have?"

It was worse than I thought. Earlier Rackleff had talked about searching the weekly papers for leads, and I hadn't put it together with a passing remark he had made back in Cambridge about bringing evidence to the new U.S. attorney. What that meant, it turned out, was that Earth Everlasting had abandoned risky tactics like tree spiking in favor of tactics that were, potentially, even riskier.

Rackleff had figured that the best way to slow the cutting of the forests was to use the criminal code. So he had
turned Earth Everlasting into a sort of pro bono detective
agency, digging out evidence that could send people to
jail. People like government officials and corporate
executives.

"We worked the strategy out with Bill and JoEllyn Belter," Rackleff said. They were the two environmental lawyers who owned the house we were sitting in. "When
you're bucking the timber companies and the U.S. government at the same time, as we were under Bush and
Reagan, civil actions get tied up for years in court. And
you eventually wind up losing anyway unless you're
lucky enough to get a pre-Reagan judge. But it's harder
for the government to ignore violations of the criminal
code, partly because they get more attention from the
press."

So the Belters armed Earth Everlasting activists with
appropriate sections of the U.S. criminal code and sent
them out to find violations. "The first solid evidence we
got was of arson," Rackleff said. "Cold Creek Forest Products hired a couple of unemployed loggers to set forest
fires in the Carswell area."

"How do you make money on a forest fire?"

"You burn an area where it's illegal to log, and get it
declared salvage. Then the timber companies are allowed
to log it."

"Log what?"

"Whatever's left, which is plenty. Often the best trees
aren't burned. Maybe only a small part of the tract is
burned."

The original lead on arson had come from one of those
weekly papers. A reporter had a lot more information

than his paper would print, and so he turned it over to Earth Everlasting.

"Ben Schecter was his name," Rackleff said. "He was only a couple of years out of Oregon State. His father had a small trucking outfit, two or three trucks, in Carswell, but the son had become a committed environmentalist at college. It killed him."

"Killed him how?"

"After we more or less forced the Forest Service investigators to charge the two men, the son was arguing with his father over the case one day. Finally he threw it right in his father's face that he himself had been the one who fed us the information. The father tossed the son out of the house and evidently told half the town about it. One of those towns where logging is the only industry and there's a lot of rage. Some unemployed loggers followed him out of a dance and beat him so badly he never regained consciousness."

"What happened to the guys that killed him?"

"Nothing. Nobody saw anything."

"I come from a little, crapped-out town like that, and in fact everybody knows everything when something like that happens."

"Of course."

"So the father must know who killed his boy."

"Probably, but he doesn't blame them. He wrote a letter to the newspaper his son worked for. It amounted to a defense of the loggers who attacked his boy. He blamed Earth Everlasting for his son's death, and in a certain sense he's right. If it hadn't been for us, his boy would still be alive."

"If it hadn't been for those loggers, too."

"That's true. The combination made the explosion, but both ingredients were necessary."

"What kind of a guy is the father?"

"Loud, angry, confused."

"Great."

As we went on, there turned out to be more and more lawns to toss dynamite on. Rackleff's people had gathered evidence against Cascadia Timber Company and Dixie-Cascade for altering brands on trees, which was the first I knew about branding trees. It turned out you stamped a brand into the butt that told whether the log had come from private or public property. Dixie-Cascade was the company headed by Hap Overholser, the big Louisianan who had debated Rackleff at the JFK School.

Earth Everlasting had gathered evidence against Cascadia for timber rustling from the national forests and against Cold Creek Forest Products for arson. Cold Creek turned out to be a subsidiary of Dixie-Cascade. Rackleff's people had brought charges against Pacific Northwest Pulp and Paper for bribing Forest Service officials with prostitutes and free vacations. Against the Forest Service officials who took the bribes. Against Willauer & Bradford, Inc., for illegal export of logs. Against Tonsasnot Reforestation Industries for misgrading of timber.

And on and on.

"Who was the comic who used to ask the audience if there was anybody out there he hadn't offended yet?" I said. "Mort Sahl?"

"I don't know," Rackleff said. "I don't think I've offended the Brotherbund yet, though."

"Yeah, well, they seem to be sending you death threats, so maybe you made a clean sweep after all."

Rackleff smiled. "Maybe I did."

"Speaking of that, what does the FBI say about the letters?"

Rackleff glanced at his watch. It was a bottom-of-the-line Casio, like mine. "They'll be here in an hour," he said. "You could ask them."

"Here for what? Didn't they already talk to you?"

"After I took your advice and showed them the letters, yes. Now that someone took those shots at the house, they want to talk to me again."

"You told me over the phone they were helpful when you went to them about the letters. What did they do?"

"They said they would look into it. By helpful I just meant that they took the threats seriously and acted concerned."

"Did they say anything about this Brotherbund?"

"Pretty much the same thing that was in the papers. That there was no proof the letters were genuine, but that they were keeping an eye on all the skinhead groups."

"How did the papers hear about the letters? From you?"

"No, from the U.S. attorney's office, when their press person was responding to questions about the shooting. They asked him about possible motives, and he mentioned the letters. The *Oregonian* ran a story about the letters and the shooting, although not a very long one."

"Back East they wouldn't even mention a drive-by shooting at all, unless somebody got hit," I said. "But you're a name. The wires must have moved a few lines, anyway, because Hope saw it in the *Washington Post*."

"It's funny," Rackleff said. "Something seems like a huge, important thing to you, and then you look at the story in the paper and it's no more important than an out-of-town baseball game."

"Papers aren't very good at figuring out what's important."

"Still it tends to put you in your place."

"I better find a place myself, speaking of that. I don't want these FBI guys to see me when they come."

I WAS WATCHING THROUGH THE BLINDS IN THE
Belters' upstairs bedroom when the car
pulled up outside. It was a dark blue car,
a couple of years old. I don't know the
makes of cars, but it was the kind of anonymous, lower-middle-of-the-line car that you see on the interstates with
a lone driver, always a man. The backseat is usually
rigged as a closet, with the salesman's clothes hanging
from a rod.

The two men who got out of the car could have been
salesmen, too. The driver was in his late twenties or early
thirties, the passenger in his fifties. They both wore navy
blue suits and white shirts and red ties. When you
thought about it, they were dressed as American flags.
The older man might have been the VP in charge of sales
for the whole division, everything west of the Rockies. He
was of medium height, not exactly fat but getting close
to plump. His cheeks were definitely plump. His hair was
still dark, except for patches of silver at the temples, and
combed back flat. He wore glasses that vaguely suggested
aviator glasses. The lenses were just barely tinted gray,
the closest an FBI man could probably let himself get to

4 7

the Tonton Macoute look. The younger man didn't need glasses yet, and didn't have the little patches of white hair. But in twenty years he would be his boss's twin.

As they came toward the front door, I went over to the second-floor landing and sat down on the rug, leaning against the wall. From there I could hear what went on in the living room, and would still have time to duck into a bedroom if anybody headed upstairs.

"Mr. Rackleff?" a voice said from the hall. "Paul Honig. We've talked on the phone. This is Special Agent Coulter."

"Pleased to meet you," Rackleff said. Special Agent Coulter mumbled something. "Come on in and sit down."

"Any more letters?" Honig asked after everyone was squared away.

"No, not since the ones I showed to the people at your office. Have they made any progress on who's sending the things?"

"It's under active investigation."

"But no luck yet?"

"You can be sure it's a high-priority item with us, Mr. Rackleff. Particularly since the shooting incident, and naturally all along, even before. Sending death threats through the mail is a federal offense. Also we take a very serious view of anybody potentially tampering with a federal witness."

"You think the threats are from somebody who wants to keep me from testifying?"

"We're not excluding any possibilities."

"I suppose it's possible. Testifying on what, though?"

"We're working on a number of things. What have you been involved with that might have offended the Brotherbund?"

"Nothing that I can think of. But we've involved ourselves in a half a dozen or more things that other people and groups would like to see us out of. Mr. Garber's office has the information."

"I'm aware of that. As I'm sure you're aware that the normal procedure would have been to involve the Bureau."

"I assumed that's what we were doing. You're both in the Justice Department. Isn't the United States attorney the department's senior official out here?"

"I doubt very much if you're really that naive, Mr. Rackleff. Why not just go to the president?"

"I would have, if I felt it was necessary and I could have got in to see him. It's done every day, isn't it?"

"There are channels, Mr. Rackleff, as I'm sure you're fully aware. When federal laws are allegedly violated, citizens normally go through the Bureau, not the office of the U.S. attorney. And investigations of those alleged violations are normally carried out by the Bureau, not by private individuals such as yourself. We're the ones who are competent to carry out these types of investigation. We're not subject to intimidation the way a civilian is. You should have requested us to carry out any investigations."

"Isn't the U.S. attorney the one who requests you to carry out investigations?"

"That's exactly right. He requests *us* to investigate. He didn't request *you* to investigate, did he?"

"Since he didn't have the information to base a request on, we took that information to him."

"How do you know he didn't have information? Did somebody in my office tell you what information we have on what cases? We have hundreds of cases working at any one time. That information should have gone straight to us."

"It did go to you, didn't it? What's the difference whether it came in the front door or the side door."

"We *are* the front door!" Honig said, his voice starting to rise. Then he got control of himself and went back into bureaucratic mode.

"We're the ones who evaluate raw information brought to us from civilian sources," the FBI man said. "When and if the information meets established criterions for being passed on to the appropriate parties in the office of the U.S. attorney, then we pass that information on as appropriate."

"But in the end the decision to prosecute or not to prosecute is made by the U.S. attorney, right?"

"Technically that is correct."

"And so we gave him preliminary information that he could base a decision on," Rackleff said. "Some of our material he didn't see fit to act on and some of it he did. We're going around in circles here, Mr. Honig. We're not saying the big thing that we both know."

"Which is?"

"We took our information directly to Mr. Garber because we wanted to get action on it. We didn't take it to your office because our experience in the past has led us to believe you would have buried it."

"The Federal Bureau of Investigation is not in the business of suppressing legitimate information on violations of federal law."

"More circles, Mr. Honig. The thing about circles is that they never get you anyplace. I'm on notice now that you're mad because I went over your head."

"It isn't that at all."

"Okay, it isn't. Don't you think we ought to move on to whatever brought you out here? Look, I've got some

5 0

coffee ready, tea or soda if you prefer. Orange juice. Can
I get you folks anything?"

"Nothing," Honig said.

"Special Agent Coulter?"

"No, thanks."

"I think I'll make myself a pot of tea, then."

I heard the door to the kitchen open and close. I had
arranged it with Rackleff to take a good while with the
tea, rattling and clanking around to show that he was
paying no attention to the FBI agents.

"Does this jack-off think we're morons?" I heard the
young agent say. "Does he think he can pull an end run
around the Bureau?"

"He's already done it, hasn't he?"

"Only because that asshole is dumb enough to buy his
flimsy evidence and the Bureau isn't."

"That asshole being Frederick C. Garber?"

"Well, yeah. Sure."

"Mr. Garber is the U.S. attorney appointed by the presi-
dent for the state of Oregon and confirmed by the U.S.
Senate. He is the ranking representative in this state of
Attorney General Reno, who runs the Justice Department.
Of which the Federal Bureau of Investigation just happens
to be a part."

"Well, yeah. Of course."

"Now, look, Doug, you're a good man. And this asshole, so-called by you, is not your direct-line superior,
which is me. But he damned sure outranks you, doesn't
he?"

"Yes, sir. I only thought . . . just between the two of us."

"How the hell do you know what's between the two
of us and what isn't? Maybe there's a reporter hiding in
the closet for all you know. You see my point? My point
is respect for the office."

"Yes, sir."

"That said, Doug, you're certainly entitled to your personal opinion as long as you keep it personal. Same way I'm entitled to mine. For all you know maybe we've got the same private opinion. And maybe I'll tell you what my private opinion is, a few months from now. Because that's when I'll be retired. But you, young fella, you've still got twenty, twenty-five years in the Bureau to go. You follow me here?"

"Yes, sir. I'm sorry, sir."

"No problem. You're a good man."

I heard the kitchen door and then the pantry door as Rackleff came back with his tea.

"You're sure you won't join me?" he said. "The water's hot. Won't take a minute."

"I'm fine," the young agent said.

"Mr. Rackleff, there's something you ought to know about the FBI," Honig said. "The Bureau is not political." I couldn't see him, but it sounded as if he was keeping a straight face. "We don't make the law, we just enforce it."

"But you can't enforce all of it," Rackleff said mildly. "You must have to prioritize."

"Not on any political basis."

"We're probably just using the word in different ways. For me, any government decision to spend limited resources on one thing rather than another is political in nature."

"Mr. Rackleff, if the Bureau let politics enter into law enforcement, why would we be here?"

"I don't follow you."

"You don't seem to think that the Bureau gives a damn about the environment, and here we are trying to protect a big environmentalist like you just the same way as we'd protect any other citizen regardless of his views. Also regardless of the fact that this same individual has gone to the U.S. attorney and accused the Bureau of harassment. Which number one it isn't so and number two it won't keep us nevertheless from doing our job of investigating these death threats and shooting incidents against a witness in upcoming federal trials. So let's get on with it."

"Fine," Rackleff said. "What do you want me to do?"

"Whatever's to be done, we'll do it. We know the areas you've been active in and what potential individuals that you might have given cause to commit these hostile types of activities against you."

"Which is a good-size crowd," Rackleff said. "But the only ones sending me death threats are the skinheads. Why them?"

"We're working on that."

"Do you keep an eye on this Brotherbund outfit?"

"We keep an eye on all extremist groups with a potential for violence."

"What's their philosophy, beyond racism and anti-Semitism? Why would they threaten an environmentalist?"

"We can't comment on ongoing investigations."

"The papers always mention a Max Wilhoite. Who is this Max Wilhoite?"

"He's the assistant manager of a gym over in southeast, off Division, when he's not running around playing Nazi on the weekends. He calls himself the Leader."

"What's he the leader of? How many people are in this Brotherbund, anyway?"

"They claim two hundred and fifty members. It's probably more like twenty."

"Is he somebody I should worry about, or is he mostly noise?"

"He was arrested once for burglary when he was a

juvenile. Since then he's been acquitted twice of assault charges. We consider him armed and dangerous."

"Were these serious assaults, then?"

"Gang fight type of activity with a racist element. Neither victim was hospitalized except on an outpatient basis. However, we consider him dangerous on other grounds."

"What grounds?"

"We can't comment on suspicions and ongoing homicide investigations. Take my word for it. He's dangerous."

"Well, what should I do?"

"Exercise normal caution, the same as you would after dark or in a dangerous locality. We'll take care of the rest."

"Will somebody be keeping an eye on me? Special Agent Coulter?"

"We don't have the manpower to provide regular security, but we'll take measures as appropriate. Notify us as to any travel plans or other unusual movements in high-risk environments."

"Such as what?"

"Such as public appearances, rallies, demonstrations."

I watched out the window again as they left, trying to memorize the appearance of both of them. I did the same for the car, although it was probably out of the motor pool. Still, I noted the number. If I was going to be watching Rackleff's back, I didn't want to get all excited over stalkers who were nothing but FBI agents doing the same thing I was.

"Were you able to hear everything?" Rackleff asked when I came downstairs.

"Oh, yeah. Plus what they said when you were in the kitchen. I don't think they like you, Robert."

"I don't like them very much either, which should help you convince Hope I'm not a saint."

"Why? Are saints supposed to like FBI assholes?"

"I imagine so. After all, those two can't help what they are. They're frightened of being different, so they join the biggest gang they can find. Most people join gangs. I formed my own little gang, if you want to look at Earth Everlasting that way. It makes me feel safe, too. But eventually I wound up in the same business as Honig after all, didn't I? Both of us sniffing around after people and trying to put them in jail."

"You're not in the same business," I said. "You chose to pick on big guys and he chose to pick on little guys. There's all the difference in the world."

MY SECURITY ROUTINE FOR RACKLEFF WAS
based on the theory that the best security
of all is when people can't find you.

5

For a week in and around Portland, we
had shifted from one supporter's house to another every
couple of days, with me making the arrangements from
pay phones. Rackleff would park his van or truck, whatever you called it, a good distance from the house. I
would have prepositioned the green pickup in sight of
the house, but three or four blocks away. I would watch
to see if anyone was sitting in parked cars or cruising the
neighborhood, and after a little bit Rackleff would walk
toward me. If he was still all alone, which so far he always
had been, he would hop in with me and off we'd go to
a parking spot around a few corners from our night's
lodging. He'd walk to it with his overnight bag and so
would I, staying well behind him to check for tails. Again,
there never were any.

And unless whole squadrons of skinheads or cops or
timber company spies were on the job, there probably
never would be any. I used to know a spook in Laos
who spent a tour teaching surveillance techniques, among

other things, to the Moroccan secret police. If he was right, tailing somebody who suspected you were doing it was practically impossible without a lot of expensive stuff like beepers and helicopters and radio communications and a fleet of cars traveling before and behind and along parallel streets.

Only the police or the FBI could handle anything that elaborate, and I didn't imagine that either of them really cared that much. Still, they might care enough to tag along if they knew our plans. That was why I used pay phones. It was also why we ignored Honig's request to keep the Bureau informed of our movements. The FBI talks to a lot of unpleasant people. Sneaks, Mafiosi, skinheads, Klansmen, police spies, Roy Cohn, Walt Disney, you name it. You never want to touch the FBI. You don't know where it's been.

And so we didn't take the one piece of advice Special Agent in Charge Honig had given us: to keep the Bureau informed of our travel plans.

Which at the moment were taking us toward the Pacific Coast.

Rackleff's van was fifteen minutes ahead of me on Route 26. I was clattering and rattling along in the pickup. The rattling didn't bother me a bit. I grew up with old pickups, and they're supposed to rattle. It's a sign of health.

The old green Ford was completely anonymous, with an empty rifle rack in the rear window and a big tool chest bolted along one side of the eight-foot bed.

The rains had stopped and the windows were open. A few more days of driving in the warm sun and I'd have a truck driver's tan on my left forearm. A few small white clouds dotted the blue sky. You could see their shadows on the fields. Tidy farmhouses sat on the swells of the rolling land, often well back from the road. The fields were light green from the new crops or chocolate brown from the plow. The sky was robin's egg blue, the barns were red, the evergreen forests were almost black, the huge, ancient trees shading the farmhouses were just turning to the deep green of summer. It was a landscape out of a children's picture book, peaceful and pretty and so neat it seemed unreal.

The way we had planned the trip from a security point of view, Rackleff was supposed to stop at the first pull-off he could find past a little town called Necanicum Junction. I would drive on by till I was out of sight, and find my own place to park. Then he would continue on his way, and I would fall in behind him again after having checked to see if he had picked up any tails up to that point.

Maybe this was overkill. Maybe all this rigmarole was silly, but there were things about the threatening letters and the drive-by shooting that bothered me a lot. On the surface the letters didn't seem to amount to much. As my Secret Service friend said, there were nuts in every crowd. Enough of them send letters so that practically everyone in the public eye gets nut mail. But only the tiniest fraction of the letter writers take that next step, the John Hinckley step.

But this writer had taken a peculiar intervening step in firing those warning shots. Something other than nuttiness seemed to be going on, although I couldn't figure out what. That was why I had set up this silly game of hopscotch when we traveled. It seemed better to overreact than to underreact.

All at once, in the distance, I saw something worth overreacting to.

It was Rackleff's van, pulled over to the side of the road a good ten miles short of our agreed rendezvous. I took my foot off the gas to give me time to think. It could have been a simple breakdown, a rest stop, anything. I was close enough now to see that the rear doors were open. I saw a form inside. I downshifted and rolled up behind, opening the door with the idea that I might want to jump out, let the pickup ram the van at low speed, and try to take advantage of the confusion.

Then I saw that the figure was Rackleff, and that he was waving hello. I braked to a stop, cut the motor, and sat for a moment till my own motor had slowed down. Rackleff jumped down from the van and came up to me.

"Hi," he said, just as calmly as if I hadn't been about to charge the enemy single-handed and save his life. "I was keeping an eye on the road for fear you might miss me. Something here that it suddenly occurred to me you should see."

I hadn't focused on it, but now I saw a sign over his shoulder that said, WORLD'S LARGEST SITKA SPRUCE TREE.

"Sure, let's take a look."

"No, just you," Rackleff said. "I've seen it before, and it's too depressing to see again."

I headed down a short road, not much more than a hundred yards long. A camper and a minivan and a couple of cars were parked at the end, all with out-of-state plates. A man wearing Bermuda shorts was walking toward the minivan with his wife and his son and daughter, both children in the least attractive period of human life, from thirteen to fifteen.

"That's really something, huh?" the man said. "Enough wood in that baby to make six houses."

"Big woops," said his son.

I practically never miss my father, but for a second

there I wished the old bastard had been handy. He would have smacked that kid cross-eyed.

The baby in question rose up for 216 feet in front of me, according to a sign so weathered it was nearly unreadable. The giant tree's circumference was given as 52 feet and six inches. Its crown spread was 931 feet, which was more than three football fields and seemed impossible. Maybe spread meant circumference or area instead of diameter, though.

Anyway, the crown spread was the least impressive part of the World's Largest Sitka Spruce Tree, here in Crown Zellerbach's Clatsop Managed Forest. The most impressive part was the trunk, which rose up limbless for fifty yards or so. The crown spread seemed insignificant, so far above that to look up at it made you feel like you were falling backward.

"Estimated to be over 700 years old," the sign said, "this spruce contains over 55,000 board feet of lumber, enough to build six two-bedroom houses. But that will not happen. This tree, and others in the area, are permanently protected from harvesting."

A few dozen other giant spruces and firs were scattered around the open grove, but most of the growth was alders and other low, small junk wood. Among them were hundreds of huge, rotting stumps of trees that had been managed right out of Crown Zellerbach's sad forest. Little trees were growing out of the giant stumps, though, so that things would probably be back to normal in six or eight hundred years.

I took an untended path to another grove nearby. Old outhouses stood along the path, with green paint peeling off them. One was turned over. Saplings grew out of the corrugated standpipe, pushing their way up through a mulch of rusted cans and bottles green with moss. Trucks had made muddy passages through the few large trees that had so far escaped management. The rest of the trees were represented by moldering piles of stripped bark. Farther on the grove ended in a dry, open area cluttered with the litter of lumbering—stumps and dead branches.

I turned back, into the open shade of the thinned-out grove. When I got to the world's largest Sitka spruce tree, I spotted a sign I had missed. It was nailed to a tree. It said, "Cut no trees or shrubs in park area." Like the rotting outhouses, the sign seemed to date from the 1940s or 1950s.

The male kid was standing with one foot on a raised root of the giant Sitka spruce. "HahahaHAha, hahaha-HAha, hahahaHAha," he was braying to his sister. "That's the Woody Woodpecker song!"

I left before my parenting instincts could take over.

Rackleff was still sitting in a camp chair in the back of his van, going through the contents of a folder from his boxes of files.

"You're right," I said. "It's depressing."

"Isn't it, though? There's an incredible sadness about it. The outbuildings rotting away. The words on the signs and the condition of the signs themselves. The standing trees and the stumps. Dissonant messages."

"Tell you the message I got," I said. "Park management isn't the fast track at Crown Zellerbach."

OUT OF AN EXCESS OF CAUTION, I HAD RACK-
leff drive back toward Portland while I
waited at the little park. Nobody special
followed him east, and nobody special
seemed to be behind him when he came back again a
little later as instructed, heading west. I waited fifteen
minutes after he passed and pulled out.

By now most of the road was forested, which surprised
me. I had expected to see scalped hills, clear-cuts in all
directions. I got my answer when I stopped to take a leak,
and afterward wandered a few yards down the dirt road
where I had pulled off the highway. The forest ended and
there were my clear-cuts, checkerboards that made the
hills ugly as far as I could see.

I told Rackleff about my little side trip when I came up
with him at our rendezvous outside Necanicum Junction.
"The timber companies leave a fringe of trees along the
highways, kind of like hedges," he said. "They're called
fool 'em strips."

When our little two-truck caravan hit the coast, with
Rackleff way ahead, we turned south on the coast highway. The scenery on 101 was okay, but nowhere near as

spectacular as I had expected. The Pacific was gray, not blue. Enormous rocks stood out of it here and there, but mostly the ocean stretched off unbroken till Japan.

We were headed for a town called Agnes Beach, where Rackleff was supposed to check into the Seaview Motel under the name of Robert Morley, Morley being his middle name. Then he would park the van out of sight from the highway and wait for me in his room.

There had been some moderately upscale towns along our way, but Agnes Beach turned out to be low-rent. So did the Seaview Motel. When I drive my own car, I always carry a nylon equipment bag full of extra blankets and pillows, and a 200-watt bulb for reading. But now my cheapo motel kit was back in Cambridge.

I paid in cash as always, on the general theory that paper trails are bad things to leave behind you. On the same theory, I registered as Bartley T. Berger and put down a license plate number that was one digit off.

The management had taped handwritten instructions onto the old dial phone in my room. I followed the instructions with no hope, and I wasn't disappointed. Then I tried starting with an eight instead of a nine, with a zero before the area code, and following that with a one instead of the zero and then without either a one or a zero. This made a total of six tries or maybe more, since I probably repeated one or two of the combinations without knowing it. All I got was idiot recordings or just a dead line. And all I wanted was to direct-dial a collect call from Oregon to Washington, D.C. Somewhere out there was the information superhighway, but I couldn't access the operator. I finally called the desk, and the clerk got me an operator from some off-brand phone company, and she passed me on to an AT&T operator, but not without a fight.

"Bethany," Hope said when the secretary had got her to the phone. "What are you up to? What's happening out there? All that stuff. Come on, tell me."

"This a good time? You got a minute?"

She did, and so I told her about the weird routines I had got Rackleff to agree to, and about the Schecter boy, who had been beaten to death for informing, and what little I knew about the skinheads, and about the FBI's visit to the Belters'.

"You know these lawyers, the Belters?" I said.

"I know of them. I think she has a little inherited money. They're able to do a lot of pro bono stuff, anyway. Some civil rights stuff, but mostly the environment."

"Are they all right?"

"Far as I know. Why?"

"Right now I'm a professional paranoid. I ask myself who knew Rackleff was in the house the night of the shooting, and naturally the Belters are on the list."

"You're not saying they had their own house shot up?"

"All I'm saying is that you can't damage a house much with a few bullets and their bedroom is in the rear."

"Why would they have done something like that?"

"Probably they didn't. I'm just looking at all the possible contingencies, however remote. Isn't that what lawyers do, too?"

"Shut up about lawyers, Bethany. Some of my best friends are lawyers."

"One of mine is, too. How about Olympic National Park?"

"What about it?"

"We were going to have a vacation together, me and my lawyer friend. Remember? And yesterday Robert was telling me about Olympic National Park."

"Olympic National Park, huh? Gee, I'd have to think about that for a while. Okay, I accept."

"Good. When can you come out?"

"Pretty much any time, but aren't you tied up with Robert?"

"I don't think it's going to take much longer. I'm going to talk to the skinhead and I'm going to look into the father of this Schecter kid when we're down there. But I don't think I'll get much."

"Why not?"

"Because my feeling is if either of them wanted to kill Robert, they'd just go ahead and do it. I think the letters and the shooting are only psychological warfare, and I don't think these guys are quite advanced enough for psychology."

"Death threats and drive-by shootings aren't very advanced."

"It's the letters that are advanced. Maybe advanced isn't the word, but peculiar. The wording is a little wrong. The tone is off. They read like nut letters but they don't look like nut letters. And this Louis Schecter and this Wilhoite guy, why would they write nut letters anyway?"

"I don't know about Schecter, Bethany, but Wilhoite has got to be nuts. I mean, he's a Nazi."

"Fucked up isn't nuts. Is David Duke nuts?"

"Not legally speaking, certainly."

"Or even psychologically speaking, probably," I said. "Certainly not the kind of nuttiness that makes you sit alone in your little rented room and brood and write nut letters like these."

"How come they're signed with the name of Wilhoite's group, then?"

"That's exactly it. The one thing that makes no sense to me. Once it does, I'll be able to make a decent guess about what's going on. And then maybe I'll be able to stop worrying about Robert."

"How are you two getting along?"

"Pretty good. I like him. I wish I had his balls."

"Come on, Bethany. The last thing you've got is a balls problem."

"Different kind of balls. His kind is better."

We talked some more about our maiden vacation. Hope turned out to know somebody at the Interior Department. She knows somebody practically everywhere in the federal government. So she would get the literature about Olympic National Park and find out about reservations, and probably about mean annual rainfall and protected species and recommended insect repellents as well. Judging by past performance, within the week she'd be having lunch with some guy who got Congress to turn it into a park in the first place, or ran it for the past twenty years, or wrote the definitive book on temperate zone rain forests.

After unpacking, I went to the room the clerk told me was registered to my associate, Mr. Morley, and found the door unlocked. Shower sounds came from the bathroom. I locked and chained the front door behind me, and closed the open shades. The water stopped while I was unpacking, and Rackleff stepped out of the bathroom with a towel around him.

"Your door was open, Robert," I said.

"With the water running, I was afraid I wouldn't hear you knock."

"I would have waited outside. I know this stuff seems like a Mickey Mouse pain in the ass, Robert, but I think you ought to take it seriously."

"I'm sorry. I know you said to always lock doors, but

it just never occurred to me. I don't have much to steal, and it's easy to replace."

"Thieves aren't the problem."

"I know that. I'll try to be more careful."

"You've got to watch out for little things. For instance, you parked the van in front of your own door."

"But the room is in the rear. Out of sight of the highway, the way you said."

"Put yourself in the shoes of a person who wants to kill you, Robert. Say he checks every motel parking lot in town, front and back. He sees your vehicle parked in front of one particular room, with the drapes open or a light in the window. So he busts the window in with an AK-47 and hoses down the whole room. Park on the other side of the parking lot, away from the rooms, and he doesn't know which light is yours."

"How does this person even know we're in Agnes Beach?"

"Couldn't say. Since we don't know who he is, we don't know how he knows anything. How did he know you were in Lake Oswego? Who would have known that?"

"Are you suggesting it's somebody connected with Earth Everlasting?"

"I don't have the slightest idea. But I've got various things to try."

"What things?"

"Pulling at different threads to see what comes loose. Whoever knew you were staying with the Belters that night, I'll talk with them. When we go down to Carswell, I'll see if I can get anything out of the father of this kid that got killed, the newspaper reporter for the weekly down there. When we get back to Portland I'll try talking to the head skinhead."

"Max Wilhoite."

"Yeah. Maybe he'll sell me a membership in this gym where he works."

We were in Agnes Beach to meet with a man named Lamar Purcell. "He's a very successful local business-man," Rackleff had told me. "He's been very generous with Earth Everlasting over the years." From what I had seen of Agnes Beach, though, there didn't seem to be much to build a successful business on. When Rackleff was dressed, we set off in the pickup for what I had assumed would be Purcell's office.

Route 101 through Agnes Beach was a two-lane high-way with railroad tracks running between it and the sea. Cottages and bungalows crowded up to the inland side of the road, and another row of cottages faced the bay on the other side of the railroad tracks. The beach was flat and featureless. Signs said you could rent boats for crab-bing and seal watching.

The road swung inland from the tracks and took us past swap shops, little tired motels built from cinder blocks, souvenir stores, garages, gift shops, minimarts, flea mar-kets, and bait shops. There were a couple of RV parks, a small engine repair service, a rock shop, and three or four antique shops. They all had beach glass and bottles in the windows and driftwood out front.

A scattering of larger houses sat on a ridge behind the town. Behind them were higher hills, all chopped up into clear-cut rectangles in various stages of regrowth. Here and there the loggers had left trees standing to help re-seed the slopes. The lone trees had a peculiar look, like single whiskers that the razor missed. Their trunks were bare of branches until the very top, the only part where their foliage had been able to find sun in the now-vanished forest.

"Looks like a dog with the mange, doesn't it?" I said.

"It's even more shocking from the air," Rackleff said. "Whenever we can afford to fly visiting firemen over areas of heavy clear-cutting, they come back down as true believers. That's one of the reasons we're here. Lamar Purcell has offered to buy us a small plane."

So Purcell must have been able to drag money out of Agnes Beach somehow. Even a small plane is ridiculously expensive to buy nowadays. Gas isn't so bad for the moment, but insurance has reached the level of grand larceny.

"Do you still fly?" Rackleff asked. Hope had told him that I had sometimes flown Senator Kennedy during my stint as his body man.

"I let my license lapse," I said.

I had let all the rest of my paper existence lapse back in the early Reagan years, too. Credit cards, bank accounts, driver's license, anything that would tie me into the national data base. I had created a new identity for myself in the name of Tom Carpenter, with a new driver's license and a new Social Security card. All this made me feel secure and in control at the time, in some probably crazy way.

Lately it seems less important, but I still feel more comfortable ghosting through life. There used to be a game called Conjugations, where you'd think up things like, "I am firm, you are stubborn, he is a pig-headed fool." In this case it would go, "I am private, you are secretive, he is a paranoid head case." By now I'm probably somewhere between third person and second person. I don't know whether this is progress or not. Maybe not, because I do have enemies. And I keep making new ones.

"I thought flying was supposed to get in your blood," Rackleff went on. "Didn't you like it?"

"Well, it beat driving a cab as a way to make a living. But as a hobby it's too expensive."

"Turn in where all that driftwood is on the left," Rackleff said. "That's where we're going."

"That's his office?" I asked. "This big philanthropist guy?" It was a small, one-story building, even tackier than most of the strip through Agnes Beach. A sign on the roof, made out of pieces of driftwood formed into crooked letters, said LAMARS CHAIN SAW GALLERY.

"Wait till you see," Rackleff said.

I pulled over to the side of the road, next to a bearded pioneer eight feet tall. He was carved out of wood, like all the other pioneers, totem poles, eagles, and bears that cluttered the yard in front of the shop. There were tangles of silvery driftwood, too. Huge logs, three or four feet wide, stood on end waiting to be carved. A gateway nailed together from unfinished slabs was out front, although there was no fence around the property and no gate in the gateway. A sign on it said REDWOOD TREES AND LIVE BURLS. This wasn't redwood country as far as I knew, so they must have been trucked in from farther down the coast.

"That's him," Rackleff said, raising his voice so I could hear him over the growl of a chain saw.

The man with the chain saw was of medium height, thin and wiry. He wore a work shirt so faded that the black and violet checks had almost blended into one pale color. His canvas apron was shiny black with oil and dirt. On his head was a greasy motorcyclist's cap, with a small brown ponytail sticking out from under it. Safety goggles, sideburns, and big noise suppressors made it hard to see

his face. He stood in the middle of a circle of brick-
colored sawdust.

The man and the sawdust circle and a half-carved five-
foot bear were all under a small, square awning held up
by tent poles. The awning had green, salmon, and white
stripes and had probably once been bright and festive.
Now it was faded. Like the man's clothes, it was overlaid
with the brick color of the sawdust. To one side of the
circle of sawdust was a waist-high pile of shavings and
tanbark. A plywood sign leaned against it, with FREE
spray-painted on it.

The old Stihl chain saw growled and whined as Lamar
Purcell worked with his back to us. I had put in enough
time on the woodpile as a kid to know that he was
damned good, although I would have known it anyway.
There's something about an expert at work that tells you
he's an expert even if you don't know how to do the
job yourself.

The saw slipped between the bear's legs and the pitch
of the motor changed as the teeth ripped up into the
crotch. Rackleff winced right along with me. It was every
boy's nightmare, sliding down the banister that turns into
a razor blade.

Done castrating, Purcell moved around to the other side
of his bear statue and finally spotted us. He killed the
saw and somehow slid his goggles and earmuffs and cap
off with a single swipe of his free hand. The dust-free
circles around his eyes made him look like a character
from *Little Orphan Annie*. His smile flashed and made another patch of white.

"Hey, Robert," he said. "How you making it, man?"

"Fine, Lamar."

"This is your teeth, huh?"

"My teeth?"

"The man watching out for your sorry ass."

I wasn't happy that this stranger knew my business, and I must have showed it.

"I told Lamar you were looking into the threats," Rackleff said. "He was the first one I asked about the letters, and he was the one who suggested I look up somebody like you. So then I called around until finally ..."

"Till finally somebody or other told you about me."

It took Rackleff a second to get it. "Right," he finally said. "Till somebody or other did. Look, I'm sorry, but this classified information business isn't the kind of thing I'm good at. I trust Lamar. I trust you."

"Trust but verify," I said.

Lamar grinned again. "It's cool, Robert," he said. "This guy and me been the same places. We'll get along."

He stuck out his hand and said, "I'm Lamar something or other. Purcell, actually."

"I'm Tom something or other. Carpenter will do."

"Let's go inside," Lamar said. "Fuck this bear. He's been waiting a long time to come out of that log, let him wait a little more."

Inside were clocks, boxes, and tabletops made out of burls and redwood slabs. Tangles of driftwood and roots sat on the floor. Thick coats of polyurethane made the finished pieces gleam wetly.

Besides the boss, the only other employee was a large woman in her forties wearing a Mother Hubbard straight from Woodstock. Her graying blond hair hung down Earth Mother style. She was in a tiny office staring at a computer screen so that I couldn't see her face. It was hard to imagine big bucks coming out of a two-person shop full of driftwood and carved animals. More than hard.

"Robert says you're thinking about getting him a plane," I said.

He looked at Robert the same way I had earlier, as if he wondered how much more Robert had told me, and why. "It could happen," he said. "We had a pretty good year last year."

He led us into his own office, which was a low room built onto the back of the shop. The floorboards had been sanded only by years of foot traffic. The desk was a big door sitting on a couple of two-drawer filing cabinets. Purcell sat in an old brown swivel chair, and we sat on a couch that looked like he had rescued it from the sidewalk on collection day. I knew the look. I had furnished my own apartment in Cambridge from the same store.

"Sometimes we worry too much, you know what I mean?" Lamar said. "I think that sometimes. Yes, I do. Probably people like me and you, Tom, probably we worry too much. Robert here, he doesn't worry so much and he gets along pretty good. He was in *People* last year. I wasn't in *People*, were you?"

I shook my head. I didn't think Lamar wanted to be in *People* any more than I did.

"Well, maybe we ought to think about what Robert was saying just now. He was saying he wasn't worried about either of us. He was saying he trusted us. What did you say, Tom? You said trust but verify. And what did I say? It's cool, I said. Which it is. Cool. What I'm thinking, though, is that what Robert was saying is he trusts both of us since we haven't fucked him yet. So we're already verified as far as he's concerned. You see where I'm coming from, Tom?"

He didn't wait for me to answer. He went right on.

"Yeah. We're already verified for each other because

Robert verified us for himself, so maybe we can go the modified hangout route, what do you think?"

"Maybe so."

"So do you think they're trying to kill this poor bastard?"

"I don't know yet. It's possible."

"Can you stop them."

"I don't know."

"You're not carrying a gun." It wasn't a question, so he knew how to tell. My shirt was tucked in, for one thing. Still, my pants and my shirt were fairly loose and could have hid a gun. But an experienced man can usually spot the bulge as the other person moves around. One of my Secret Service pals claimed that the weight and bulk of even a small gun made a man carry himself a little differently—not much, but enough so that a trained eye could pick it up.

"No, I'm not carrying a gun."

"Want one?"

"I think they just bring trouble."

"There's no shit about that. Guns bring trouble. They definitely do. Plus they make you stupid. You ever notice that? The stupidity part?"

"I think it's a tendency they've got, yeah."

"Well, what are you going to do, then? How are you going to save his ass?"

"We're trying to fly below the radar."

"Phony names? Pay phones? Sleep different places? Like that?"

"Like that."

"I can dig it. You can probably do it, no problem. You, Tom something or other, you could. Me, I more or less could if I had to. Robert, though? Robert's in *People*. Robert most definitely cannot do it. It's a whole different thing when you're in *People*. For instance let me give you an example. John Lennon."

Lamar was right, of course. John Lennon had still been a public man, no matter how hard he tried to hide. He had keys, an address, appointments, appearances, probably an office and secretaries and a schedule. Maybe he walked the dog, went out for groceries. So some guy who never had a life was able to wait around outside and take Lennon's for his own.

"We're flying low just for now," I said. "Once I get a routine set up and Robert gets used to it so he'll do it by himself, I'll turn him loose and go try to find out which lawn to throw the bomb on."

I told Lamar Purcell my story about the union organizer in Mississippi.

"Probably this union guy's retired by now, huh?" Lamar said. "Too bad. I could use him."

"I could use him, too."

"Hey, now you *are* him. So which lawns look good to you?"

"It's more complicated than it was for the Mississippi guy. There you were talking about a small power structure, probably four or five guys that ran the town. Robert, here, he's pissed off people all over the state that probably never even heard of each other. Even if you could bomb all of their lawns, where would it get you? You'd just be telling the guy who did it that you didn't really know which one he was."

"Yeah," said Lamar. "What's more, you'd be telling the cops exactly who threw the bombs."

That was true, too, although it hadn't occurred to me until he said it. Lamar definitely had more of a feel for this kind of thing than you'd expect from a chain saw sculptor.

"Without getting into exactly what your business is, Lamar, would you happen to know people in various parts of the state that might be able to give me a hand in this?"

"Robert has a rough idea what my business is. Tell him, Robert."

"I'd rather have you tell him, Lamar."

"I'm sort of a banker, agricultural loans. Bridge loans, what they'd call them on Wall Street. When a farmer is temporarily exposed and needs cash to tide him over. Like suppose he's sold his crop in advance but he needs money to get it in the ground, take care of it, get it harvested, like that."

"These would be cash loans? Pretty steep interest on them?"

"Well, it's sort of supply and demand. Certain places, Florida say, a guy like me would be competing for customers with the regular banks. Here I'm pretty much the man."

"Business has been good, you said?"

"Pretty good, yeah. As logging jobs go down the tubes you get a lot of interest in alternative crops on public lands."

"Public lands?"

It turned out, which I should have thought of, that the big advantage of public lands was that the government couldn't very well confiscate them if agents found your marijuana growing there. Same thing with land owned by the huge corporations. "You let the timber companies clear your fields for you, then you move in with your crews," Lamar said.

"On TV you see these foresters planting seedlings all over the place as soon as the bulldozers drive off," I said. "Wouldn't all these foresters cramp your style?"

"Tell him, Robert."

"The timber companies have to replant, it's true," Rack-leff said. "But it isn't much like the TV ads. From the corporation's point of view, if it's public land it doesn't even belong to the company. And if it's private land, the men running the company today will be long dead by the time the tract is ready for harvesting again. So they look at the bottom line and hire the cheapest replant crews they can get, which often means Mexican contract labor. The labor contractor has got a bottom line, too. It's in his interest to finish the job as quickly as he can. He's paid by how many seedlings he plants, not how many come up."

"Fuckers dig a half-ass hole and jam those seedlings down in it any way they can," Lamar said. "Makes what they call J-roots. Even if a J-root doesn't get washed out in the first rain, it won't grow."

"Doesn't the Forest Service or somebody come around and check it?"

"Never happen," Lamar said. "Practically never, any-way. Maybe right after, to see that the job was done. From then on, a clear-cut might as well be the Sahara desert. No good for nothing. Nobody ever goes there. Well, prac-tically nobody. Like I say, there might occasionally be some moonlight farming going on."

The farming could get pretty elaborate, as Lamar Pur-cell went on to explain it. The operators hired their own crews, who would move up to an isolated clear-cut and dig random holes among the stumps and slash, so no straight lines of plantings would show from the air. They might have to truck in good dirt to fill up the holes, and probably a generator to pump water up from a creek. As the plants grew, clipping crew chiefs would move in with men to kill all the males, so the plants would flower with-out being fertilized. And then came the harvest, and the drying, all of it labor intensive. Nobody had invented the marijuana gin yet.

"Most of these guys aren't the sort of guys that look ahead," Lamar said. "They make a big score, they're not too likely to set aside operating funds for next year's payroll. So next year they look around for someone like me to front them the money."

"These are the guys I could talk to?" I asked. "Guys in different areas of the state?"

"Well, not so much in the rimrock country in the eastern part of the state. Too dry."

"Aside from that, though. Would they be likely to know what's going on with the timber companies, industry groups, whoever the hell it might be that's after Robert?"

"Hey, these guys are born and raised in these small communities. They know everything. They're not considered like criminals. More or less it's like they're legitimate businessmen."

"You don't have any Bible Belt problems? With that antigay bullshit you had on the referendum out here, I got the impression this was Falwell country."

"Well, you got to understand the psychology. These small, dirt-poor communities, these are people that know they're being fucked. They're being fucked by the cops and the schools and by the lawyers and the doctors, the big chain stores, the papers, the TV. The government doesn't give a rat's ass for them. The Republicans and the Democrats just take turns ramming it to them.

"Now maybe these are just small people, but they're not stupid. They know they're not going to win. They know they got no friends. Who's on their side? Fucking Kiwanis Club? Fucking Better Business Bureau?

"Only their little church, that's all. That's the only place that gives a shit for them. That's the only club that will let a loser like them in the door. That's the only family they can find. Of course they got certain rules in this family, like maybe you can't drink or swear or play cards or go whoring around. If your kids want to read the dirty parts in *The Catcher in the Rye,* tough shit. The high school librarian inked out those words, and you got to wait till the bookmobile comes to town. If you opened a saloon in their town, these people would crawl all over your ass. If you sold pot outside the junior high, they'd probably lynch you.

"But they hate the goddamned government even worse, remember. Hate the cops, hate outside authority. These are Robin Hood guys, not sheriff guys. You can raise whatever you want in your backyard or theirs, as long as you ship it someplace else to sell. They'll even help you raise it, cover for you, tip you off on raids. Particularly if you spread the money around a little."

"Like you," Rackleff said.

"Well, yeah."

"What do you do?" I asked.

"Little things. I'm the main one that puts on Agnes Beach Days every year, a kind of like community festival. I buy uniforms for the teams, maybe build a ball field or something."

"Something like the emergency room," Rackleff said.

"Maybe a few pieces of equipment for the new emergency room, yeah. Behind the scenes, I'm never in the papers. But a little place like this, word gets out. Look, it's business, that's all. Same as investing in politicians, which I also do. You take your judges, your prosecutors, your sheriffs, they all need help when they run for office. Later on, if there's any slack at all, they'll cut it for you."

"And investing in college students?" Rackleff said.

"A couple of bright kids, their parents up against it,

they need help with the tuition? Hey, you got it, folks. Just don't say it's me. Tell the rich kid your Uncle Harry died. Shit, it's just PR."

"Like the support you give to Earth Everlasting in cash that nobody ever knows about? Lamar, the truth is you're a sixties idealist."

"Will you get off my fucking case, Robert? I'm a businessman."

THE PLANE PURCELL HAD IN MIND TURNED OUT
to be a Cessna twin that he had taken in
part payment of a debt from a grower
down in Winston, which evidently was
near someplace called Roseburg. The arrangement was
that the grower would give the plane directly to Earth
Everlasting, so he could get the tax write-off for a charita-
ble deduction. But it would have to be done discreetly,
so that nobody would know but the IRS. Apparently Winston was the kind of place where they ran a person out of
town on a rail if they thought he was soft on spotted owls.

Once they had settled how this could be done, Lamar
hollered for the woman in the other little office and asked
her to fire up some Red Zinger for us. Lamar and I had
lived through different sixties. While he was developing
a taste for herbal tea, I was working on green tea in the
soup kitchens of Vientiane. But in both places, the wom-
enfolk brewed and fetched the stuff with no questions
asked.

"Have you ever seen a clear-cut close up?" Rackleff
asked me.

"Not to actually walk through, no."

"It's the next best thing to seeing the devastation from the air," Rackleff said. "Are there any particularly good specimens nearby, Lamar?"

The one Purcell took us to was north and east of town, way up in the hills. For a while we were on blacktop, a secondary road that served a scattering of small houses and mobile homes. Then we were on a dirt road where there were no more houses, and then for a long time we were on a logging road only wide enough for one vehicle at a time. The road was old and had been overgrown, but now the saplings had been bent and broken by truck tires and bulldozer treads. The leaves on the flattened growth were still green. Around a bend we came suddenly on the clear-cut, so suddenly that I almost ran the pickup into a small yellow dozer. A twin to the yellow dozer sat at a dangerous-looking angle, halfway up a steep hillside. No one was around to watch the equipment.

"Some of those red hots in your outfit," Lamar said to Rackleff, "they'd take advantage of a situation like this."

"I hope not," Rackleff said.

"Man, they'd dump sand into the oil filter pipes in five minutes flat, and pretty soon those dozers would be scrap."

"I won't say they wouldn't do it. I won't even say I wouldn't sympathize with them. But if they were my people, they'd be doing it against orders."

"Have I been missing something, Robert? What I remember, you been known to spike a tree or two in your day."

"Not for more than three years. We had a three-day retreat and went all over the issue of ecotage. The end result was that we renounced all forms of violence, including tree spiking and disabling equipment."

"Oh, yeah? I never heard that."

"It was in the papers."

"Well, that's why, then. I don't see the papers much."

"It wasn't exactly headline news. We only make head-lines when there's confrontation. The papers don't give much space to a six-point nonviolence code adopted by a bunch of tree-huggers."

"How about those three guys I heard about in Estacada last year, they weren't your guys? They were framed? What?"

"They had worked with us in the past, but they burned those trucks on their own."

"I don't know, man. Two gypsy truckers, that was their life savings that got burned up there."

"I know it," Robert said. "I asked a man in Hollywood in the movie business, a producer who's been good to us, I asked him for the money to replace those trucks."

"Was that in the papers, too?"

"I wouldn't have told the papers, but the way it turned out, I didn't have anything to tell them anyway. We made the offer to the two truckers, and they turned us down."

"Dumb shits."

"That's how high feelings are running, on both sides."

"Gets tricky, doesn't it?" Lamar said. "You didn't burn their trucks but you offer to replace them so they can get back to hauling the timber you're trying to save. They tell you to go fuck yourself, so the timber gets saved anyway. Only not really. I guess somebody else just hauls it. But it's still pretty complicated."

"It's complicated, all right," said Rackleff. "It's easier for the Estacada three, or for Mr. Overholser at Dixie-Cascade. They just choose sides and stop thinking."

"I'm not even real sure which side I *am* on," Lamar said. "That stuff I carve into bears, it's a renewable resource all right. Only it renews pretty slow. So there I am outside my shop, whacking up logs that have been around at least since the Civil War, easy. And inside I do my real business, which it so happens is also a renewable resource. Result of which I can afford to do a little something now and then to help guys like you save the old growth. Which if you ever really did save it, I'd go broke. You can't grow pot in the shade."

"Grow anything out here, it looks like," I said, rooting around with the toe of one of my Red Wings. The loose soil on the hillside was a deep auburn, the color of tanbark but finer and richer looking.

"You'd think so, wouldn't you?" Lamar said. "But it's loose and there's no ground cover to hold it, and it's only a few inches deep. Once the crews slick off a hillside like this, the gullies start up. A season or two of rains and you won't be able to grow shit up here. All this topsoil will be in the Pacific."

We started up the hill, using the zigzag path the bulldozers had made. On both sides was a giant jackstraw tangle of logs and branches and roots. Plastic Day-Glo strips marked the boundaries of the cut. Beyond that the dark woods rose up immediately, without the usual fringe of underbrush that normally grows at the edge of forests. Among the four- or five-foot-tall stumps grew ferns and sorrel, shade plants that would probably die soon in the sun. Sap still ran from broken stems. Everything looked fresh, as if the cover had been stripped off it only moments before.

"These guys look like they just stepped away for a minute," I said. "They going to mind if they come back and find us?"

"As a rule they'd be pretty edgy if they saw strangers around their machines," Lamar said. "But whoever they are, I'll probably know them. And they'll certainly know me."

"Otherwise what would happen?"

"Otherwise, it could get pretty nasty. Particularly if they knew who Robert here really was. You got a big name around here, Robert, and basically it's mud."

"I'm used to it," Robert said. "Not happy about it, but used to it."

"So it's good that Tom's got you registered under another name. Something you should have been doing all along."

"I know, but I don't think I'll do it anymore."

I opened my mouth to say something, but decided it could wait till later. Lamar probably noticed, since he changed the subject immediately. Why should he get in the middle, between Rackleff and his nanny?

"You can see the whole process here," Lamar said. "Most of the slope they've skidded the logs off of. Up top there, the trees are still on the ground and they'll probably get to them later on today, or tomorrow. Not much left to do except haul the logs off, and that'll probably be the end of it.

"I know the cheap shit that owns all this out here, and he won't bother to put in seedlings. It'll just turn into what you might as well call an uninhabited desert, no good for nothing for nobody. Just briars and scrub, once the trees are skidded out of here. No more use to people than it is to the spotted owls."

Lamar Purcell had invited us to supper. His house was one of the ones on the hills back of town, and it only looked fancy by comparison to the bungalows and cottages down by the sea. Meanwhile we went back to the motel, partly because there was nothing else to do in

Agnes Beach and partly because Rackleff wanted to do his laundry. He traveled with two changes of clothes, and he washed one by hand each night. Next day he hung the spare set in the back of the van to finish drying.

I had meant to wait till he was done with his wash to tackle him about traveling under his own name, but the hell with it. I followed him into his room and I started in while he was running water into the tub.

"What did you mean back there, you don't think you'll do it anymore?"

"Do what?"

No reason he should remember, after all. I was the one who had been making a big deal of it in my mind, not him.

"Register under another name when we're on the road."

"Oh, I see. I just don't feel comfortable with it, that's all."

"What's the harm in it?"

Rackleff kneaded at his clothes for a minute, soapsuds coming out between his fingers.

"Have you ever read John Woolman's *Journal?*" he asked at last.

"No."

"He was a Quaker from New Jersey who traveled through the colonies in the 1700s, speaking against slavery."

"And he registered under his own name?"

"I'm getting around to it, Tom. Bear with me."

"Okay."

"Woolman never wore clothes that had been dyed, because he thought dye was a way to hide dirt. What he said was, 'Through giving way to hiding dirt in our garments a spirit which would conceal that which is disagreeable is strengthened.' "

A little late, I worked out the connection between Woolman and the light-colored clothes Rackleff always wore. "Is that why you have to do your laundry every day?" I asked. "Because it's undyed?"

"Sounds crazy, doesn't it?"

"Who am I to talk? I do four hundred sit-ups every other day. I'm stronger, you're cleaner. Probably we're both crazy."

"Probably we are."

"How does it all work out to registering under your name at motels, though?"

"Using another name is sort of like dyeing your clothes," Rackleff said. "At least that's the way it seems to me."

"You're concealing the dirt?" I said. "I don't follow you here, Robert."

"Not dirt, exactly. But what I do is disagreeable to a lot of people. To them it's dirt. I think they have a right to know it's there. Or I'm there, rather."

"I'm still not following you."

"I don't blame you. The analogy isn't exact. But I feel that if I choose to take positions that cause hostility, then I shouldn't try to escape the consequences by pretending to be someone else."

"Then if you don't mind me saying so, what the hell am I out here for?"

"I was frightened. I'm still frightened, but I don't think I ought to let myself give in to it."

"Jesus, Robert," I said, and after a moment a thought came to me. "Are you a Quaker like Woolman?" I asked. "Is this some kind of a Quaker thing?"

"I'm not a Quaker, but I admire them. I've been moving

our group closer to Quaker ethics. That's what I was talking to Lamar about, this nonviolent manifesto. Along with a number of other groups, we've adopted what we call a Peaceful Direct Action Code. Part four is pretty simple, pretty direct. It says, 'We will not run.' "

"You're not running. You're about to go to Carswell, Robert. Carswell is where a bunch of loggers beat one of your people to death. The dead guy's father lives there, and he's a mean son of a bitch who blames it all on you. Whatever you're doing, Robert, you're definitely not running."

What he was doing, in fact, was a bodyguard's worst nightmare. The truckers in Estacada had turned down the Hollywood producer's money, but the money was still there. Rackleff had learned that his dead informant had a younger brother about to graduate from high school, and he intended to offer to pay for the boy's college education.

"Let me handle it," Bill Belter had said when Rackleff brought up the idea during one of our strategy sessions in their kitchen. The kitchen was safely out of sight from the street, in case of another drive-by. "That's what lawyers are for. Neutral middlemen."

"Young Ben Schecter died because he helped me," Robert said. "This is something I have to do myself." I didn't know about Woolman and his undyed clothes at the time; I thought Rackleff wore natural-colored fabrics for some whole-earth reason. I didn't know yet that undyed cloth and living a monk's life out of the back of a van and carrying the whole world's responsibility on his own shoulders all made a curious kind of consistent sense to him. At the time I just thought he had a death wish, wanting to visit Carswell. The farthest he would give in to our arguments was to allow Bill Belter to set up the meeting with Louis Schecter in the office of the weekly newspaper

that his son, Ben, used to work for. With all sorts of people around, there shouldn't be much danger of violence
during the actual meeting.

Lamar Purcell inclined to the death wish theory, too,
when we told him at supper that we were heading out
for Carswell the following morning. "Robert, this is crazy
shit," he said. "You understand that, don't you?"

"I understand it. But I feel I owe that father the oppor-
tunity to meet me face-to-face."

"That father as good as killed his own son, Robert. I'm
sorry, but it's bullshit that there's some good in everybody. A man like that is solid prick, wall-to-wall."

"Even so," Rackleff said, and that was that.

Leaving Agnes Beach the next day we played our hopscotch game till I was convinced nobody was behind us.
From then on Rackleff led the way, with me hanging just
far enough behind to keep him in sight.

I wasn't worried about the meeting with Louis Schecter
in the newspaper office. What worried me was that we
were meeting the following morning in a private home
with a couple of local greenies from the community college who were still funneling information secretly to Earth
Everlasting. That meant we would be spending the night.

About an hour's drive out of Carswell Rackleff stopped
for gas, and I pulled in behind him.

"Robert, I've been thinking," I said as he filled up.
"This Schecter knows you're going to show up at the
newspaper office at four o'clock, and he knows you're
going to leave there sometime. So it's easy to find out
what vehicle you're driving, and where you're staying the
night. So why don't we ask this Milford guy if you can
spend the night with him?"

Ernest Milford was the publisher of the *Carswell Free*

Enterpriser. I didn't figure anybody was likely to invade the home of one of the town fathers.

"I can't expose him to that," Rackleff said. "Look what happened to the Belters' house."

"Well, will you at least let me register you under another name, then?" I said. "Just this once? That way we can drive out of town till we're sure nobody's behind us, then sneak back in and spend the night in peace."

I knew *sneak* was the wrong word as soon as it was out of my mouth.

"I don't mind the driving part," Rackleff said. "But I haven't changed my mind about the other business. I won't sneak around under another name."

I didn't bother to argue. If he had decided that the ethical thing to do was to walk around with a target on his back, my chance of changing his mind with the logic and consistency of my arguments was zero. Under the circumstances it didn't matter much, though, since my own ethical code had a lot more give to it. I had figured out a way for both Robert and me to have clear consciences.

The *Carswell Free Enterpriser* had the type of board-and-batten facing above the ground-floor windows that a lot of shops in the West have. It looked like one of the windowless false fronts on a western movie set, but in fact there was a real second story behind it. The name of the paper was spelled out in letters made of alder branches that were nailed to the false front. There were small display windows on either side of the front door, but the only things displayed were old front pages of historic issues of the *Enterpriser*. FIRE RAZES LUMBERYARD. CARSWELL CENTENNIAL SET. COUGARS COP SECOND IN STATE IN CLASS C FINALS. That sort of thing. The clippings were pasted onto colored construction paper, which was pasted onto cardboard. The corners were coming unglued.

Inside was a knee-high railing separating the public area from the desk, where a woman in her sixties sat. Before she could ask what we wanted, a frosted glass door behind her opened and a bald man with rimless glasses came out.

"Ernie Milford," he said. "I'm the cook and chief bottle washer around this place. Come on in, come on in."

The furniture was blond oak that had probably been new back in the 1920s, and hadn't been polished or refinished since. A big desk, a big revolving chair for the boss, a couple of nonrevolving chairs with arms for important guests, three more without arms for the enlisted troops, and a good-size table. All of it creating what a lot of radio announcers call a suit of office furniture. Louis Schecter wasn't due for a while. The publisher had wanted to talk with us privately beforehand.

"Sit yourself down, Mr. Rackleff," Milford said. "And Mr.—?"

"Tom," Rackleff said. "He's an associate of mine."

"Well, I hope you fellows understand that there isn't much likely to come of all this. Lou Schecter isn't much of what you'd call an open-minded fellow, and he feels real strong about what happened to his son."

"What was Ben Schecter like?" Robert asked. "I talked to him on the phone a good many times but I never met him."

"Had the makings of a fine newspaperman, but he needed seasoning."

"What kind of seasoning?" I asked, curious. As far as I knew, the kid had come up with the biggest story in Carswell since the Cougars lost the Class C finals. And this guy Milford, this seasoned newsman, had spiked it.

"Small town newspapers are different," Milford said. "Our job isn't to tear down the community, it's to build it up. In a small town, a big headline isn't everything. Give you an example. In Eugene or Portland, someplace like that, I'd put you two fellows right on my front page next week."

"What for?"

"Just for being here. Like when Nasser went to Israel, just him being there was big news."

"Like David going to the lion's den, huh?" I said.

"Exactly. Mr. Rackleff here, he's not too popular in Carswell County. I'd put your proposal to Lou Schecter in the paper, too, but I'm not going to do it. Tell you why. Because I think this money you're talking about for a scholarship. . . . How much is it, incidentally?"

"We have twenty-three thousand dollars that a donor gave for another purpose, but he's willing to shift it over to this," Rackleff said.

"Well, I don't believe Lou Schecter would take a nickel from Earth Everlasting if he was starving, that's how stiff-necked he is. So that's the story I'd put in the paper, that the famous Robert Rackleff offered a grieving man blood money for his dead son. . . ."

Robert opened his mouth but didn't say anything, maybe because he couldn't come up with the right words for the job.

"That would be my big headline," Milford said, "and it might sell a few papers or get me an award or something, but I'm not going to run it, and I'm going to tell you boys why not."

Because it's vicious, stupid, lying bullshit, I managed to avoid saying.

"I'm going to treat this visit like it never happened and I'm going to tell Lou Schecter to do the same, and he'll listen to me because he knows I know what's best for our little community here."

"Which is what?" I asked.

"Which is a defense fund for Joey Finder and Mike Souda."

"Who are they?"

"They're the two men charged with arson on the basis of the evidence Ben Schecter turned over to us," Rackleff told me. "They were hired by Cold Creek Forest Products."

"Allegedly hired," Milford said.

"Let Cold Creek defend the guys, then," I said. "Probably they can afford it."

"Oh, they can afford it, all right," Rackleff said. "Cold Creek is controlled by Dixie-Cascade."

"Your old buddy from the JFK School debate, huh?"

"That's right. Hap Overholser."

"Mr. Overholser has done a lot for this little community," Milford said. "Well, what about it? Those two boys could use a first-class defense team."

"Is this a joke, Milford?" I asked.

"No joke."

A knock came on the door, and the woman from the outside office stuck her head in. "Mr. Schecter is here," she said.

Schecter was the kind of round man who looks no particular age except grown up. The fat plumped out any wrinkles there might have been in his face, so that he could have been forty or fifty or even sixty. He held a billed cap in his hand. It had left the bald spot on his head dead white. What you could see of the rest of him was reddened from the weather.

"Sit down, Lou," Milford said.

"I ain't sitting down with that son of a bitch," he said,

looking at Rackleff. "I wouldn't even be here if it wasn't for you, Mr. Milford."

"Well, you are here, Lou. So at least listen to what the man's got to say."

"I'll listen, but I ain't sitting with the man that killed my boy."

"A lot of things came together to kill your boy, Mr. Schecter," Rackleff said. "I won't deny that I was inadvertently one of them. That's why I'm here."

Schecter looked like he had a thing or two to say about that, but Ernie Milford had told him to listen. It was plain that Milford outranked him, and by a good deal.

So the round man shut up while Robert Rackleff made his offer to send the younger Schecter son, Bert, through college.

"You can take your blood money and stuff it," Lou Schecter said at the end.

"Nobody needs to know where the scholarship came from, if that's what's bothering you," Rackleff said.

"Going to college is what ruined my other boy," Schecter said. "A lot of professors filled his head full of foreign bullshit, made him forget where he come from."

"Foreign?" Rackleff asked. "At Oregon State?"

"There's still some of us in this country that knows what it means to be an American. There's people ready to fight for the Christian white man, and more of them than you think. Even right here in Carswell."

"Skinheads, huh?" I asked.

"I said enough. I ain't saying no more."

I looked at the publisher. "The Brotherbund been active locally?"

"We don't need any more outside agitators here," Milford said. "Lou's just talking."

I would have asked Lou about it but there was no use, now that Milford had shut him down.

"What about a general scholarship open to any deserving local kid?" Rackleff asked. "It could be named after your boy."

"He stopped being my boy the day he started squealing to you tree-hugging sons of bitches."

"No need for that language," Milford said.

"You do the talking, then, Mr. Milford. Tell them what we decided they can do with their money."

"I already told them."

"We?" Rackleff said. "You're in favor of this defense fund, too, Mr. Schecter? You'd rather use the money to defend hired arsonists than to send people to college?"

"We don't know they're arsonists," the publisher said. "They've been charged, that's all."

"We don't even know it was arson," Schecter added.

"How about it, then?" the publisher asked. "There's already a small legal fund set up for those two boys. All you got to do is add your twenty-three thousand to it. You want me to just write it up as an anonymous gift? Up to you. If I was in your place, I'd take credit for it. Be a nice gesture. Show you're sorry for the trouble you caused."

"I have to say I'm confused, Mr. Milford," Rackleff said. "Did you seriously expect that I would go along with this?"

"I thought I'd give you the chance, anyway. Lou here, he's enough of a Christian to want to hold out a hand to a couple of poor sinners. I thought you might have been that good of a Christian, too."

Ernest Milford was trying not to smile but not making a very good job of it. Probably couldn't wait to tell the boys at the barbershop about this one.

"I guess there's nothing we can do here, then," Rackleff said. "I feel sorry for you, Mr. Schecter. I feel even more sorry for you, Mr. Milford."

"Don't feel sorry for me," Milford said. "I got a real good headline out of our meeting."

We were getting up to go when something caught my eye. I pointed to an ad on the back page of a copy of the *Free Enterpriser* that was lying on the table. "Cold Creek Forest Products a regular advertiser?" I asked.

"Quarter-page ad every week," Milford said.

"Carswell must be a pretty big market for them. Sell a lot of logs here, do they?"

"Nope, they don't sell anything here," Milford said. "It's what they call institutional advertising. Just building up goodwill in the community."

"So it comes to a little more than ten thousand a year," I said to Rackleff. We had walked back to our vehicles, which were parked around the corner from the *Free Enterpriser* office. And then we had walked past them, and then we had stopped to wait for a while to see if anybody followed us around the corner.

"Something like that," Rackleff said. He had been calculating the yearly cost of a quarter-page ad from the rate card I had picked up from the lady in the outer office. "There are all different kinds of rates, depending on frequency and what page it's on and so forth. Kind of hard to figure out."

"Close enough to figure out why Milford killed Ben Schecter's stories about Cold Creek burning down the woods."

"All the big companies buy local support in ways like that," Rackleff said. "Particularly Dixie-Cascade, which of course owns Cold Creek. Hap Overholser is notoriously generous with the local media and politicians."

"Hey, it's his right as an American," I said. "Hope explained it to me once. The Supreme Court says the more money you've got, the more free speech you can buy."

9 7

I glanced up and down the street. Since nobody seemed to be paying any particular attention to us, we got into our vehicles and I led the way to one of the motels on the outskirts of town.

"Your picture's been in *People* magazine, just like Lamar said," I said when Rackleff opened the door of his van to get out. "Park around back and let me register for the both of us."

He hesitated, and so I said, "Don't worry, I'll give them your right name. I'll tell them R. Rackleff, is that all right? Just the initial? Will you give me that much?"

"Okay," he said, and smiled.

So I got us two rooms, one for R. Rackleff on the side of the building facing the road, the other for Bartley T. Berger on the other side. Back outside, I gave Berger's key to Rackleff and kept his for myself.

Of course this meant that anybody who got Rackleff's room number out of the guy on the desk would come busting into my room instead. But that was the plan, to the extent that I had one.

Robert and I went out to a fast-food place for supper, and went to our separate rooms afterward. Presumably he stayed in his, but I grabbed a couple of pillows from mine and took them out to the pickup to make myself more or less comfortable. From there I had a view of any cars coming in, as well as a view of the door of the room registered to Robert. It seemed like a good time and a good place to stay awake all night.

Carswell was pretty much a company town, and Hap Overholser turned out to control the company. Overholser was smart, rich, and mean. Lou Schecter was stupid and mean. Ernest Milford was shrewd and probably even meaner. Somewhere out there, free on bail, were the two

loggers who would blame Rackleff for getting them
charged with arson. Somewhere, too, were the men who
had beat Lou Schecter's son to death. Schecter seemed to
have been telling us that there were skinheads around,
too.

The only good news was that Rackleff had, sure
enough, been in *People*. It was one thing to beat a young
and unknown reporter to death after a dance. It was another to kill a national figure. A person could go to jail
for that.

Still I watched.

A car came in now and then, stopping at the office to
check in and then driving on down the line to park. Mo-
torists unloaded and moved in. Lights went on behind
the heavy plastic drapes. After a while, lights started to
go off, one by one. By twelve-thirty most of the windows
were dark. I walked to the rear of the building and saw
that Rackleff's window was dark, too. I walked back to
the pickup. To stay awake, I tried to think through various scenarios. If anybody knocked on the door of what
was supposed to be Robert's room, I'd slip around back
to his real room, load him and his stuff into his van, and
send him on his way. I'd follow him and meet him later
at some prearranged place down the line. On the other
hand, maybe if they waited outside, I'd . . . or if they broke
into the room and found it empty, maybe I could . . .

When at last it happened, at least it started out in one
of the ways I had foreseen. The time was quarter past
one, and the light inside the office had gone off. Two cars
turned in and stopped near the office. A man got out of
one of them and rang the bell. The desk clerk must have
been in his little back room, waiting, because after only a
moment the door opened a crack so the man inside the
darkened office could hand something to the man outside.

The door closed again. Neither one had said anything. The man got back in the car, drove without hesitation to my room, and backed in so that he was facing out. The other car, following behind, did the same thing.

I didn't like the business about facing out, presumably for a quick getaway. I liked it even less when a man got out of the second car and unlocked its trunk. He left the lid cracked open and went over to the first man, and another man who had been in the first car. So there were three altogether.

They went to the door of the room, and one of them stood on either side of it while the man with the key unlocked the door to the darkened room. He pushed the door slowly while the man on his right stood ready with a pair of small bolt-cutters, in case the chain was fastened. When the man opening the door met with no resistance, he swung it wide open and switched on the light. The three men stood in the doorway looking at the empty beds, with the pillows missing from one of them. Then they went inside and the door closed behind them.

The minute the way was clear I ran to warn Rackleff. The quickest route was through the passageway near the front office that led through the building to the rear. I had just made it around the corner and out of sight when I heard a door open and shut, and then footsteps hurrying my way. For an instant I thought one of the attackers was after me, but then I realized he couldn't have seen me. The others must have sent him to the office to find out what the hell was wrong, and get the right key if necessary.

I couldn't let him get to the clerk, so I stepped out of the corridor, practically right into his face.

"Hey, buddy," I said. "Got a match?"

Actually, I just started to say it, to give him something

to think about while I moved in. But he was too alarmed to think. He jumped back instinctively and I missed my grab.

He said something, not a word but just a sound that my sudden appearance had startled out of him. Then he raised the hand he was holding the bolt cutter in, and I knew I had him. There are dozens of different ways to deal with a weapon coming down at you, and every one of them was as automatic to me as scooping up a grounder is to a veteran shortstop. The only question was how badly I wanted to hurt the guy. The answer was badly, since he had two friends somewhere around. I broke his arm.

We both heard it snap. We both looked down at the way it hung crooked, and at the bolt cutter where it had fallen to the ground. "Jesus, you broke my arm," he said.

"You still got one to go," I said. I picked up the bolt cutter.

"What's the matter with you? You crazy?"

"Shut the fuck up and listen. You say anything louder than a whisper from now on and I bust your left arm, too. You follow me?"

He nodded.

"That's good. Shut up and keep nodding." I was patting his pockets as I talked, but all I found was a jackknife. I took it.

"Your two buddies got any guns?" I asked.

He shook his head.

I went behind him with the bolt cutters. They aren't made to cut at an angle, the way scissors do. The two blades come together parallel, like elevator doors closing. I closed them on his right ear, front to back, not quite tight enough to break the skin but too tight to pull away.

"Let's try that last question again, because if it turns out you're bullshitting me, you lose the ear. They got guns?"

This time he didn't shake his head. He couldn't, without tearing his ear.

"Blackjack," he whispered.

That was good. If he told me about the blackjack, it was likely he had been telling the truth about the guns.

"They've got blackjacks?"

"I don't know for sure. I know Harry carries one."

"Which one is Harry?"

"The small guy."

"What's your name?"

"Art."

"Art, we're going back to the room. If everything goes the way I say, I won't have to hurt anybody any more. So do your best to convince your friends. Do real good, Art. Or your ear comes off."

I could tell from the way he moved, like an old man, that the pain from his arm was kicking in. But we made it to the room, and he knocked with his good hand and told them to open up.

When they did, I just stood there behind Art for a minute letting the two men take it in. The angle in Art's arm between the shoulder and the elbow, the bolt cutters about to bite his ear off.

"He's crazy," Art said.

"Tell them to move back," I said.

"Do it," Art said. "Please do it. Jesus, guys."

They did it. I maneuvered Art around a little, and had him put the chain in the door. If anybody decided to make a dash for it, I wanted to slow him down.

"Toss your blackjack over here, Harry," I said to the smaller of the two men.

"I don't have it."

"Show me, then. Take your pants off and swing them against the wall."

"Wait a fucking minute . . ."

I tightened the handles on the bolt cutters a tiny fraction of an inch, and Art cried out with pain. "Jesus, Harry, *please!*"

"You fucking pussy," Harry said to Art. I was sorry it wasn't Harry's ear instead. But he took a leather-covered sap out of his hip pocket and tossed it over by me. I kicked it under one of the beds, out of easy reach.

"Okay, Harry, now get into that bed. Crawl in careful so it doesn't come unmade, and put your hands under the covers, down by your sides."

"Like shit I will."

"Harry," I said, "I'm going to explain just one time why I want you in that bed. Then if you don't get in, Art here, I'm taking his ear off. Next comes you."

Harry stood waiting, looking tough to make up for not really being tough.

"Okay, now pay attention. I want you in that bed because there's two of you guys against one. Once you get in that bed, it'll take you a few seconds to get yourself out. And that's all the time I need to let go of Art's ear and take care of your big buddy here."

The big buddy seemed to puff up even bigger, like a frog. "Do like he says, Harry," he said. "Soon as fuckface lets loose of Art's ear, we'll see who takes care of who."

So Harry got into the bed the way I told him, grinning and making a production of it.

"All tucked in tight?" I said, once he was. I tossed the bolt cutters under the bed where the blackjack was, and moved clear of Art.

The big guy came running at me with his hands open to grab me, which might have meant he was a wrestler.

But more likely it just meant he was a head-butter who wanted to yank me toward him, and then smash my face in with his forehead. I took his right hand and used all that momentum to power a hip throw.

When a taller man is coming at you fast and off balance, and doesn't have a clue, a hip throw can be a pretty impressive thing. He went arcing through the air, and his back hit the sharp edge of one of those long pieces of furniture that double as bureau and desk in motel rooms. It could have broken his back easily enough, but he took the hit a few inches to one side of the spine, just at the belt line. If he didn't have a problem with his lower back already, he could count on one for the rest of his life.

He wound up on the floor on all fours, making a bellowing sound from the pain. He wasn't going anywhere. Neither was Harry, who had started to get out of bed but changed his mind.

Probably I could have convinced him to tell me who had sent them, but the immediate problem was to get Rackleff as far away from Carswell as fast as I could. So I cut lengths of cord from the drapes, and tied Harry's elbows together behind him. Then I did the same to the big guy, who was in too much pain to put up any resistance.

I looked over the room's possibilities, and settled on the shower stall. I got them both into the bathroom, Harry easily, and the big guy by putting a thumb hold on him, and there I rigged them both to the shower pipe with cord nooses around their necks. They'd be all right as long as they stayed upright.

"I can't stand up," the big guy said. "My back's all fucked."

"You'll find a way."

"Christ, buddy, give me a break."

"You got your break already. I didn't beat you to death the way you would have done to Rackleff. Hold still, asshole."

I was going through his pockets to check his ID. Then I did the same with the other two guys, keeping all three driver's licenses just so they'd have to go through the hassle of getting new ones.

The guy with the broken arm, Art, was the only one of the three who showed the slightest promise as a human being. So I made him as comfortable as I could on one of the beds, running cords from each of his ankles to the corresponding leg at the bottom of the bed, and a third cord from his good hand to the headboard. I left his broken arm free, since the hand on it was useless for untying knots or much of anything else.

From my stakeout, I knew that the rooms on either side were empty—probably by arrangement with the desk clerk or owner, whichever he was. Just in case, though, I turned the TV on loud to cover up any noise. Then I went in and turned the shower on, warm so that the two guys inside wouldn't get chilled down into hypothermia. The water would keep the knots too wet to untie, even if they managed to get their hands up that high. And nobody would be likely to hear them shouting, with the water running. If I was lucky, they'd stay put till the maid found them next morning.

The last thing I did before leaving was go around the room with a damp washcloth, wiping down everything I could remember touching.

"Who sent them?" Robert Rackleff asked once he had let me in, and come awake enough to grasp what I was telling him.

"I got their names and maybe we can find out later," I

said. "Right now it doesn't matter. Only thing that matters is to get ourselves out of this county before somebody can drag us back. You take the pickup, because nobody associates you with it, and head straight for Portland. Don't stop for anything but gas."

"But that puts you at increased risk," he said.

"Robert, will you for Christ's sake listen to me this time? There's things you know how to do and things I know how to do. For now just do it, and we'll argue the ethics later."

"It just seems to me—"

"Just listen, okay." I told him my plan while he was gathering his stuff from the room. "Is that it?" I said when I was done. "You got everything now?"

"I think so."

"We're out of here, then. Don't slam the door getting in the pickup. Keep the lights out till you're clear of the parking lot. Don't look for me behind you. When you get to Portland, just sit there in that Kmart lot till I find you. It might be a long time. Now beat it."

The way the motel was laid out, there was a good chance that the man in the office wouldn't notice a pickup leaving from the rear parking lot with its lights out. I watched till Robert was out of sight, and then I ran for his van. As soon as I was around the first bend in the road, I switched on the headlights and headed for Portland myself.

Once I finally got to the Kmart where we had arranged to meet, I found the old green Ford pickup without too much trouble. Rackleff was sleeping in the cab, his head on the pillows from the motel. He came awake when I knocked on the window, and opened the door.

"Been waiting long?" I said.

He looked at his watch. "A little more than three hours."

"I tried to bypass towns the best I could," I said, "and I got lost a couple times. Wasted motion, probably. I don't think anybody followed me."

"Nobody followed me, either," he said. "I used one of your tricks. I turned into a little country lane and waited till ten cars passed. Then I got back on the main road."

"Let's find someplace for breakfast," I said. "Someplace with a pay phone. We've got some calls to make. And we've got to talk."

We found a fast-food place in the next block down, and after we ate we phoned the environmentalists from the community college in Carswell. Our meeting with them had been scheduled for an hour ago, and they were getting worried.

Rackleff filled them in, and then turned the phone over to me. I gave them the names of the three men at the motel, and they knew all three.

Eugene Drayton, the big man with a lower back problem, was a logger who had been laid off two years ago. Nobody could prove anything, but he had been at the dance the night Ben Schecter was beaten to death. The talk was that he had left the hall about the same time the young reporter did.

Harry Carlton, the nasty little punk with the blackjack, had some kind of a minor office job at a lumberyard in Carswell. One of the community college instructors had heard from one of his students that Harry was involved somehow with skinheads. The guy whose arm I broke was Art Sappington, an unemployed millworker. He was related somehow—nephew, cousin, something like that— to one of the two Cold Creek arsonists.

"So we still don't know who sent them?" Robert asked after I had got all I could out of the instructors.

"Maybe nobody," I said. "Maybe Milford and old man Schecter just let it drop here and there that you were in town. We've got to talk about that, Robert. Why you were in town."

"You know. You were in on all the arrangements."

"You didn't need to be there. You could have done it all by phone. Registering under your name is the same kind of thing. You're asking for it, Robert. Why are you asking for it? Do you want it?"

"To be killed, you mean? To become a martyr?"

"You keep going where the lions are."

"I don't think I want to become a martyr. Certainly I'm far from being a saint."

"Maybe, maybe not, what do I know? The only theory I've got about saints is that if a guy thinks he's one, he isn't."

"Probably a good theory."

"Robert, I'm asking these things because I have to know if what I'm supposed to be doing here is even possible. I don't know what it meant when somebody took those shots at the Belters' house, and don't know what those letters meant, either. But I believe those men in Carswell meant to kill you, even if I don't know why. If you don't care very much whether you get killed or not, then I'm not going to be much use to you."

"I care a great deal."

"How much do you care? Enough to quit Earth Everlasting? Enough to lay off this business of bringing criminal charges against everybody in sight?"

"Not that much, no. I had a history professor once who used to say that major social change only comes about when enough people get to the point where they'd rather die than."

"Than what?"

"Than pay taxes to King George. Than sit in the back of the bus. Whatever."

"There's a difference between sitting in the front of the bus and going to Carswell. Going to Carswell wasn't for Earth Everlasting or for the spotted owl or the blue marble. It was for you. You see what I mean? It was for some weird Don Quixote thing."

"I see. I even agree. I was thinking along the same lines driving up here last night."

"No more windmills, then?"

"No more windmills. I'll even use phony names at motels."

"Good. Then maybe we can keep you alive until we find a real enemy knight to joust at."

That night we took the small chance of staying with the Belters again. They needed to get Rackleff ready for a court appearance the following morning. I needed something from the Belters, too. They had promised me a list of all the allegations of criminal activity that Earth Everlasting had turned over to the U.S. attorney, along with the names and addresses of everyone implicated. Any one of them might be the person who was after Rackleff, the real enemy knight.

After dinner the others plotted courtroom strategy while I sat by and listened. The hearing involved allegations that employees of the Dixie-Cascade Corporation had unlawfully altered the brands on raw logs rustled from federal lands. Rackleff was to testify as to how he had come into possession of a certain videotape purporting to show the alteration of said brands by agents of the said corporation.

"Overholser's lawyers are going to claim nothing illegal happened," Bill Belter said. "And besides, the guys that were doing it were somewhere else that day."

"But our people got the whole thing on videotape," Rackleff said. "Why else would Overholser's men be sawing off the ends of logs except to get rid of the old brands and put on new ones?"

"Your people got a video with somebody on it doing something somewhere. Sometime."

"They're going to argue that the tape is a fake?"

"I would. Revenge-seeking former employee hires other malcontents to stage the whole scene. Tree-hugging pinko from the East falls for it, or maybe even hired the malcontents to do it . . ."

"They're not malcontents. They're still with the company and their faces are on the tapes."

"Somebody's faces. The quality of the tape isn't too high. Dixie-Cascade is going to trot out practically the whole evening shift at the mill to swear that the guys on the tape never left the floor that night."

"The company's lawyers would let that happen, knowing it was false?"

"Believe it."

"What about ethics?"

"Our ethics professor used to pose some dilemma or other and ask us what we would do in those circumstances if we could be absolutely sure we'd never get caught," Bill Belter said.

"And to get caught suborning perjury," JoEllyn Belter said, "you have to be a lot dumber than most lawyers think they are."

"Are you saying they could get away with this scot-

free, when we have them videotaped in the act?" Rackleff asked.

"Maybe scot-free in the short run," Bill Belter said, "in
the sense that there might not be enough to convict them
before a friendly jury. But that might not be the end of
it, now that we've got a new administration, new people
at Agriculture and Interior. Even if we lose in court, there
are follow-up things that an aggressive prosecutor could
pursue."

"Let's assume the jury doesn't believe the tape," JoEllyn
said. "It happened in Simi Valley, but that wasn't the end
of it, was it?" The Belters worked like a tag team, one
taking over from the other.

"Well, that won't be the end of it, here," her husband
said. "Not with a guy like Fred Garber as U.S. attorney.
His people know perfectly well that tape is genuine, and
they'll be mad they lost. Then what ideas can we kind of
help them along with, to continue to pursue the case?"

"For one thing," JoEllyn said, "the timber had to have
been stolen from government lands, which is theft. For
another thing, it's illegal to export raw logs from federal
lands anyway, even if you haven't stolen them—"

"The point is," Bill Belter cut in, "that none of this stuff
JoEllyn's talking about, none of these things happens totally inside the company, where they can control it. Somebody outside the company bought those logs for export,
somebody in the Forest Service probably knew they were
being cut on public lands. If we keep pulling at the string,
other things will come loose. And pretty soon Dixie-
Cascade could find itself barred from cutting on public
lands . . ."

". . . And then Overholser is really screwed," JoEllyn
picked up. "He's already cashed out most of the trees on
company land, to pay the interest on the junk bonds he

loaded the corporation down with. If he's barred from the cheap timber on federal lands, he stands a pretty good chance of losing the company."

"Pretty near time for the news," I broke in. Bill Belter went to turn it on. The Portland paper hadn't run anything about our trouble in Carswell so far, maybe because of deadline problems. But there would have been plenty of time for the TV news departments to hear about it.

They hadn't, though. "Maybe they didn't think it was newsworthy," Rackleff said once the news was over. "It would just look like an attempted burglary in a small town."

"The motel clerk knew about it," I said. "The three guys themselves knew about it, the emergency room knew about it, some hotel maid probably knew about it, Ernie Milford's reporters must have picked it up, the cops have to know. And most of them also know that the whole thing happened in a room registered in the name of a nationally known environmentalist who's already been shot at once. If the papers and the TV stations still think this is just a second-rate burglary, there's been a whole lot of damage control going on down in Carswell. In fact, my guess is that there's no official report at all, and so there won't even be a break-in to explain. Couple guys out drinking, got to fighting. One of them breaks his arm, the other hurts his back. When they sober up they're buddies again. No charges. Nothing happened at all."

"You could bring charges," Bill Belter said.

"Where would it get us?" I asked. "The cops wouldn't cooperate, everybody would lie, the prosecutor would do the absolute minimum. We'd just spend a lot of time and money, and everybody would walk in the end, anyway."

Besides which, I didn't want to be in *People.*

*   *   *

The hearing was set for ten the next morning. In what had now become our usual pattern, I hung back behind Rackleff in my anonymous pickup.

Rackleff found the last parking place near the U.S. courthouse, which seemed to be located in the very center of the local power structure. We had just passed the Portland *Oregonian* building and were coming up on the University Club. As Rackleff backed his van into a metered space in front of the club, I kept going and found an underground garage around the block for my pickup. Rackleff had gone inside by the time I walked back to the courthouse.

Inside the entrance was a metal detector with a couple of building guards to run the operation, although it was hard to see why it should be a two-man job. The machine beeped as I went through, which surprised me, since I had put my key ring in the guard's basket. When I checked my pockets, I found the jackknife I had taken from Art after breaking his arm back at the motel. It had turned out to be a Robeson, a nice little knife. I put it in the basket along with my keys, and this time the machine passed me. The guard gave me back my keys but kept the knife for me to pick up on my way back out.

I found Rackleff sitting with JoEllyn Belter outside the courtroom the guard had directed me to. As planned, they took no notice of me. I would be more useful watching over Rackleff from a discreet distance than sticking tight to him like a Mafia bodyguard. I went on inside the courtroom and checked over the fifteen or twenty people scattered around the yellow oak benches. One of them was a young woman with a notebook in her lap, probably a reporter from the paper a couple of blocks away. But she wasn't the expert on courts that I was looking for.

Instead I slid behind an old man with a long, seamed

neck sticking out of a collar too big for him. He was sitting alone. "Anything interesting on?" I asked him.

Without turning, he said, "Just a bunch of tree-huggers on a preliminary injunction hearing. But at least it's an evidentiary hearing instead of just pure legal bullshit."

This was the expert I was looking for, an old retired guy who hung around the courts all day long. I did a lot of that myself, back in Cambridge. It's the best show in any town, and it's free.

"What kind of relief they seeking?" I asked.

"This damned Rackleff fellow wants Dixie-Cascade to stop cutting in the Garton's Mountain area. Says they've been rustling logs off federal land. Old Will Bullock gonna cut him a new asshole before this is over."

"He's a tough judge, huh?"

"He's from timber country like me, old Will is. Forty-two years I spent in the woods." By now the guy had turned around.

"You sure don't look it," I lied.

"Oh, I'm older than I look," he said. "How old would you say I was?"

"I don't know. Sixty, right around there?"

"Seventy-seven next month." He stuck his hand over the back of the bench for me to shake. "Luther Bidwell," he said.

"Tom," I said, shaking. "Pleased to meet you."

While we waited for the judge, Luther filled me in on the personal histories of the marshal, the judge's clerk, the assistant U.S. attorney assigned to this case, the new U.S. attorney, who was a damned tree-hugger, too, and Bill and JoEllyn Belter, another couple of damned forest fairies. The Belters were Jews from New York City, and so was Rackleff. Luther agreed with me that they didn't look

Jewish, but you couldn't tell by that anymore. Not with plastic surgery.

In this kind of pretrial hearing, as courtroom loafers like Luther and I both knew, the plaintiff's job is to show that he's likely to win at the eventual trial. This made it into a sort of preview of both sides' cases, and it went about the way the Belters had predicted.

Robert Rackleff talked about the tape, and what it had showed. Dixie-Cascade's lawyers—five of them—argued that the tape could have been doctored, the faces weren't clear, the alleged culprits were elsewhere at the time, written company policy prescribed severe penalties for altering brands, disgruntled former employees with criminal records, and so on.

Luther had been right about Judge Bullock. He overrode most of the Belters' objections almost instantly and upheld most of the objections from the company's lawyers. He hurried things along, obviously anxious to get this nonsense wrapped up by lunchtime.

"This court is now adjourned," he said at last. "Will counsel for both sides please approach the bench."

Luther half-turned toward me and showed me his watch. "Twelve-thirty right on the button," he whispered. "Old Will Bullock runs the tightest court in Portland. They reserve him the same table at Taylor's Steak House every day, and he's never more than a minute or two late."

Most of the spectators began moving for the doors while the lawyers huddled, although Rackleff stayed behind. I waited outside on a bench in the hall, till he came out a few minutes later with the Belters. "We won't have his decision till tomorrow," Bill Belter said to me.

"We're all through here, though?"

"Robert is. JoEllyn and I are going to look through some files in the clerk's office, since we're right nearby."

Robert had a meeting in northwest Portland at two, and the plan was for me to follow him out there so we could have lunch beforehand.

I let Rackleff go ahead, and I dropped farther behind when the guard couldn't find the pocketknife he had confiscated from me on the way in. He couldn't find it because the other guard had put it in his basket.

By the time I got outside the courthouse, I saw Robert climbing into his van. He was going to wait for me as usual. When I pulled up, he would take the lead while I watched the rear. I turned away toward the parking garage.

I only got a few yards when the blast came.

AT FIRST THERE WERE LITTLE CLINKING AND
rattling sounds as debris fell down on cars
and pavement. Then there was silence, except for traffic noises. For a few seconds
everybody on the sidewalk was as stunned and motionless as I was. Smoke was coming from the shattered
windows of Rackleff's van, although no flames were visible. The walls were bulged out. The door on the driver's
side was open, so I could see Rackleff behind the wheel.
At last my brain dropped into gear and I ran to help him.

Black, greasy smoke filled the cab. Fire could break out
any moment, and secondary explosions would be next. I
threw Rackleff's limp left arm around my shoulder,
grabbed his left hand in my right one, and hauled him
out into the street. My only thought was to put something
large between us and the burning van, and I headed for
a Chevy Suburban parked a couple of cars back. I got
him behind the Suburban and kneeled to lower him to
the ground.

Then I saw.

His right leg was gone from above the knee. His left
leg was still attached, but hanging from midthigh like the

loose end of a flail. All that held it were a few rags of red muscle and a glistening white tendon. A trail of blood led from the truck to us. More blood pulsed with every heartbeat from the stump of the right leg.

I took Rackleff's hand from around my neck and propped him in a sitting position against the Suburban. When I let go of the hand I had been clutching, it fell like a dead thing into the blood that was puddling on the sidewalk. But his sagging head lifted slightly.

"Robert!" I said. "Robert! Can you hear me?"

His eyes didn't open but sounds came from his mouth and soon sorted themselves into words. "Why?" he said, very clearly. Then, "Oh, mother, it hurts." His words disintegrated back into just sounds of pain, and then even the sounds stopped.

I saw polished black shoes in front of me, and looked up to see a uniformed policeman. "All right, sir, would you please stand back?" he said. "We'll take care of this." Behind him was his partner.

When I stood up, whatever had been powering me finally wore off and I started shaking. The cop was on his knees, trying to keep out of the blood and do CPR at the same time. His partner stood by, glad to leave him to it. Scared and horrified people stood by, watching from a few yards back. Sirens sounded in the distance. The black smoke still rolled out of the van, but no flames showed.

"Were you in the vehicle with him?" the second cop asked.

"No, I just pulled him out."

"Are you all right, sir?"

"I'll be okay. I just need to sit down."

"We'll need to talk to you, so don't go far."

"I won't," I said, but far was just where I wanted to go. The crowd opened to let me through, and I sat down on some nearby steps to satisfy the cop. Once he had turned his attention back to the injured man and the arriving medics, I headed for the corner. And once around it, I started to run.

I slowed down and looked myself over as I approached the parking garage. The blood that soaked my pants felt thick and sticky on my skin. But the pants were black denim, so the red hardly showed. Rackleff had said that the nature of dye was to hide dirt. Now it hid his blood.

I stood close to the cashier's booth as I paid him, so he couldn't see my soaked pants while I waited. At last I heard the popping and missing of the old pickup's engine as it came up the ramp. Neither the attendant nor the cashier seemed to be staring when I got into the pickup. Thank God for dye.

I drove slowly, still shaky, until I was miles away and came across a McDonald's. Inside, I went directly to the men's room and locked myself in the only stall.

I took off my shoes and socks and pants. The socks I just set aside and didn't bother with. But I rinsed and squeezed my pants legs in the toilet bowl, flushing and repeating until the water was only pale pink. The shoes were navy blue sneakers, and weren't much of a problem. The blood washed off the rubber part easily, and didn't show on the canvas. When I came out, a man was waiting.

"I thought maybe you drowned in there," he said.

"Sorry," I said. "Some kind of a bug." When he had closed the door of the stall behind him, I wrapped my bloody socks in paper towels. On the way out I dumped them in a litter bin. Whoever emptied the trash would just twist the big plastic liner shut and never look inside.

From McDonald's I asked directions to the nearest Goodwill store, and there I bought clothes. I didn't want to go back to the Belters to get my things. I didn't want to go anywhere near the Belters or anybody else associated with Earth Everlasting until I could sort out what was going on, and probably not then, either.

I picked out three pairs of socks, a pair of boots that weren't too badly worn, a sweater, underclothes, a couple of shirts, an old navy blue sweat suit with no name or logo on it, a denim jacket, and a raincoat that felt so soft that the weatherproofing was probably gone. But it was the best I could find.

I paid, asked for a bag to put my old clothes in, and went back to the booth to change. In the mirror I looked properly anonymous. In the parking lot there was one of those big donation boxes the size of a Dumpster, for when the store was closed. I dropped my bag of old clothes through the slot. My bags of new old clothes went in the huge toolbox in the bed of the pickup.

Next I called the office of Belter and Belter, attorneys-at-law. They were in conference. "Look, could you write this down and take it in to them?" I said to the woman on the phone. "Believe me, it's worth interrupting them. Let them know that Tom needs to talk to them urgently, now . . . No, just Tom is enough. The Tom who was at last night's conference. That's important. Last night's conference. Will you do that for me? You have my absolute word that this is a message they'll want to get right away, no matter who they're talking to. They won't be mad you interrupted, Scout's honor. Really. Will you? Okay, great."

In a moment she came back on to say Mr. Belter would speak with me now. "Bill," I said quickly, before he could even get through "hello." "You know how I am about phones. Do me a favor. Go to somebody else's phone as quick as you can and call this number." I gave him the number on the pay phone I was using, and then stayed in the booth with the receiver to my ear but the hook down, to keep anybody else from tying up the line. A couple of minutes later the ring came.

"That was fast," I said.

"I'm calling from another office on the same floor."

"You've heard what happened, haven't you?"

"We heard the explosion while we were going to the clerk's office, and finally somebody came rushing by and told us a bomb had gone off."

"Do you have any idea how he is?"

"He died on the way to the hospital."

"I thought he might. The blood was pouring out of him."

"You saw him?"

"I pulled him out of the van."

"Oh, my God, so you're the man. Do you know the police are looking for you?"

"I figured they would be, when I ran."

"Why did you run, then?"

"I don't have anything to tell them about the explosion that they don't know already. I didn't even see it. Just heard it."

"Why not tell them that?"

"Listen, will you be my lawyers? You and JoEllyn?"

"Do you need a lawyer?"

"I need lawyer-client confidentiality if I'm going to talk to you."

"All right, we're your lawyers."

"Advise me not to flee."

"Of course you shouldn't flee."

"Okay, I'll take it under advisement. Of course there's nothing to flee from yet. I'm not charged with anything. There's no reason for anybody to know I was even in Oregon, let alone at your house. I don't know why anybody would ever think to ask you about some anonymous stranger that ran away after an explosion."

"How about the people down in Carswell? They know you were with Robert."

"They know somebody was. Robert was registered under his real name. I wasn't."

"I see."

"The other thing is that the people down in Carswell tried to kill Robert and then covered up the whole thing. And next thing you know he winds up dead. I don't think they're going to make much noise about our visit."

"I'm still confused, Tom. What are you up to?"

"I want to find out who killed him. But I don't want anybody to know I'm trying to find out, or that I even exist. Among other things, I'm afraid somebody might be trying to set me up for the bombing."

"What makes you think so?"

"It's just one of a lot of possibilities. But there were odd things about the timing of the explosion, odd things about the shooting, odd things about the letters. The only straightforward thing so far was when those guys came after Robert in Carswell. That hung together and made sense to me. Nothing else does."

"How do you plan to find out what's going on?"

"You don't want to know. I don't have the responsibilities you have, so I can do things you couldn't do."

"Where can I get in touch with you?"

"I don't know."

"If there's any way at all I can help . . ."

"Just the pickup. Can you see to it that nobody at Earth Everlasting turns it in as stolen?"

"I think so. I'm Robert's executor, and I'm the general counsel for Earth Everlasting. Which will basically mean I'll replace Robert until things are sorted out."

"One more thing. Assuming all the files and records in the van were destroyed, would that cripple your investigations?"

"Were they destroyed?"

"I don't know, but whoever blew up the van might think they would be."

"Well, the answer to your question is that there might be a few things we wouldn't be able to find, but not many. Most of what we had went to the U.S. attorney's office, and I have copies of all of that here. But I see your point."

"I thought of it because Robert always talked about having his office in his hat, more or less," I said.

"He liked to say that," the lawyer said, "but I always tried to make sure that was a bit of an exaggeration."

"That's it, then, Bill. I've thought over the advice you gave me, and now I guess I'll flee."

My next stop was a lot where a guy sold new and used truck caps out of an office in a trailer. I bought a used one, to match the beat-up truck it would go on. But it had all the features, such as they were. Small screened windows to give a little air, and a lock on the back door that would keep my valuable possessions safe. He helped me heave the thing up onto the back of the truck and then fasten it into place. Now I had a roof over my head.

Next I went to a surplus store to get some valuable possessions: a sleeping bag, utensils, a small butane stove, a duffel bag, and a poncho to back up the raincoat I had my doubts about. And I bought a couple of seventy-five-inch foam sleeping pads with waffles on one side. Fit the two waffled sides together and you've got as good a mattress as there is.

I locked everything up inside and headed for a place called Powell's City of Books, which claimed in the yellow pages to be the biggest new and used bookstore in the world. It would have to be, to stock the weird stuff I wanted. And it was.

It took up a whole city block. They handed out maps at the entrance so you could find your way around. It took a little looking, but eventually I found two books of the type I needed. They were called *Home Workshop Explosives* and *Improvised Radio Detonation Techniques*. I also found something I had been a long time looking for: Thurman Arnold's *The Folklore of Capitalism*. My own copy was all full of highlighting, and I wanted a clean one to give to Hope. I thought she should read—actually, I thought everybody should read—the chapters where Arnold argues that government taxes and corporate profits are essentially identical.

That night I tried to read one of the bagful of paperback mysteries I had also picked up in Powell's but my attention kept slipping. I was in the laundry room of the first campground I had come to, heading west from Portland along the same road Rackleff and I had taken to the coast not long ago. Since I had forgotten to buy a lantern, the laundry room was the only place I could read. But since I couldn't seem to read, there wasn't any point watching clothes tumble in the dryers anymore. So I went back to the truck, made myself a kind of chair out of the foam pads, and watched the life of the campground.

I suspected I'd be spending a good deal of time in campgrounds for a while. They're even more anonymous than motels. Give a phony name and nobody will ever find you. There must be millions of Americans who live almost totally off the books, drifting around RV parks and campgrounds. If they're tied to the national database at all, it's only because their Social Security checks or their pensions or their dividend checks need to find them. They are the new nomads, nameless and restless and rootless, as elusive as gypsies.

People came and went to the laundry, the game room, the snack bar, the showers, the little convenience store that took up half the main building. A few of them nodded as they saw me looking out the open door in my truck cap, but nobody said anything beyond hello. That was fine with me. I had all the friends I needed, on the other side of the continent. For now I just wanted to be part of the scenery.

Next morning Rackleff's murder was all over the Portland paper. I bought a copy at the campground store, along with a razor and toothbrush and other small things that I had forgotten to get in the city. The main story said:

Nationally known environmental activist Robert Rackleff was killed by a car bomb yesterday outside the United States courthouse here.

No one else was killed or injured in the thunderous blast that shook Sixth Avenue just before noon, although windows were cracked in both the courthouse and the nearby University Club.

Rackleff was dead on arrival at Portland Medical Center, according to police. The victim's right leg was blown off by the explosion, and his left leg was almost severed, police said.

Rackleff, the founder of Earth Everlasting, was leaving the courthouse after testifying at a hearing into charges of altering timber brands leveled against the Dixie-Cascade Corporation by the U.S. attorney in Portland.

"This is a tragic loss for the American environmental movement," said Congressman Roland Perlmutter

(D-Ore.) in a prepared statement. "Almost single-handedly, Robert Rackleff stymied countless efforts by timber interests to clear-cut the priceless ancient forests that are our common heritage. I call on local, state, and federal law enforcement officials to spare no effort in bringing his murderer or murderers to justice."

Authorities are said to be working on a number of leads. "Mr. Rackleff was the subject of several death threats which were already under investigation by this office at the time of the alleged murder," said Paul Honig, chief of the Federal Bureau of Investigation's office in Portland.

"We took those threats very seriously, and had warned Mr. Rackleff to notify us of his movements, but he chose to disregard our request."

Honig said the FBI was working closely with Portland police to determine whether the bombing was linked to any of several criminal allegations that Earth Everlasting has brought against timber companies, Forest Service officials, and private individuals charged with brand-altering, timber rustling, arson, and other criminal acts.

"Threatening witnesses in a federal criminal proceeding is a felony," Honig stated. "Several other violations of federal law may have also been involved in this alleged bombing."

Honig said FBI bomb experts have reached a preliminary determination that the bomb was triggered when Rackleff attempted to start his vehicle, a van that was heavily damaged by the initial explosion and the fire that followed. Firemen were able to extinguish the blaze before flames reached the fuel tank.

A passerby pulled Rackleff from the driver's seat

and dragged him to shelter, witnesses said. Police arrived on the scene within minutes and administered first aid to the victim. While they were doing so, the passerby disappeared.

"My understanding is that this individual was instructed to stay in the vicinity," Honig said. "We are very interested as to why he did not." Honig denied that the man was a suspect, but said he was wanted for questioning.

Honig said the threats to Rackleff's life were in the form of letters from a skinhead group that he would not identify. The largest and most active of several such groups in the Portland area is called the Brotherbund. Several of its members are said to be suspects in the slaying of a Nigerian street vendor who was kicked to death last October.

"We keep a close watch on all hate groups," Honig said. "If one of them has been involved in these threats, we will know it very shortly." Honig said that while skinhead organizations focus primarily on white supremacy, skinheads have also sought recruits in logging communities where unemployment is widespread.

"This type of individual is known to fish in muddy waters," Honig said. "We have reports of recruitment activities by white supremacy groups in many areas of the state where employment is heavily impacted as a result of environmental regulations."

The story went on to fill most of an inside page, but not much more was added. There were two more stories inside, too. One was a profile of Rackleff. He had been just short of forty, older than he looked. He came from Doylestown, Pennsylvania. His father was a retired stockbroker. Robert had gone to Swarthmore, and then served with the Peace Corps in Morocco.

Apparently he had been impressed to learn that in the time of Queen Elizabeth, Morocco had been green and rainy enough to grow most of Europe's sugar. Then men with their goats and sheep had turned the country into semidesert. So when Rackleff got back home he went to the Yale School of Forestry, where he concluded that the most important problems to solve were not scientific, but political.

After graduating in 1980, he moved to the Pacific Northwest and began to work with tiny, shadowy groups even more militant than Earth First! He was jailed for ninety days once for trespassing, which had consisted of chaining himself with five colleagues to a giant tree in a northern California redwood grove scheduled to be leveled. He was arrested three other times, for tree spiking and sabotaging heavy equipment.

"His rigid principles wouldn't permit him to lie, either to his own lawyer or to the court," the *Oregonian*'s reporter wrote, "but they permitted him to remain silent during police questioning and before the court, which was then obliged to enter a plea of not guilty on his behalf. Rackleff was acquitted every time."

Soon Rackleff broke with the eco-terrorist wing of the movement. It wasn't clear from the story whether he objected to their potential for violence, or whether he just thought their tactics were unproductive. At any rate, he founded Earth Everlasting and set out to use the law against the timber companies instead.

"Rackleff's group was small," the *Oregonian* said, "and the operation ran on a shoestring. But his influence was far greater than the size of his organization. In a very real sense he was the organization, and its strength grew out of his personal charisma.

" 'He was the conscience and the soul of the environmental movement,' said Steven Gilligan, the executive director of Greenpeace. 'He was our Gandhi, and our Martin Luther King, Jr. Like them, he combined moral authority with a genius for tactics. His loss is a tragedy for the environmental movement.' "

I thought of him sitting on the ground, broken and pulsing out his life's blood. Oh, mother, it hurts.

He had known all along that someday it was bound to hurt. Maybe that was what was behind nonsense like going to Carswell. Maybe at some secret level Robert Rackleff had just wanted to get it all over with.

I thought back to our talk in the motel at Agnes Beach, after I had lost the argument over registering him under assumed names. He had hung his laundry up to dry, and we had just caught the end of a TV dramatization based on the 1964 murder of the three civil rights workers in Philadelphia, Mississippi.

"Poor bastards," I said. "They should have tossed away the key on those peckerwoods that did it."

"I wonder," Rackleff said, surprising me.

"Why do you wonder?"

"The killers were victims, too, really. Like the men who beat Ben Schecter to death down in Carswell. Like Schecter's father. Like dogs in a cage."

"Dogs in a cage?"

"If you administer electric shocks to dogs in a cage, they don't attack the experimenter. They attack each other."

He paused, and when he started talking again it was as much to himself as to me.

"Towns like Carswell are like cages. Hundreds of little

cages, all over Oregon and Washington. Idaho, Montana. The shocks come from men in places like New York, Boston, Houston. Tokyo, London. Overholser has closed three of his mills and moved them to Mexico, for instance. One of them wasn't far from Carswell.

"The big companies are already in the middle of abandoning the Northwest and moving most of their operations to places like Alabama and Georgia, where the trees grow faster. The only reason they're even bothering to cut on federal lands out here is that the Forest Service sells them the timber for next to nothing.

"But in the little cages, all the dogs know is to bite each other. Loggers lose their jobs, and Ben Schecter dies. More shocks come from out of nowhere, more pain. The fighting in the cages gets worse. What can you do?"

"Just what you're doing," I said. "Shock the experimenters back."

"Is that the best thing?" he asked himself. "Will that get anybody out of their cages? Those peckerwoods in Mississippi, as you called them, suppose they had gone to jail. Would it have made them understand that poor whites and poor blacks spend their lives in the same cages, getting the same shocks from the same jailers?

"That's what Martin Luther King was trying to make people understand, what Jesse Jackson is still saying. King's idea wasn't to send anybody to jail, it was to go to jail himself. His idea wasn't to use the law to punish people, it was to change it so people wouldn't get punished.

"What's my idea? It's not love, it's revenge. If I shock people, why should I be surprised if they shock me back? Don't I deserve it?"

He sat for a long moment, staring across the room. All along, he hadn't been looking at me. At last he said, "The worst of it is, it's not even working. I'm not even saving the forests."

My whole life has been a long preparation for being utterly useless at times like this. Robert wasn't looking for disagreement or even agreement, he was looking for love. I don't do love well.

All I could think of to say was, "I hope you feel better," so I said it. He nodded, and tried a smile.

"Will you be able to sleep?"

"Oh, yes," he said. "I can practically always sleep."

"Well, get some sleep." I put my hand on his shoulder in a gesture that must have seemed as stiff and awkward to him as it did to me.

R<small>ACKLEFF, IN THAT NIGHT OF DEPRESSION,</small> <small>HAD</small> *10*
been right about one thing. Somebody he
had been trying to shock had sure enough
shocked him back. And it had happened on
my watch, and I was beginning to suspect I could have
prevented it. It was my turn for doubt and self-loathing
now.

Before leaving the campground, I telephoned Hope at
her office. "Are you all right?" she said the instant she
came on. "I got your message on the machine last night,
but are you really all right? Where are you? What
happened?"

Once I had covered all that, I asked Hope if she knew
that Rackleff had suffered from depression. At least that's
what it had sounded like to me.

"I didn't know, but I'm not surprised," she said. "Had
there been any trigger?"

"Not unless it was the death threats. But that wasn't
what he was talking about. He was worried because he
wasn't Martin Luther King, Jr. He hated himself because
he wasn't perfect. Like you sometimes get."

"Like you do, too," Hope said. I had had my own bad
spells, although not for a good while now.

"I've got plenty of reason to hate myself just now," I said.

"Oh, no, Tom," she said. "Are you slipping?"

"Back to the heavy drinking, you mean? No, just a few beers like always."

"But not depression?"

"Some, but I'll probably be okay. It'll take a while to get over the bombing. I washed his blood out of my pants in a toilet in McDonald's."

"My God, Tom."

"It's funny. All the times I used to be down, when I'd whine to you about what a totally inadequate and worthless shit I was, there was a kind of person I had in mind that I wanted to be when I grew up. Robert was a lot like that person. Disciplined, directed, selfless, tolerant, even-tempered. And then I kill him."

"Come on, Tom."

"I know. I'm just telling you how it feels."

"You want me to come out?"

"No! I mean, no. I don't know what I'll be doing, but very likely it'll be something you shouldn't be involved in."

"There's nothing you can do for him now," Hope said. "I wish you'd come back."

"I can't, though."

"I was afraid of that."

I drove along from the campground toward Agnes Beach, feeling the old feelings of bitter self-loathing and self-contempt. "Dumb, dumb, dumb," I kept saying to myself. I was rapidly convincing myself that I could have foreseen the bombing, and should have.

I pushed the old pickup right along, because I knew I had a good chance of feeling better once I got to Lamar Purcell. It wasn't anything special about Lamar, just that you make an effort to override depression when you're in company, and often the effort works.

"You might be making too much of that meek and mild shit with Robert," Lamar Purcell said. We were drinking some kind of rose hip stuff in his house. "I had this old lady once, she practically meek and milded me to death. Finally got to where I had to move to San Francisco to get away from her. Told her I was going out to score some acid and never came back."

"I know what you mean," I said. My ex-wife had been patient and long-suffering. Never angry and shouting, always forgiving, always understanding. Only a few small sighs, sometimes, and then she would considerately leave the house till she got through crying, and then she would come back with a gentle smile. You wanted to knock her through the wall.

I wondered how long a woman would have lasted with Robert Rackleff, watching him scrub the evil out of his undyed clothes every night. Let me do that, she would have said, and Oh, I'm used to it, he would have said, and things would have started downhill right from that point. Finally she'd have to run away to keep from braining him with the steam iron, and he wouldn't have the least idea why she left.

"You're telling me Robert wasn't really so meek and mild?" I said.

"He was meek and mild like a starfish. You know how a starfish does a clam?"

Well, no, I didn't. Never even thought about it.

"He wraps himself around that clam and just starts to pull on him real gentle. But he never stops. Clam eases up for a second or two, and the starfish takes up the slack. Couple days later, the clam finally says fuck it, by now

I'm most of the way open anyway, might as well give up and let the goddamned starfish eat me."

"Is that how he got that airplane out of you?"

"Pretty much. I'm an old tie-dyed hippie, right? So already I'm in favor of his program, you know? I give him a dollar here, a couple dollars there, and that gives him that first little bit of slack. Pretty soon, I'm like, man, how would you feel about an airplane? I'm pretty sure I got one here somewhere, let me just look."

"So probably he'd be even more persistent with people who were against his program."

"Persistent, stubborn, whatever word you want to use. Robert was always polite, never got mad when you said no. But he never got discouraged, either. Always came back at you. And that was if he was on your side."

"Who might have wanted to blow him up?"

"Hey, he might have got blown up by anybody. Movement like that, a lot of weirdos climb aboard. When he first came out here, Robert fooled around a little with eco-defense, you know what I mean?"

"Tree spiking?"

"That kind of thing, yeah. Sabotaging heavy equipment, stuff like that. After a while he decided it wasn't the way to go, but not everybody agreed. There was some bad feeling about it in the organization, you know?"

"Yeah? How bad?"

"Not bad enough for what you're thinking. The tree spikers, they're basically nonviolent people. Even when they're crazy, they're not that kind of crazy. Or most of them aren't."

"Was there bad feeling toward him in the environmental movement at large?"

"I wouldn't know. I never heard about any."

I hadn't, either. At least there hadn't been any echo of it in the newspaper accounts of his death.

"How about in Earth Everlasting itself?"

"A palace coup or something? It was mostly him. You didn't join because you wanted a corner office someday, you know? You joined because you wanted to be like one of Robert's followers."

"There must be membership lists, though. Bank accounts. Officers. Donor files. Nonprofit papers. Maybe it's a foundation, with assets."

"What's your point?"

"That there'd at least be something to take over, even without Robert."

"I guess there's all that stuff. The lawyers could tell you."

"You know the Belters?"

"Him I know, not her."

"What do you think of him?"

"Regular white-bread lawyer. Not the kind I hire, but hey. Different strokes."

"As far as I can tell, he inherits. He's the executor. He's got all the papers in his office."

"You don't trust him?"

"I don't know who to trust. I'm out here all alone."

"It's tough," Lamar said. "I was that way here, when I first came up from California."

"Now that you know people, who do you think could have blown him up?"

"Got to be somebody in the timber industry or somebody fronting for them. Lobbyists. Company security. Industry councils. Cops. Maybe Forest Service cops. They got hundreds of pot commandos, the Forest Service. The pricks got nothing to do now that they think they've burned up all the pot in the National Forests. They're getting bored, so they're starting to kick a little tree-hugger ass."

"You don't buy the skinheads, then?"

"Sure, why not? I just forgot to put them in. You can rent them out for whatever you got in mind, I hear. Plus they're crazy fuckers, although who am I to talk, huh? Maybe I know a crazy fucker or two myself, the line of business I'm in."

"It wouldn't surprise me."

"In fact one of my crazy fuckers was telling me an interesting thing the other day, Tom. A grower over in Carswell. He says a kid he used to work with got his arm broken in some trouble at a motel."

I nodded. When I was done telling him about it, he nodded, too.

"Teach 'em to fuck with the Lone Ranger, huh?" he said.

"Maybe it didn't. Maybe they kept going till they got him."

"I doubt it. The dead reporter's old man has the name of being a mean son of a bitch. He took a chain to one of his drivers a few years back and left the guy blind in one eye. But he's dumb. He might have organized something as dumb as that shit they tried at the motel. But blowing up a van way off in Portland at just the right time, with the right guy in it? That's a real stretch, Tom, considering the guy's a total cement head."

"Everybody in Carswell isn't a cement head, though. For instance this publisher struck me as being a shrewd little rat."

"I'm not saying there's no Carswell connection. Just that it probably isn't Lou Schecter."

"What about the people on this list?" I asked. Lamar took the list the Belters had made for me the day before the bombing. There were eighteen names on it, from all up and down the state.

"What's it a list of?" Lamar said after he had scanned it.

"People who face criminal charges because of information turned over to the U.S. attorney's office by Earth Everlasting."

"A lot of money on this list," Lamar said. "Overholser alone is supposed to be worth a half a billion. Mind if I keep this?"

"Why not just write down the names so I can hold on to it?"

Lamar jotted down the names and handed the list back to me. "There you go," he said. "I wouldn't want my handwriting and fingerprints lying around either, not if I was a mystery man like you."

"Am I a mystery man?"

"Sure, you're all over the news," he said. "The mystery man that pulled Rackleff out of the truck and ran off. Naturally, they want to talk to you."

"No great reason to talk to me. Plenty of witnesses to crimes disappear. They just don't want to get involved."

"Still, the only suspects they're talking about on the news are the mystery man and the skinheads. Maybe they think you're a skinhead with hair."

"I don't understand about those skinheads," I said. "Why would they send Robert those nut letters?"

"You could ask them."

"Yeah, I thought about that."

Once I got back to Portland the boss skinhead wasn't hard to find, not with a name like Max Wilhoite. I knew he worked in a gym, so I just started down the list of gyms in the yellow pages and asked for Max at each one until somebody said, "Hold on, I'll get him." Then I hung up and drove out there.

Jim's Gym was off Southeast Division Street, on a block where private homes were mixed with a thrift shop, a bingo hall, a furniture refinishing shop, a couple of small Vietnamese restaurants, and a bicycle repair shop. The trees and the flowers saved the neighborhood from the monotony of a thousand other similar drab neighborhoods in the arid parts of the West. Here, though, laurel hedges bordered the street, and large trees—spruces, firs, cedars, sycamores, and walnuts—shaded the houses.

But the gym baked unshaded in the sun: a one-story, flat-roofed building that had probably started out as a small warehouse or market. There were a couple of glass-brick windows off to one side of the door, but for the most part Jim's Gym was windowless.

The name, the neighborhood, and the building itself all suggested that you had come to the wrong place if you were after aerobics, leotards, carpeting, StairMasters, NordicTracks, and plastic-covered pastel dumbbells, color-coded by weight.

Sure enough, inside I found heavy industrial rubber matting on the floor, and barbells and dumbbells with black cast-iron plates on them. The customers wore sweats with no sleeves and the legs torn off to make them into shorts. Most of them wore leather lifting belts that had turned dark brown from years of perspiration.

The nearest thing to a suit was the guy who finally noticed me standing in the door and came up to see what I wanted. He wore clean, white gym shoes, and a blue tracksuit with MAX and ASSISTANT MANAGER stitched on the jacket. He had a round, bald head that needed a shave. He was just around my height, a couple of inches short of six feet, and a little more heavily built. I put him at around 195, 200.

"You one of those reporters?" he said, chest and chin up and out. Bristling.

"Huh?" I said stupidly. "Reporters?"

"It's nothing," he said, smiling as he slipped from Schwarzenegger to Dale Carnegie. "Just been a bunch of damned reporters around is all. I don't know what for. Can I help you?"

I told him I was interested in membership, and would he mind showing me around the place.

"What do you do, Tom?" he asked while we were looking at the showers and locker room.

"I'm an architect. Just been out on a site." This was to explain my general lack of elegance, and still make him figure I had money.

"What brings you out this way?" In other words, what was a nice boy like me doing in a place like this?

"I'm looking for a real gym," I said. "Not one of those goddamned singles clubs with a juice bar and that shit. I used to be in pretty good shape and it's time I got back."

So we talked the talk for a while, one sweaty gym rat to another, and then I asked him about membership fees.

"Sounds reasonable," I said when he told me. "You got yearly rates?"

"Same as by the month. Most people just go by the month."

"Reason I ask, I want to kind of trick myself into working out regular again. If I paid for a couple years up front, I'd have enough invested so I'd have to use the place. That sound crazy to you?"

"Don't sound crazy at all. Sounds like good sense to me."

"Hey, Max," one of the guys with the wide leather belts

hollered across the room. "The cable on this goddamned thing is binding again. You want to come take a look at it?"

"Go ahead," I said. "I've got to get back to the job, anyway. Listen, what time do you close down?"

"Nine o'clock, except five on Sundays."

"Why don't I come back at nine, then, when we'll both have more time. Give us a chance to take care of the paperwork. I'll bring my checkbook along."

It would also give me a chance to get ready for our little talk by doing some reading on explosives. Reading was getting to be a problem with my new life-style. It was too dark and too hot in the back of the truck, and too bright and too hot up front in the cab. I missed my La-Z-Boy recliner at home and the reading lamp behind my left shoulder.

After wriggling around in the front seat of the pickup for a while, I finally gave up trying to find a comfortable position and searched out a branch library. It felt odd to be taking books into a library, but these particular books wouldn't be on the shelves. No tax-supported library would carry titles like *Home Workshop Explosives* and *Improvised Radio Detonation Techniques*.

First, though, I took a look at the newspaper. There wasn't much new on the bombing. The FBI had taken the lead on the case, on grounds that the killing was an attempt to obstruct various federal cases being looked into by the Bureau and the U.S. attorney. Arrests were imminent. The *Oregonian* mentioned the mystery witness but left little doubt that the main suspect was an unnamed skinhead leader. I turned to my texts on explosives.

Meanwhile it was story hour in the branch library, and in the next room a woman was reading *Charlie and the Great Glass Elevator* to a dozen or so preschoolers sitting around her on the floor. Every time she came to the word *mister* she would stop and say, "Mister Who?" and the kids would shout back, "Mister WONKA."

This supplied regular reality checks for me as I tried to read about dual-tone multifrequency transmitters and nitroglycol, which has the advantage of being three or four times less sensitive than nitroglycerin itself. "This should be very reassuring," I read, "to all the timid hearts contemplating entering the explosives manufacture field."

"Mister WONKA!" the kids hollered.

The library closed at five, which gave me plenty of time to drive out to a multiplex and catch the new Clint Eastwood, *In the Line of Fire.* The first Clint I ever saw was when I was a kid assigned to the army attaché's office in Laos. One night in the ARMA house they showed *Hang 'Em High,* which we hated to see end to such an extent that we beat on a big table with our folding chairs until they bent and the table broke. Drinking had been going on in the establishment.

Clint peaked in *High Plains Drifter,* probably the best movie ever made, and he bottomed out in the two orangutan flicks. What the hell, anybody can have a couple of off days. But he was back in form for this new one, which fit right into my present situation, since it was about a bodyguard who lost his client. It gave me hope to see that Clint made up for his lapse eventually. And it gave me hope to look at him still up there on the screen, the once and future Clint. It feels good to know that no matter how old I get, Clint will always be older and still busting heads.

I was back out at Jim's Gym a few minutes before nine. I parked in the next block, faced so I could see the door. A couple of guys left singly, and then a bunch of three left just after nine. The lights were still on inside. I waited a few minutes, and when nobody else came out I walked to the gym. The door was locked, but Max Wilhoite came to open it when I knocked.

"Oh, good," I said. "I was afraid I might have missed you."

"Me, too. I was getting afraid you wasn't going to come."

"Oh, I was coming all right. I was just held up, is all. Look, some of your equipment is since my time. Would you mind walking me around the stations, showing me how they work?"

And so we did that. Wilhoite took off his assistant manager jacket for the demonstration, which was reasonable enough, but he stepped over the line into asshole when he took off his T-shirt, too.

Max had the kind of build that comes out of a gym, not out of the genes. The major sign is biceps out of proportion to the rest. Bodybuilders go nuts for biceps, which are mainly for show. Think how many times you need your biceps in any kind of work or game. Very little, compared to back, hands, forearms, abdomen, and legs. Especially legs. I couldn't see Wilhoite's legs under his pants, but it was a good bet they were puny compared to his torso. Gyms are full of varsity bodies with JV legs.

We started on the pull-down machine, which works another vanity muscle, the latissimus dorsi. The lats are what you use every single time that life puts you in a spot where you have to spread your hands really wide apart and pull yourself up to look over an eight-foot board fence. To be fair, they're also what you use if you do the breaststroke a lot.

"Why don't I go first?" I said. "That way you can check my form and then show me the way I ought to be doing them." There was only one machine I needed to get him on, but it would be a good idea to tire him out a little first. I mounted the bench of the lat machine and made a considerable show of grunting and jerking at a 140-pound load, which was a lot less than I could comfortably handle. As I had hoped, Wilhoite added another eighty pounds and showed me how a real man did it. In the process, he gave me a good view of the boils scattered across his upper back and shoulders. You see that kind of acne a lot in gyms. It comes from steroids.

As we made the circuit of the machines, I kept asking things like how much he could handle on this one, and how many reps could he do at that weight, and how many sets of reps, and how long would it take a guy to . . . , and so forth. Wilhoite responded well to all this flattery, not working himself to failure but building up lactic acid in his muscles nonetheless. He didn't have too much pep left when we got to the decline bench.

"I never saw one like this," I said. "What's the point of it?"

"Works your lower pecs," he said. "You just do it like a regular bench press, except your torso is slanting down."

I climbed aboard the thing, which was basically a slant board with a barbell rack at the lower end where your head was. Wilhoite loaded the bar with the modest weight that I could be expected to handle, and stood behind the rack, where he could be my spotter. A spotter stands by while the other guy lifts, ready to step in and help the lifter if he lowers the weight and can't get it back up again.

In my performance so far, I had been pretty wobbly but always just able to get the bar back up and safely onto the rack where it belonged. This time I let it look as if I had worked to failure and needed a spot. Wilhoite grabbed the bar in the center with one hand and took up enough of the strain so I was able to raise the weight to arm's length and lower it into its cradle.

"Son of a bitch," I said when I had finished pretending to get my breath back. "That one is hard."

I helped load more plates onto the bar, and Wilhoite took my place to show me how the thing was done. I moved behind the bench to spot him. His system so far had been to pump out reps rapidly, quitting before he showed much sign of weakening. But I had been around gyms enough to know that when he was knocking off he had only two or three more reps left in him, certainly no more than four.

I stood ready in my role as junior partner as he started. "Wow," I said when I judged he had reached the right point. "How many more you think you could do if you had to?"

Probably four, although neither of us would ever know.

After three, I let him get a few inches into the lift, the hardest part of it, and I put both my hands lightly on top of the bar. He was near the limit of his strength, and it didn't take much to make the bar settle back down on his neck. He couldn't do much objecting, because now 220 pounds of weight were pressing on his windpipe. I wasn't pushing down on the bar, but I wasn't pulling up on it either. The only reason I kept my hands on it was to stop him if he tried to escape from under by heaving up on one end or the other.

As the last of his strength left him, the bar dug fractionally deeper, and still deeper. He was making strangled noises, and his upside-down face was turning bright red.

I let it go on for a few seconds more, and then helped him clear the bar barely off his neck. But I only lifted a little. He had to keep straining to hold the bar up. His arms quivered, and ridges stood out on his pectoral muscles.

"What . . . doing," he got out.

"I'm fucking with you, Max. Only two places this bar can go is your neck or your face. Tell me about the bombing."

I took up more of the bar's weight, so he could get his breath enough to talk. After a moment he said, "Hey, come on. You guys already know."

"What guys would that be, Max?"

"You . . . ," Wilhoite started out, and then it struck him that there was something wrong here. "Just guys," he finished, so I let the bar settle down again on his Adam's apple till I thought he might be ready, and then I eased the load.

"Who did the bombing, Max?"

"Jesus, I did it, all right? Let me up."

So I did.

I made him work to raise the weight, but I gave him just enough help so that he finally managed to clear the brackets with it. The instant he was safe he let go and the barbell clanged down onto its support. He lay there on his back, too exhausted to move, while I waited. At last he rolled himself off the bench, ending up on his knees, and then he used the weight rack to help him get to his feet. He could have reached out and grabbed this pussy that had sneaked up on him, but he wouldn't do it yet. Not till his arms stopped quivering and his breathing got back to normal and his fear could turn into manly outrage. I stood where I was, hands loose and open, arms a little bent, waiting.

But he still surprised me.

I HAD BEEN SO READY FOR ATTACK THAT FLIGHT *11* caught me flat-footed. He had two or three steps on me by the time I readjusted. I caught him in the locker room, where he was scrabbling for the zipper on a gym bag. He was already bent over with his back to me, so I just barreled into him. At the same time I reached through his crotch, grabbed the front of his belt, and flipped him. He landed on his back with his head toward me, a position that offered me all sorts of opportunities. The one I took was the neck. It had worked pretty well the first time.

I was on him before he could figure out how he suddenly happened to be flat on his back on the floor, with his shaved head locked between my legs. The head scissors is highly illegal because it is dangerous and it hurts. So I put out full pressure for a little bit, to show him what could happen. His face turned red, and he began to make those noises again. I slacked up a little, just keeping a tight enough hold to make sure he wouldn't go anywhere. I smiled down into his face to show him something funny was about to happen, and I reached up for the gym bag. It was heavy, which explained why he ran for it. I pulled a gun out. I couldn't say what kind of a gun it was, except that it was a big, black one.

I used to own guns before I grew up, though, so at least I knew enough to be able to swing the cylinder out and shake the bullets loose. I put them in my pocket and tossed the gun to the other side of the room. Wilhoite followed it with his eyes, like a dog tracking a stick through the air. I found his wallet in the bag, and I stuck that in my pocket, too. He started to say something, but I tightened my legs so he couldn't.

His towel and clothes weren't interesting, and I threw them on the floor. On the bottom of the bag I found a clipping from a catalog. It showed a heavy, clunky, lace-up boot. "KICK-ASS DOC MARTENS armor your feet with thick, waterproof 6 oz. leather and steel toes!" the ad copy said. I started to read aloud: "And these babies aren't just for stompin', they're for ridin', too! When you've got your legs wrapped around a thousand-plus cc's of hot, throbbing crotch rocket, and a tar crack feels like a pot-hole, you better be in your leathers . . . right down to your feet!"

I looked at Wilhoite, who didn't seem to be blushing. Probably skinheads don't blush. " 'Crotch rockets,' Max?" I said. "Your mama let you read this shit?" He still didn't blush.

"Answer me," I said, grabbing his nose and twisting it the way kids do. "Your mama know you read this shit? How about Hitler? Hitler know about these crotch rockets?" He made a move with his arms, which were both free, but he couldn't reach my face with my legs in the way. And the instant he moved I tightened on his neck.

"Understand something, asshole," I said. "There's nothing you can do to me. After a while I'll let you up and you can give it a shot if you want, see for yourself. Right now you just lie there and listen to what I'm asking you. You give me the best answers you can or I'll clamp down on you till you pass out. Understand?"

He didn't answer, so I clamped down for just a little.

"Understand?" I asked again.

"Yes," he said.

"Okay, what's cyclonite?"

"I don't know."

"Try."

"That shit Superman eats in the comics?"

"How about RDX?"

"I don't know."

"C three? C four?"

"That robot in the space movie? The one with Garth Vader?"

"How about TNT?"

"Everybody knows TNT."

"That what you used for the bomb?"

"Sure."

"How did you ignite the charge?"

"Blasting cap."

"What number?"

"One."

"Number one?"

"One blasting cap."

"Yeah, but what number. You know, from one to eight."

He paused, and then took a chance: "Number one, like I said."

"Okay, you can get up now, Max."

I unlocked my legs from around his neck and got up myself. He lay there a minute, like an animal does for an instant when you set it free, before it realizes that it can go now. I went over and picked up the empty gun while Wilhoite got to his feet.

"Well, we settled a few things there, Max," I said. "You don't know shit about the comics and you don't know shit about movies and you especially don't know shit about bombs. Come on, I got something to do out in the gym."

He followed me out, keeping a good distance between us. I stopped by the pull-down machine and asked him, "What's your best on this?"

"Two-sixty."

I pulled the pin out of the stack of weights and put it back in farther down, at 240.

"Let's see," I said.

While he was getting ready, settling his thighs under the bar that would keep him from rising up in the air when he tried to lift more than his own weight, I released the cylinder on his big revolver and let it hang open. When he had raised the stack of weights as high as he could, I reached in and put the revolver under them.

"Hey," he said, holding the stack in the air, "what the hell are you doing?"

"I'm helping you bust your gun, Max. I don't think you're a good person to have a gun."

He was letting the weights down slowly, but even then there was a good chance he would deform the cylinder hinge so that it wouldn't close properly. He stopped the stack short of the gun and held it there. He let go when I smacked him in the back of the head with the heel of my hand, as hard as I could.

"We going to have to go around again, Max, or are you going to drop that stack for me?"

He lifted it up, and let it fall like a guillotine from as high as he could get it. I made him do it four more times before I was satisfied that the gun was junk. Then I sat down on the bench next to the pull-down machine.

"What's the biggest guy I saw in here this afternoon?" I said. "Two-sixty, two-seventy?"

"Something like that."

"Okay, now. If I was to hit that guy in the back of the head like I just did to you, it would hurt him just as much as it hurt you. Same thing if I kicked him in the balls, or busted his arm, or broke his nose. You understand what I'm saying?"

"I guess."

"No, you don't. I'm saying that no matter how much muscle you got, everybody bleeds the same. Everybody hurts the same. Hurt them enough, everybody dies the same. That's my lesson for you, Max. You can push more iron than me, but I can whip your ass all day long. I know how to get past your muscles and hurt you. So you can tell me what I want to hear up front, or we can go around for a while and then you'll tell me anyway. Either way is okay with me."

"Some of my guys are coming to pick me up any minute."

"Don't be fucking ridiculous. Come on, let's get going here. Where we start out is that you didn't blow up that van, so the question is why you told me you did?"

Wilhoite didn't know anything about explosives, and he didn't know anything more about this particular bombing than anybody could have learned from the papers.

"I was just bullshitting you," Wilhoite said.

"I know that, Max. Okay, let's try something else. How do you spell *vengeance?*"

"Huh?"

"Don't you know the word?"

"Sure I know it."

"Then spell the son of a bitch."

"I ain't much on spelling."

"How about *scourge?*"

"What's that?"

"You don't know the word?"

"No."

"You knew it when you wrote those letters, didn't you?"

"What letters?"

"When was the last letter you wrote?"

"Mostly I phone."

"The last letter, Max."

"Long time. I don't remember."

"Did you ever write a letter to anybody?"

"I never really had to."

"So you never wrote a letter in your whole life?"

"Not really."

"So you couldn't have written a letter to Robert Rackleff?"

"I never wrote him no letters, no."

"Is there anybody in the Brotherbund that sends out letters?"

"I guess so. Must be."

"I'm talking about official letters from the club or whatever you call it. Do you have like a club secretary?"

"Nobody wouldn't send no official letters out without me seeing it."

"Rackleff got death threats in letters that supposedly came from the Brotherbund."

"They said Brotherbund on them?" He sounded like it was really news to him. So far, the papers hadn't specified any one skinhead group.

"That's what they said. Looks funny, doesn't it? First

the letters come, then somebody shoots at the guy's house,
and then somebody blows him up."

"I can't help how it looks."

"Oh, you've been helping. We're getting places."

"We are? Where are we getting?"

"Look at all the shit we know now. We know you
didn't bomb Rackleff but at first you said you did. We
know you didn't send him any letters, but somebody
did."

"I didn't say no such things."

"Sure you did, Max. You just didn't know what you
were saying."

"I don't know who you are, but you can't prove nothing on me."

"Look around you, Max. You see a judge here, jury, any
of that shit? Just me. I say what's proof and what ain't."

The whole business of shooting at the house had bothered me. So had the letters. The thing was wrong-side-to.
If you wanted to blow somebody up, you went ahead and
blew him up. If you wanted to take credit for it, you sent
a letter to the papers afterward, not before. Things were
needlessly complicated. Plainly somebody else was ma-
nipulating Max, who had the brains of a Guernsey cow.

"You said 'us guys' already know about the bombing,
Max, remember? Let's go back to that. What guys?"

"I don't know. I was just talking."

"Just happened to have a barbell on your neck, so you
were casually shooting the shit? Come on, Max. Help me
out here."

"I don't even know who you are."

"I'm working for the family. Rackleff's family. Main
thing, though, is that I'm not one of us guys. Us guys
being the ones that you thought I was, the ones that are
setting you up for this bombing."

"You don't know shit."

"Listen and see whether I know shit. This is a pretty big favor you're doing, letting somebody set you up for a murder charge. Not like loaning your lawn mower to somebody or giving him a ride home from work. So these guys must have had your dumb ass really hammered into a crack. Who could that be, Max? Who could push around a guy in your position, a guy that heads up his own organization? Has to be cops, doesn't it?

"See how this sounds to you, Max. Cops come to you and say, Hey, Max, we got your ass good on this one, whatever it is. Dope? You guys are dealing maybe?"

"The Brotherbund doesn't touch drugs."

"Then that Nigerian you stomped last fall? Something, anyway. They got you on something and you and the cops both know it. Maybe they could say a word for you, even drop the charges, if you helped them out with little stuff now and then. No big deal. So it goes along like that except pretty soon they're squeezing you harder and harder.

"Who's doing this shit to you, Max? Who's turning you into a fink for the cops. Pot commandos from the Forest Service? DEA? ATF? FBI? Has to be some kind of federal cop. The whole thing smells federal."

"Nobody's doing nothing to nobody."

"What do they really want out of you, Max?"

"Nothing."

"Who's making it look like you killed Rackleff?"

"Nobody."

"Then why did you tell me earlier that you did?"

"You were fucking strangling me."

"Now that I'm not strangling you, you didn't do it?"

"That's right."

"Can you see why I'm confused, Max? Is it possible

that you did it as a favor for the cops, and then they kicked you out of the boat and told you to swim for it?"

"If the FBI wants to whack somebody, they just whack him. Why would they need me?"

"Who said anything about the FBI?"

"You did."

"I said DEA and pot commandos, too."

"FBI is just the one you think of."

"It's the one you thought of, all right. Let's assume FBI, then. The FBI doesn't mind killing people, you're right. But they have a regular procedure for it. They set up a raid or a siege type of situation where they've got the guys outnumbered a hundred to one. Like Idaho or Waco. As soon as the press isn't looking, they open fire and kill everybody inside. That way nobody can say who shot first."

"I wouldn't know," Max said.

"That's right, you wouldn't. Believe me, though, the FBI wouldn't risk its own men to commit an outright murder."

And of course this is what bothered me. Federal cops are bureaucrats and they rise by covering their ass. It practically never gets to deliberate, individual murder, and when it does, it's usually overseas. Where, as General Westmoreland was once stupid enough to say on camera, human life is cheap. Even then the job is practically always contracted out, which was a thought.

"Of course they might contract it out to some civilian," I said to Max. "A guy like you could run all the risks in the world and why should the feds give a shit? I'm just thinking aloud here, Max. But how does it strike you so far?"

I didn't give him a chance to answer, but he was paying attention.

"The trouble is, though, you didn't do it. Not that you wouldn't have, but you don't even know how it was done. You maybe don't even give a shit who actually did do it, Max, but you ought to. You're in trouble. Did these cops say they'd make a lot of noise about charging you but then they wouldn't really do it?"

He didn't answer, but he was still paying attention.

"Did they say they couldn't really bring you to trial even if they wanted to, because then you'd tell the court who hired you? Did you believe that shit, Max?"

"If somebody was ever to say something like that to me, I'd believe it, sure. Because it would be true."

"Sure it would be true, as far as it went. They'd never bring you to trial. But that doesn't mean they'd just let you walk, Max. Not with what you'd have in your head. You'd be the only one that knew who really blew up Rackleff. So Max, you're fucked."

By which I meant he was dead, but he still didn't understand that.

"That's how much you know," he said. "I'm not fucked."

"Tell me why not."

"You're so smart, tell me this. How can a person be two places at the same time?"

"You're telling me you were someplace else when the bomb went off?"

"Maybe I was, maybe I wasn't."

"And fifty people can swear you were in the gym at that exact time?"

"Actually it was my lunch break."

"With Hillary and Bill?"

"Very funny. I was halfway across town when the bomb went off and I can prove it."

"How many miles?"

"Too far to set off any bombs. Try like maybe five miles."

"Well, that's a little long for a small FM transmitter. You'd want to use an auto-alarm paging transmitter or a VHF scanner. Probably the scanner. You can get up to thirty-five miles on those."

"So?"

"So can you prove that at twelve-forty P.M. you didn't press a button anywhere within a thirty-five-mile radius of the U.S. courthouse?"

"As a matter of fact, yes."

"How are you going to do that, Max? Were you in jail at the time?"

"You could prove it without being in jail. Pictures prove it."

"Pictures don't have the time on them."

"Some pictures do."

"What pictures?" I said, and the answer came to me as soon as I asked it. "Money machines, Max? Like that?"

"Like that," he said, sounding pleased with himself. Old Max, not so dumb after all.

I thought it over, how it would fit together from the point of view of whoever had been pulling his strings. Maybe they had told him that the deal was for him to go to trial and sit tight until things were looking really bad for him. Then he whips out this secret photo and the judge turns him loose and the whole courtroom stands up and applauds. Poor, dumb Max.

"Think how it's going to go in real life, Max," I said. "You say to the judge, 'Excuse me, Your Honor, all that's well and good except I was halfway across town at the time having my picture took.'"

"And here's the picture right here, Your Honor," Wilhoite said, holding out his hand, as if he were giving the thing to the judge.

"Have you actually seen this picture, Max?"

"I don't need to see it. I know where it is."

"You think the bank's going to give it to you?"

"That's what lawyers are for. I tell him where to look, he'll look."

"Yeah, right. The lawyer goes to the bank and the bank says tough shit, those pictures are on an endless loop that erases itself as it goes along. Or we only keep them till the check clears. You think the bank has a big warehouse they keep all those pictures in forever?"

"It wasn't a bank. I was cashing a check in a market."

"Still. How long you suppose they keep those pictures?"

"I never thought about that."

"Well, here's something else you never thought about either. How did you know exactly what time to go in and get your picture taken?"

"You tell me, if you know so much."

"Okay, I'll tell you. Whoever set the bomb off told you when he was going to do it."

"What's the difference, as long as it was the right time?"

"Think, Max, think. You're in court now, picture it. You just told the jury that you couldn't have set the bomb off, because at twelve-forty you were having your picture taken in a grocery store. Take a look, folks, here it is. See?

"Now up jumps the prosecutor and he says, 'Tell me something, Mr. Wilhoite, did you happen to be wearing clothes that day? You did? Well, did those clothes have pockets in them? I don't see those pockets in the picture. In fact I don't even see your hands. Are you aware that radio waves travel through fabric, Mr. Wilhoite?' "

"Well, I'll be a son of a bitch," Wilhoite said, and I hurried right along to give him more to think about.

"Never thought of that, huh, Max? See the beauty of it, though? All along you figure you've got an airtight alibi. Then suddenly the air leaks out of it, and then it gets even worse. The prosecutor twists it all around to use your alibi against you instead of for you.

"He asks you to explain the coincidence that you happened to arrange it so as to be standing in front of a camera miles away at roughly the same time a guy gets blown away that you've been sending death threats to. How many times a month would you say you cash checks there, Mr. Wilhoite? How many remote-control bombs would you estimate were set off in the Portland area in the last five years, say? Okay, now what would you estimate are the odds that you would happen to be standing in front of a camera with a timer at the exact time this particular explosion occurred? And so on and so on. You see where I'm going, don't you, Max?"

"None of that wouldn't happen," Wilhoite said. "If it started to go like that, I would just say in court who really told me to keep my mouth shut while they pretended like I done it."

"Exactly, Max. Now you got my point. You're walking around with information that could send these guys to jail. You're in the driver's seat here."

"Fucking-A."

"Jesus, Max, wake up and smell the coffee. You think the federal government just walked up and put its balls in your pocket by mistake? You think you can go to them now and say, Look, guys, I decided I'm not working for you anymore and by the way, I want you to drop that Nigerian thing you got me on. Also how about loaning me five bucks till payday? In your dreams, Max. You're never going to get as far as a courtroom. Whoever these guys are, they don't have any problem that a dead skin-head won't solve."

I went over this a couple more times, from different angles but always pointing out that Max Wilhoite practi-cally had to be next after Rackleff on the list. The thought plainly hadn't occurred to him before; thought wasn't something that came easy to him. But at last I caught him nodding agreement at something I had said. So it was sinking in.

"Max," I said, "I'm not asking for names here, but at least give me an agency. Are these guys FBI?"

"I didn't say nothing."

But he screwed up his face something horrible and pro-duced a wink. God knows what movie it came from.

"That's the way, Max. You didn't tell nobody nothing, and nobody can ever say you did."

By now we were just two guys sitting on neighboring benches in a gym, no hostility or threatening body lan-guage on either side. Going over alternatives, like a couple of lawyers working for the same client.

"I could make a deal with them," Wilhoite said. "Like they could put me in the witness protection program."

"I wouldn't make any long-range plans like that, if I were you. I'd think short-range, Max. Very, very short-range."

"You mean like . . ."

I nodded.

"They wouldn't kill a guy that cooperated with them, would they?"

"These are not grateful people, Max. You're not a per-son to them. You're nothing but a skinhead, not even human. You're a thing to them, the kind of thing they spend their whole lives putting in jail and then joking about it in the locker room."

"They come after me, they're going to have to walk through a whole fucking army of my men to get me."

"They'd love that. You think you're the only informer they've got in the Brotherbund? If you holed up somewhere with your guys they'd know where you were in about twenty minutes. Twenty minutes after that they'd seal off the block and start setting up fields of fire. They *want* you to go to ground, so they can kill all of you at once. Flak jackets, gas masks, loudspeakers, tanks. Janet Reno would go up another ten points in the polls."

"What am I supposed to do, then?"

"The smart thing would be to take tomorrow off and do a little detective work. Before we can figure out what to do, we've got to know more about what's going on."

"What kind of detective work?" he said.

And so I outlined a useful day for him, finding out answers to various questions I had. Better for him to go poking around than for me to do it. I was a mystery man, and I hoped to keep it that way. We made arrangements for me to call him after lunch at the house of a cousin of his, a non-skinhead cousin. It was a good working assumption that Max's home phone and the gym phone were tapped.

"One more thing you might want to do, Max," I said. "Wipe that gun down and get rid of it so at least the bastards can't tie you to the shooting at Rackleff's house."

"Yeah, good idea. I was going to do that."

"I figured you were, but I thought I'd mention it."

"Listen, let me ask you one last thing, though," Wilhoite said. "When we were going around the stations before, you had to be bullshitting me, right? You could have lifted more?"

"I could have lifted more, sure. But you would have still beat me."

"Yeah, right, that's what I thought. That's exactly what I been telling myself."

"IT WAS LIKE YOU SAID IT MIGHT BE," MAX WIL- **12**
hoite told me over the phone when I
reached him the next day. "It's not a videotape thing they got, it's more like a camera-
type thing only it prints the time and the date under your
picture, too. When they cash your check, you know? So
what they do is throw everything out after thirty days
unless there's a problem like the check bounced or something, so they're supposed to still have the picture of me
only they don't, and that's the thing. Because this
cocksucker come and took it."

"Which cocksucker?"

"The FBI cocksucker. Honig."

"*Honig?*" I asked, amazed. I spelled it for him.

"I guess that's how you spell it," Wilhoite said. "I never
seen it written out."

"First name Paul?"

"I don't know. Special Agent Honig is all I know."

"When you call him, how does the secretary answer
the phone?"

"I'm not supposed to call him. He calls me. Or sometimes just comes by."

"With another guy? Young guy?"

"Always alone."

"What does he look like?"

"Just an old guy, out of shape. Gray at the temples."

"Glasses?"

"Yeah. You know him?"

"I think I saw him around."

"You there?" Wilhoite said after a while.

"I'm here. Just thinking."

I was thinking that a special agent in charge might well decide to go along when one of his agents called on a semifamous environmentalist who had been getting death threats. But it was inconceivable that under normal circumstances he would involve himself, personally and alone, with a skinhead informant. Guys like Honig were senior bulls in the bureaucracy, with scores or hundreds of special agents under them. They moved paper and called meetings; they didn't do actual work.

"How do you know it was Honig who got the picture?" I said at last. "Anybody can flash a phony ID. She remember his name?"

"No, but who else would have known about the picture?"

"Good point. I think you better call him up, Max."

"Like I said, I'm not supposed to call him except it's an emergency. He gave me like this fake name to tell whoever answers."

"You don't think this is an emergency? Why did he grab that photo, Max? He took it so you wouldn't have any insurance against a double-cross."

"I don't get it."

"If you've got the picture, you can always prove you're innocent. If they've got it, they can always lose it. What's the fake name you're supposed to use in an emergency?"

"Richard Roe."

"Jesus. Well, anyway, you see why it's time for Richard Roe? Tell Honig just what you told me about what you found out at the grocery store."

I stopped and backed up. Richard Roe was a guy who needed things spelled out slowly and fully. "Don't tell him that you told me, understand. Don't mention me at all. Tell him you got nervous so you went by this grocery store. You wanted to be sure they hadn't done anything with the picture. And the girl said the FBI took it, and you want to talk about why, and you want that picture for yourself in case your lawyer ever needs it.

"He'll say he'll hold on to it for the lawyer. No matter what he says, keep telling him you've got to talk with him about the picture and the whole situation or you don't know what you'll do. Act upset, pissed off. Tell him you'll meet him at the gym after it closes, say at quarter till ten. Tell him you want to know the whole story about those death threat letters, too."

"Damn right I do. He never told me he was going to send no official letters with the Brotherbund name on the sons of bitches. Had to have been him, because for sure none of my guys sent no letters. Which I knew they never did anyway, but you said to ask around, so I done it."

"Max, there's something pretty goddamn peculiar going on here, and you and me are going to get to the bottom of it. Here's what we'll do . . .'"

By nine-thirty that night I had set myself up more or less comfortably in a shower stall at Jim's Gym. It was the only place we had been able to find where I could stay hidden and still listen to whatever Honig had to say to Wilhoite.

I had had Wilhoite decorate the set a little, by putting

his boom box next to one of the weight benches. He had spread a towel out on the bench itself. The idea was that he would answer the door when the FBI agent came and take him back to the bench where he had been working out. He would turn the music off, and I could eavesdrop.

And it would have been a good idea, except for Wilhoite's taste in music. There I was sitting on the chair I had dragged into the shower stall, trying to enjoy an article in *Muscle Monthly* about how some guy blitzed his pecs. And there was Max Wilhoite a few yards away, blitzing his own pecs to the sound of Megadeath and the barbells clanging and Max grunting like a sow giving birth.

What with all that going on while I was trying to absorb the fine points of Man Mountain Dan Marley's daily routine for getting really ripped, pec-wise, I didn't even hear the knocking at the door. All I heard was Max hollering to hold on, he'd be right there.

"What the hell is that you're listening to?" the FBI man said as he followed the skinhead into the gym. "For Christ's sake, turn it off. And put your shirt on."

"Hey, I happen to be in the middle of my routine, okay?" But he switched off the music.

"The hell with your routine," Honig said. "Now what's this shit all about? What in the hell makes you think I'm at your beck and call?"

"You're here, ain't you?"

"I don't appreciate the tone of that remark."

"There's things I don't appreciate neither, Honig."

"Special Agent Honig."

"Whatever. Anyway, what's going on that you've got my picture from the store? What's going on you're sending out official letters with the Brotherbund name on them? Wasn't nothing like that in our agreement."

"Our agreement is what I say it is, you pathetic little dirtball."

"Hey—"

"Shut up. On the evening of October twelfth you and your other dirtballs bought corn dogs from a Nigerian street vendor and subsequently refused to pay him. When he insisted on his money, you surrounded him and beat him till he fell to the ground. Then you personally did a cute little trick that you picked up from German skinheads called sidewalk cracking. You stamped on his head till you heard the bones crack.

"The only reason you're not in jail on murder charges is that I personally have convinced the U.S. attorney that the evidence against you is not yet sufficient. He is not aware that I have your videotaped confession to what I have just stated in my personal safe, with a blank space at the beginning of the tape where I can insert a Miranda warning and whatever date seems appropriate to indicate that the confession just came into my hands."

Honig was silent for a minute, no doubt drilling Wilhoite with a terrifying bureaucratic stare. "End of story, Max," he then said. "End, of, story."

"Still," came Wilhoite's voice, "it ain't fair."

When people start saying things ain't fair, they've already given up. They're just whining. Whining wasn't supposed to be in Max's script. He was supposed to be goading the FBI man, threatening to go to the newspapers, talk to lawyers, disappear into some skinhead underground. Jerk Honig's chain until he laid all of his cards on the table so I could read them.

"In this life you don't get fair," Honig said. "You get justice."

"At least you could have told me you picked up my picture from the market."

"Why bother? I was going to give it to you for safekeeping anyway."

"Huh?"

"It's the proof of your innocence in the bombing, after all. I thought you'd feel more comfortable if you had it in your possession. I've got it right here in my briefcase."

"You do?"

I heard the two clicks of a briefcase being opened.

Then I heard an explosion.

My first instinct was to duck, and so I did. Max was bellowing like a bull. I got hold of myself and tried to make sense of things. Honig's next shot, if I gave him time to look around the gym, would probably be at me. I stepped silently out of the shower and eased over to the shower door to peek out.

Honig's back was to me. He held a revolver loosely in his right hand, all his attention on what was in front of him. Wilhoite was hugging himself as if otherwise he would fly apart, and he was twitching back and forth on the floor. Maybe the bullet had hit his spine and sent his nervous system into spasm; maybe he was trying to get away from the pain. He screamed as he flopped around. Blood showed bright red against the whiteness of his bare arms and torso. The smears he was leaving on the floor hardly looked red at all, against the black rubber matting.

I grabbed a wet towel out of a canvas laundry bin beside me. They were the flimsy, cheap towels you find in fleabags and downscale gyms. I made a quick and dirty mask out of it, the way train robbers do in westerns.

I had the gun out of Honig's hand before he knew I was there, before he could even tighten his grip on it. Probably he wouldn't have held on to it anyway. He seemed to be stunned at the noisy, messy havoc he had created by just pressing on a little metal thing. He didn't even turn around to see what had happened to his gun.

"Jesus," he said. "Now what am I supposed to do?"

"Try cracking him," I said. At last he turned his head and saw me in my makeshift mask.

"Who are you?" he said, coming back into focus.

"First time?" I asked, motioning at Wilhoite with the gun.

The FBI man nodded. It would have been the first time for practically every FBI man, and for practically every cop, too. No matter what TV makes you think, most cops go through their entire career without firing at anything but a target.

"Now you know," I said. "Don't you, killer?"

"Let me explain the situation so you know what's going on here," Honig said. "I'm a special agent of the Federal Bureau of Investigation. I was attempting to arrest this man for murder when he attacked me. If you'll just return my firearm, we can find a phone and call for an ambulance."

"I don't think there's any hurry."

Wilhoite had stopped thrashing around and lay still for a minute. The blood was coming from a hole almost in the center of his chest. He tried to raise himself on his elbows but was only able to get his shoulders a few inches off the floor. "Don't!" he begged to whoever or whatever might be listening, and he collapsed back on the floor. His head made a solid whump, like a stone dropping on the ground. His face had been drawn with the strain of trying to rise up and speak. Now it was slack with the mouth a little open, like a mouth-breather sleeping. But his chest wasn't moving and his eyes weren't closed.

"Looks like you did it," I said to Honig. "Nice work, killer."

"We'll still need the ambulance," he said. "Give me the gun and I'll call them."

"Fuck that," I said. "Take your tie off."

"Wait just a minute, here. I'm the special agent in charge of the Portland field office of the FBI. My identification is inside my—"

"I know who you are. I want your tie."

"Now, listen—"

"Aw, for Christ's sake," I said, and tossed the gun away so my hands would be free. I took a half nelson on him with my left arm. With my free hand I wrenched his tie off. Then I put him on the floor while I tied his arms together above the elbows. They were average arms for a bureaucrat in his fifties, soft and without strength.

He wasn't fighting, but he kept bitching and complaining, fussing and hollering all the time I was packaging him up. So I hoisted him up on the bench, grabbed the shirt Wilhoite had taken off for his workout, and wrapped it around Honig's head.

Maybe he would shut up like a canary if you put a hood over him. Even if he didn't, at least I could take the towel off my own face. To keep the shirt in place, I worked Honig's belt off him and wrapped it around the general area where his mouth had to be. He was plump enough so that the belt went around twice and I could still buckle it. The belt kept the shirt in place, all right, but it didn't stop him making muffled noises about what deep shit I was going to be in if I didn't let him go.

"Shut up, will you?" I said, and smacked him hard on the back of the head with the heel of my hand, the way I had done with Max the day before. "I've got to concentrate on something." He shut up.

Whatever Honig had been up to with Max Wilhoite, he was plainly in it alone. If I left the FBI man with the body and called the cops, he would be in very serious trouble. But he'd probably be able to lie his way out of the worst of it. He might have a much tougher time explaining his adventures to his bosses in Washington, and most likely his career would be ruined. But how much difference would it make to him? Back at the Belters' house, I had heard him tell the young agent that he was closing in on retirement anyway. They would bust him a grade, turn him loose with a pension, and hope nobody ever heard from him again.

And their interest in finding out who had killed Robert Rackleff would immediately become nonexistent, for fear a senior Bureau official would turn out to be implicated in it somehow. They'd shove it all off on the dead skinhead and close the case, which was probably what Honig had in mind to do all along. What if there were no dead skinhead, though? I thought about that for a moment but couldn't see any real advantage in taking Wilhoite's body off somewhere and making it disappear.

On the other hand, what if Honig were the one to disappear? That had a lot more promise. He and I would have plenty of time to reason together, and probably he could tell me exactly who had killed the man I was supposed to keep alive, and how.

Meanwhile, somebody would open up next morning and find Wilhoite's body with Honig's bullet in it. And maybe I could arrange for them to find Honig's gun, and Honig's briefcase. But why would he leave them behind, if he had fled under his own power? And what would he flee in? He had to have a car parked outside. I thought about it until everything seemed to fit together in a workable way. It meant a busy few hours, but it could be done.

From any rational point of view, the plan I had just come up with was insane. It only made sense if a man like Robert Rackleff had died in your arms, calling for his mother and telling you how much it hurt.

And if you felt your own stupidity had killed him. Which you couldn't help feeling if you had set up an elaborate system to make sure nobody was following the dead man's van, but never thought to check the van itself.

I might get away with it, but I might not, too. If I didn't, I could count on spending the rest of my life in jail. And anybody involved with me could expect jail time, too, even if their involvement was limited to merely knowing my whereabouts.

I thought about Hope, visiting me at some federal prison. I thought about going so deeply underground that I wouldn't even be able to risk letting her know I was alive.

I looked at Max Wilhoite, and I remembered the agony he had died in. I thought about Robert Rackleff's leg, hanging by a few scraps of sinew and tendon. In the end his clothes had been dyed after all, red with his life's blood.

I could only think of one way to make it up to him.

Honig's car was parked outside. It was a 1993 Mercury Grand Marquis, loaded, which would normally get stolen in a hurry if I left the key in it. The trouble from a thief's point of view was what it was loaded with—the siren, the red flasher stored under the front seat, the public address system, and the empty shotgun rack on the ceiling. I decided on leaving it in the airport parking lot instead. From that decision a lot of other things followed logically.

By the time I left the Grand Marquis parked by a walkway in one of the lots at Portland International Airport, the car was really loaded. Max Wilhoite's body was in the trunk, along with the ruined gun he had used to shoot up the Belters' house. The shotgun that had been in the trunk was propped up against the passenger seat, in plain sight. Under the front seat was Honig's gun, wiped clean of fingerprints. A single bullet was missing. Since there was also a single bullet in Wilhoite's body, a connection might occur to somebody. They had some pretty sharp guys in the Bureau.

I locked up with the headlights left on, so some Samaritan would be sure to take a look in the front seat before long. Then I walked across to the loading area and took a cab to downtown Portland. I got out a couple of blocks from the Marriott Hotel. I went into a side entrance, went out the main entrance where the cabs waited, and took one of them to an intersection in southeast Portland not far from where my truck was parked.

Back at the gym Honig was naturally right where I left him, which was blindfolded with bandages I had found, and handcuffed to the Universal machine. The trunk of his Bureau car had been full of interesting things, three pairs of handcuffs among them. There were also leg irons, plastic ties for hands and feet, a stun gun, Mace, and a cute little set of thumb cuffs. Since Honig probably hadn't personally arrested anybody since the 1970s, given his rank and age, it was pitiful that he would carry all this junk around.

I on the other hand, like any normal kidnapper, had a logical and legitimate need for restraining gear. In fact I had added to my collection from the gym's supply closet. It apparently served as a lost-and-found, too, so I stuffed an old gym bag with an Ace bandage, a couple of rolls of duct tape, a roll of steel cable, and a bunch of dirty, smelly sweat clothes that people had left behind at the gym. They were for Honig. The army started the process of turning you into an obedient, ass-kissing moron by making you wear its clothes, and I figured I might as well try the same technique on the special agent in charge.

Once I had locked Honig into the toolbox of the pickup, bound and gagged and blindfolded, I went back to the gym for a last check. The floor showed no visible trace of Wilhoite's blood, and the towels I had used to mop up with were safely stowed in the back of the truck. I had wiped my fingerprints off every place I could remember touching, although it was probably overkill. The gym would get opened somehow tomorrow, and after a day or two of workouts nobody would be able to sort out the jumble of prints. There wouldn't be any reason to try, either, since there wouldn't be any reason to think that the skinhead had been killed here. When I couldn't think of anything I had forgotten, I turned off the lights and let myself out the back entrance.

BY DAYLIGHT I WAS SITTING IN THE CAB OF THE truck way up back of Agnes Beach, wondering what to do about the chain in front of me. It ran across the logging road from one side to the other, spiked into big trees at each end. There was a padlock in the middle, and a private property–no trespassing sign that said violators would be prosecuted. It wasn't a threat that would mean much to a guy who had just kidnapped the top FBI official in the state of Oregon. But I needed to get through the barrier without it looking as if I had.

It came to me after a while that the padlock on the chain was the same kind as the cheap Master Lock model I had found on the toolbox, with the combination scratched into the paint beside it for the benefit of the memory-impaired. It was 10-16-4, as I knew without looking. I am memory-burdened and can remember phone numbers, combinations, and even long conversations without trying.

As far as I can tell, memory hasn't got any more to do with intelligence than good spelling does. Having near-total recall helped me scrape through school with practically no effort at all, but apart from that it hasn't been much use. I'd rather be able to whistle through my teeth, those real loud whistles that make everybody jump.

Intelligence is something different. It's connecting, it's standing things on their head and seeing them in a new way, it's seeing patterns other people can't see. For instance, it's figuring out how to replace a Master Lock padlock on a light chain when you don't have a bolt cutter or a hacksaw among the tools you took out of the box to make room for a special agent in charge. With intelligence, it finally dawns on you that you don't have to worry about the locked padlock. Instead you take a pair of pliers and snip the chain links on either side of it. Then you run the hasp of old 10-16-4 through the next two links of the flimsy chain and snap it shut. Then you dial 10-16-4 to open it again, because of course the pickup is still on the wrong side of the fence.

Once I got it all sorted out, though, I was pleased with my work. I could go back and forth at will, but any casual trespassers would be turned back by the chain. Any legitimate visitors who tried the old combination would just figure the padlock was broken and cut the chain. If I was inside the barrier at the time, I might hear them coming. If I was on my way back from outside, the chain on the ground would warn me I was driving into trouble.

Once we got to the clear-cut that Lamar had shown to Robert and me a few days before, I went exploring. Honig was safe in his toolbox. So far he hadn't made a sound. He could be dead, and in a way it might have been better if he was. Certainly burying him out here and slipping back to the East Coast was the low-risk option for me. I didn't think I'd feel much guilt over his death, either. Maybe a little, just as Honig himself had been uncomfortable watching Wilhoite die from his bullet. Maybe not even a little. Honig plainly had something to do with Rackleff's death—had either done it himself, or had it done, or could have stopped it.

A couple of hundred yards up the steep slope I found what I was looking for. The bulldozers had uprooted a stump, leaving a huge root wad upended to the sky like a ten-foot platter on edge. Where the tangle of roots had been torn loose from the ground, a saucer-shaped hole was left. Up the slope was another huge root wad, blocking the view from the top. You wouldn't be able to see anything or anybody in that shallow hole until you climbed right up beside it.

Back at the truck I opened the toolbox and immediately pulled back. It smelled like a New York doorway in there. "Pissed your pants, huh?" I said. "You're disgusting, shithead. Come on, get your ass moving and get those filthy clothes off you."

He got up slowly and painfully. He was a mess. His summer-weight dark blue suit was dirty and greasy from the toolbox. His eyes and mouth were taped, and he was handcuffed. He fumbled blindly and bumped his head on the truck cap when he tried to stand up. It brought blood, but just a little. He mumbled something that sounded like he wanted the duct tape off his mouth. I paid no attention. Ignoring logical and legitimate requests is part of basic training. The cadre's style is autistic. The cadre has the power of speech but doesn't use it to answer questions. The cadre only orders.

"Get down off of that truck, shithead. You deaf?"

After a while he found his way to the ground. I uncuffed him and told him to take his clothes off. After a while I said, "Did I tell you to take MOST of your clothes off? Take your wet panties off, too, Mary."

If the FBI had a gym, Honig didn't use it. Without his

clothes he was soft and white and round-shouldered. I tossed him the abandoned clothes I had grabbed from the gym's supply closet—a sweatshirt with no sleeves and a pair of sweatpants that had been torn off at the knee. He fumbled blindly into the clothes, getting the shirt on backward. For his feet, I tossed him a pair of abandoned flip-flops from the gym. Then I loaded him up with various supplies and we started up the hill, me behind telling him to go left or right, watch out for this or that. Always it was shithead. The cadre gives you a new name right off the bat. All control cults do.

After carrying two loads of supplies up the hillside Honig gave out. His color was bad, he was sweating heavily, and he kept falling down. So I let him sit on a cooler while I figured out what to do with him. Simple was best. I shackled the FBI man's ankle to a thick root inside the root wad.

I wrapped the Ace bandage around my head until only my eyes showed, and then took Honig's blindfold and gag off. I yanked the duct tape fast, but it still hurt. He yelped and I could see why. Patches of his eyebrows were stuck to the tape. It took him a moment to blink and focus. Even then he probably couldn't see too well, since his glasses had got smashed somewhere along the way. Still my mummy getup registered on him very satisfactorily.

"Who *are* you, for God's sake?" he said. "What do you want, anyway?"

Naturally I didn't answer him. I took a half-gallon milk container full of water out of the cooler and put it in his reach. There was a plastic leftover dish in the cooler, a Tupperware kind of a thing shaped like a bowl. It had canned spaghetti in it, left over from yesterday, but it was good enough for a trainee. I left it for him, and disappeared from his sight behind the root wad.

"Hey," I heard him calling as I climbed back down the hill. "Hey! Where are you going?"

He missed me already. Maybe it was the Stockholm Syndrome.

There were state campgrounds all along the coast, so a lot of camping supplies had to have found their way to the area. I found most of what I needed in a pawnshop in Neskowin and the rest in a Lincoln City army-navy store. Then I went to a supermarket and loaded a cart with nourishing swill. Eating habits were something else the army changed when it set out to make a new you.

Once everything was stowed away in the back of the pickup I went to one of the wall phones outside the market in the sun. The deal with pay phones seems to be to make them as uncomfortable and inconvenient as possible to use, maybe so they won't get to be gathering places. Or maybe just out of meanness.

"Lordland," a woman answered. "God bless you." It was one of those sweet southern voices, respectful and playful at the same time, that make you want to rush right out and get married.

"We have a collect call for Wanda Vollmer from Sister Mary Margaret?" my operator said. "Will your party accept the charges?"

"I don't believe we have a Sister Mary Margaret."

"It's *from* Sister Mary Margaret, ma'am. Isn't that right, sir?"

"That's right," I said. "I'm her secretary."

"I'll put you through to Miss Vollmer's office," the sweet lady said, sounding out of her depth. Presumably they didn't get too many calls from nuns at Lordland, which was a very Protestant theme park and religious foundation near Newport News. Wanda Vollmer was the one who ran it, but she had briefly gone by the name of Mary Margaret before she got the job. Only a few people knew that.

"We'll accept the charges," said somebody at last, in a new voice that was just as sweet. "Is this Sister Mary Margaret's secretary?"

"Yes, it is."

"One moment, please."

"Hey, asshole," said a new voice, perhaps not quite as sweet. "Can't you pay for your own goddamned phone calls?"

"Nice to hear from you, too, Wanda. Actually, I wanted to be sure there wouldn't be any way to trace this phone call back to me."

"Oh, yeah," she said, immediately serious. "What's wrong?"

"I need you to pass a message along to Hope."

"Okay," she said. No questions about why I couldn't just call her myself. Wanda would figure that if I didn't explain something, I must have a good reason not to. Maybe someday I would. Meanwhile, an old buddy was an old buddy regardless.

"The message is the vacation is off till further notice. I'm still where she thinks I am, and I'm still okay. Am I going too fast? You getting this down?"

"I got it. Go ahead."

"She shouldn't call anybody out here to ask about me. That's particularly important. No phone calls made from her line or any other line to anybody connected with me. Okay?"

"Got it."

"She shouldn't worry. If she doesn't hear from or about me, it means I'm okay. The minute I'm not okay, she'll hear. And tell her I love her."

"That's it? That's the message?"

"That's it."

"You understand that this is a stupid message, except for that last little part? This message is going to worry the shit out of her."

"I know it will. But I can't think of any other way to do it without dragging her down with me if I fuck up. Don't tell her that, of course."

"I won't."

"Thanks, Wanda. How's it going with you?"

"Fuck how it's going with me. You need anything else? Money?"

"I'm all right for money. I'm living real cheap."

"Tell me about it. You're the cheapest bastard I know."

"Thank you for those words."

"Listen, you know your own business, Bethany. But I got a feeling you're into something that's really big-time stupid. I'd think about catching the next bus out of town."

"You're right all the way around, Wanda. But I still can't do it."

"Fuckin' men," she said.

After the call, I sat in the truck for a while feeling bad about what I was doing to Hope. "It's for your own good," always sounds fishy. So does, "This hurts me more than it does you." But neither of them sounds half as phony as a line by Richard Lovelace that my freshman English instructor told us was the key to understanding chivalric love. It was supposed to have been said to a woman called Lucasta by some grown-up adolescent riding off to war. It went, "I could not love thee, dear, so much, Loved I not honour more."

If anybody had bothered to ask Lucasta what she thought of that proposition, she probably would have answered in the same words as Wanda. Both were in common use at the time.

I made sure that the padlock's dial was still set on eight, where I had left it. Also I had left a dry twig lying across one of the tire tracks coming up to the chain barrier, and nothing had run over it. So I undid the lock and drove on in.

I spent a couple of hours settling in. At the end of it, I had cleared a hidden parking spot for the truck behind a tangle of brush at the bottom of the hill. A camouflage tarp broke up the straight lines of the pickup, so that you couldn't easily spot it unless you went around behind the brush. Anyone not specifically looking for a truck in the area would go right on by it, or so I hoped.

Just inside the wood line on the north side of the clearcut, I set up an observation post behind a huge fallen log. It gave me a view of Honig tied to his root wad, a hundred yards or so across the hill. He couldn't see me behind the mossy log, but he could hear me chopping and pounding as I made myself comfortable. I wanted him to know that I was off in the woods somewhere, maybe watching. He hollered to me a few times, but gave up when I didn't answer.

At the end I had a little two-man tent set up in case it rained or the bugs got too bad for me. I wasn't worried about the bugs getting too bad for Special Agent Honig. Bugs were why I had given him only cutoffs and flip-flops to wear. I also had a camp chair set up where I could pass the time reading. By just raising my head I could see over the log to check on Honig. I had picked up an old pair of binoculars at the pawnshop to do the checking with. They didn't bring him in large as life, but at least they'd let me know if he was hurting himself or getting away. Apart from that, I didn't much care what he did.

So I settled down with Thurman Arnold's *The Folklore of Capitalism.* I always read with a pen handy, so I can advise the author as necessary. Reading Spencer, for instance, I fill the margins with helpful suggestions like, "Get a clue, Herb." But since this copy was eventually going to Hope, I kept it relatively clean. Here and there, though, I marked passages for her special attention.

How, for instance, can you fail to love a millionaire corporate lawyer like Arnold who writes, "Fraud, however, is a difficult thing to define in the ethics of trading, which are essentially the ethics of deceiving the other side. Therefore, in this country today it has become practically impossible actually to keep a man in jail for any other kind of debt than alimony, to which the ideology of an investment risk had never been attached."

Donald Trump better watch his step with Marla.

The thought would have gone into the margin for Hope's benefit, except that Honig had started hollering in a really serious way. I was too far away to hear individual words, but he sounded agitated. I put my pen in the book to mark my place, and put on the ski mask I had bought to replace my makeshift Ace bandage mask. The bandage had a disgusting wintergreen smell like my old high school locker room. I left Thurman Arnold for later and set out through the slash piles and the giant ferns and the stumps.

"For Christ's sake, I have to go to the bathroom," Honig said when I came up to him.

"What bathroom? You're in the field, shithead."

"What am I supposed to do?"

"Use your eyes. What's that thing there?"

"That bucket?"

I didn't say anything. The cadre doesn't answer dumb questions from trainees.

"What about paper?" he asked at last.

I let the question sit in the air for a long minute, and then answered it with a parable. The parable was true, a story I once heard from a reporter who had just returned from Cambodia. This was after the Vietnamese had closed down Pol Pot's slaughterhouse in spite of protests from civilized nations like the People's Republic of China and the United States of America.

"You're in Cambodia now, shithead," I said. "There's no paper in Cambodia. Did you know the Khmer Rouge killed Americans, too? One of them was a young guy named Harry Groves Williamson, from the state of Maine in the northeast part of the United States. That's how his confession started out. It was sixty-two pages long. He just couldn't stop writing. As long as he was writing he wasn't being tortured, I guess that's how it was.

"Anyway, his confession said he was pretending to be an innocent sailor, crossing the Pacific solo in his little boat. But he knew perfectly well he was in Cambodian waters. He was actually a CIA spy. It was there in his confession, page after page. Guy had been everywhere for the CIA. Saigon, Chile, Eastern Europe, Angola. He was even at the Bay of Pigs. He would have been eight at the time.

"The place they took him was called the Tuol Sleng schoolhouse. The Khmer Rouge guys kept records on everything, just like the Nazis. Something like twenty thousand people went into that schoolhouse. Seven came out alive. They had this manual for interrogators that said the enemies could never escape from torture. The only question was how much of it there would be. It's an interesting manual. Tells you all kinds of good things. Mostly low-tech stuff, of course, because the power went out all the time."

I stopped talking and just sat on a stump watching him through the holes in my ski mask. He seemed to have understood my parable, because he didn't ask for paper again. He didn't say anything. So I got up and went back to my camp and Thurman Arnold's book.

It would do Honig good to think about the Tuol Sleng schoolhouse for a while. Bringing up Indochina tends to make people think about crazed Vietnam vets, even though the Vietnam vets they see around them every day are no crazier than anybody else. But people believe what they hear, not what they see.

The setting sun was still hot on our mountainside. The bugs were beginning to come out in strength. For me it was an irritation. For Honig, with his arms and legs and head bare, it was going to be a lot more than that. Gnats, deerflies, horseflies, blackflies, and mosquitos were a big part of my plans for him.

So was mess call. I got a couple of containers of freeze-dried trail rations and carried them out into the clear-cut to Honig. I emptied the stuff into the bowl that had held the spaghetti, and poured water on top of it. I stirred the gray mess with a spoon and handed it to Honig.

"Humping the boonies, I used to tell myself if I ever got back to the world I'd never go camping again," I said. "And I didn't, till now you made me."

He poked at the mess with his spoon, and tried a taste. "I can't eat this," he said.

"You'll get to where you will," I said. I took the bowl from him and emptied it on the ground.

"That'll draw flies," he said.

"No shit."

I took a pair of his own cuffs and fastened his hands behind him. "What are you doing?" he said.

184

"You don't want your supper, you don't need your hands to eat with."

I sat and watched.

After a while he said, "What do you want from me, anyway?"

"Sir."

He looked up and wrestled with it a while. This was going to be even tougher for him than field sanitation had been. At last he said, "Sir."

"I want to know what cyclonite is, fuckface."

This took him a long time, too. At last he said, "I don't know."

"Sir."

"I don't know what cyclonite is, sir."

"What's RDX?"

"I don't know what RDX is, sir."

A fat fly landed on his forehead. It wandered around unconcerned while he jerked his head to dislodge it. The fly crawled down his forehead and started to detour around his eyebrow. Halfway along it decided on a short cut and climbed over the little obstacle, and headed down the left eyelid. Honig's frantic blinking alarmed the fly slightly and made it crawl away to the corner of Honig's left eye. Honig screwed up his eyes, and at last the fly flew off, but only for a few seconds. Then it landed on his plump cheek, and started moving toward his mouth.

"They lay eggs on you," I said. "That's where maggots come from. You don't get maggots on live people, though, do you? I wonder why that is. I mean, you'd think the eggs would hatch just the same, wouldn't you? I guess they must, come to think about it. Because you hear about them in wounds, don't you? Maggots, I mean. You got a little cut there where you bumped your head getting out of the truck, maybe that's what's drawing them."

Honig got busy with his left shoulder, trying to hunch it up high enough to scare the fly off. Finally the fly wandered off.

"At least cuff me so my hands are in front of me," he said. "Sir."

"Give me a reason, shithead."

"I don't know what you want, sir."

"I want to know about cyclonite and RDX."

"I don't know what to tell you, sir. I never heard of them."

"Maybe it'll come to you."

I went back to the wood line and watched for a while. He kept twisting and wriggling to get away from the insects. When the light got too bad to read, I went back down to the pickup and had my own supper. It was better than Honig's but not by a whole lot.

For breakfast I gave Honig Grape-Nuts and water after taking his handcuffs off. Grape-Nuts can soak up an amazing amount of water. This time he got some of his meal down, not that he really needed it. He could have lived for a week off the fat in his cheeks alone.

Honig's face had turned pink from the sun yesterday, and today it would turn red. Salt-and-pepper stubble was showing on his face. Wherever his body was exposed—head, hands, neck, arms, legs, feet—the insects had left angry lumps. There must have been nearly as many lumps on the rest of his body, too. The loose sweat clothes wouldn't have kept insects out.

"Listen," Honig said, and paused. "Listen, sir, I can't help you if I don't know what you want. Tell me what this is about and we can start working together, okay? What is your goal here?"

"I want to find out what cyclonite is."

"Okay, no problem. Sir. We can start from there. I was thinking about it last night and I remembered hearing about it somewhere. I think it's an explosive."

"What about RDX?"

"I'm not sure, but I think it's the same thing. Just a different word for it."

"How come you didn't tell me that last night, shithead?"

"I told you. I didn't remember at first, till I got to racking my brains about it."

"You're jerking me around. You don't want to jerk somebody around that's got you tied to a tree. Have a nice day."

I read and watched from my observation post for a while, but then I got bored and worked my way down quietly through the woods and back to the truck. I got bored there, too, so I went walking down the logging road till I found some blackberries in a clearing. They were as big as the end of my thumb. I picked until I had a handful, and then ate it in a couple of big bites and picked again. By the time I had enough, the palm of my eating hand was purple.

I went on down the road, seeing squirrels and chipmunks and little birds. It was a half an hour's walk to where the chain stretched across the road. My various telltales were undisturbed. On the way back, I stopped again at the clearing where the blackberries were.

Halfway across the clearing I heard the quick, startling rustle of a snake, and saw the flash of movement as it disappeared under a sheet of bark. I turned the bark over and saw the snake, motionless in hopes it wouldn't be noticed. It was a small gopher snake. People mistake them for rattlesnakes sometimes, which gave me an idea. I caught the snake and forgot about the berries. Back at the truck, I put the little snake in a milk carton and took it up to my lookout post with me.

I went out to check on the prisoner, taking more water with me. He'd need plenty of water, out in the sun. I refilled his bottle and turned to him.

"You ready now, shithead?" I asked.

"Look, sir, I know what you've got to be thinking. You overhear a dispute between an agent of the federal government and a friend of yours—"

"I wouldn't have pissed down Wilhoite's throat if his heart was on fire."

"Well, I was mistaken, then. I thought he was—"

"He was your friend, not mine. You were the one doing business with him. I don't give a shit you killed him. For me it was like the Army-Navy game. If I had my way, both of you would have lost."

"I got the impression you were in the army yourself."

"That doesn't make me a fan."

"Who are you, then?"

"You keep thinking you're still somebody that asks questions. Only now you're somebody that answers them. Answer this one, shithead. How come you didn't want me to find out that you knew about explosives?"

"It's simple, honest to God. I thought you were in the Brotherbund."

"So?"

"I didn't want you thinking I bombed somebody and then tried to blame it on your leader."

"Doesn't make any sense. You're still jerking me around."

Flies swarmed all over the Grape-Nuts that Honig had left. I dumped the big blob of cereal out of the bowl, and for a moment the flies buzzed around in the air to rethink the situation. Then they settled back down on the new

pile of Grape-Nuts. Myself, I went back to the shade of
the woods, had a bottle of iced Rainier Ale from my little
cooler, and lay down on the springy forest floor with a
handkerchief over my face. I even managed to nap for a
half an hour or so, before the bugs finally woke me.

I put my ski mask on and went back out into the sun
again, to see what effect the insects were having on my
special agent in charge. Maybe they had helped him rethink his situation, too, although he didn't seem too
bright. Like half the bureaucrats in the world, business
and government both, he had most likely risen by ass
kissing, claiming credit for the work of others, blaming
them for his own failures, taking no initiatives, and duck-
ing responsibility whenever possible. If he had any brains,
he'd still be a street agent.

Honig's hair had been smooth and neatly combed when
he was fresh caught. Now it was matted and filthy, with
twigs and pine needles in it. I wondered if I should shave
it off, which was another thing the military did to cut you
loose from your moorings. But I didn't want to share my
razor with him, so the hell with it.

He began in again with something he had been trying
all along, although usually I'd shut him up before he got
very far. This was how important he was, and how powerful the Bureau was, and how much trouble I was in,
and how he might be able to help me out of it.

"Shut up about that shit," I said when I got tired listening. "You'll never get out of Cambodia. You'll never
have any power again, ever."

So he shut up for a while, but then he tried another
approach. I had just been sitting there, looking expression-
less at him.

"I have to confess I had you all wrong at first," Honig
said. "Seeing you in that skinhead gym gave me the

189

wrong idea about who you were. It should have occurred to me that you were there for the same reason I was. You're a private investigator, aren't you?"

I didn't answer. Although I was certainly private and I was certainly investigating, the only license I have is to drive. And even that one is presumably invalid, since it isn't in my own name.

"I guess you're working for Earth Everlasting?" Honig went on. "Or for the family? Possibly the family?"

"I'm working on payback. I had a lot of respect for Robert."

"I did, too. You don't necessarily have to agree with somebody to respect them."

"You're a lying goddamned scumbucket. I heard you talking to your little brown-nose assistant when Robert was out of the room. You hated Robert's ass."

"I wouldn't go so far as—"

"Just shut up. None of your bullshit does any good anymore. You're fucked."

"What does that mean I'm fucked, if you don't mind my asking?"

"I've got a pretty comfortable little camp over there in the woods, and I got nowhere special to go, nothing special to do. Not now that you killed Robert. He died in my arms, I'm that guy. The mystery man you told the papers about."

Honig said something under his breath that might have been sweet Jesus. Something about Jesus, anyway.

"So I'm just going to sit back there in the woods and watch what happens to you. Sunstroke? Maybe some kind of infection or blood poisoning? Maybe it'll be diarrhea. Already you stink of piss, and you got the flies and all, going back and forth to that bucket. Maybe you'll just drain to death out your asshole."

"You're making a terrible mistake."

"I don't think so. It feels right to me."

"That isn't what I mean."

"It really does feel right, watching you wriggle around out here. It's making me feel like I'm doing something about Robert."

"What I meant was you've got the wrong man."

I ignored that, and went on talking.

"Robert was a really nice guy. The kind of life I always had, I never had the occasion to meet anybody like him. I would never have told Robert exactly what kind of life I had, because I wanted him to respect me. But it doesn't make any difference if I tell you, because you're an asshole that's not going anywhere.

"All I got to live on is my disability. I used to camp a lot, travel a lot. I'd meet people, maybe give them a lift with my truck. Something would come over me, like I was standing outside myself looking at what I was doing to them. It's hard to explain.

"I thought I was all over it once I hitched up with Earth Everlasting and started to look after Robert. Robert was younger, but it was funny, I looked on him like he was a father, only not a father like my real father. A father who would take care of me and teach me and stuff instead of hurt me all the time.

"With Robert I could just be myself all the time and there wouldn't be that other person doing things while I watched him. Robert would be watching me instead. Only now he's dead and I feel like I have to do things again."

"I can understand that," Honig said, in the false way people talk to a drunk or a looney. "I can certainly sympathize with it. But you've got the wrong man."

"You keep saying that, but it's just more bullshit. You know about bombs, you know about nut letters, you were doing business with that skinhead. If he did it, you did it, too."

"But he didn't do it."

"Who did?"

"We can work together and find out."

"We, huh? You and me? You and the FBI?"

"I represent the FBI."

"Not anymore. You just represent one guy tied to a stump waiting to die."

"I can make it a lot easier for you. You've broken laws, but you were under great strain. There's mitigating circumstances here."

"Nobody knows I've broken any laws but you, and you're never going to tell."

"There's no possible way you can get away with this. Nobody in the whole history of the Bureau has ever kidnapped an SAC."

"They still haven't, as far as anybody knows. I organized the whole thing to make sure of that. Your buddies are looking for you because I left your car out at the airport with Max in the trunk. Along with your gun. They're looking at passenger lists, talking to flight crews, checking your relatives and anybody else you might have holed up with. I don't have to tell you what they're doing. Passports, customs, credit card checks, the usual shit. But they're not thinking about anybody being kidnapped, shithead. What did you think, I sent them a ransom note?"

This was all news to him. He knew I had gone off somewhere with Wilhoite's body, but I hadn't told him what I had done with it.

"What they've been telling the papers is that other skinheads must have killed you and dumped you somewhere," I went on. "But that's your bullet inside Max. What they've got to really think is that you murdered him and ran. So they won't look very hard, for fear they might find you. From the Bureau's point of view, you're better off hiding in Mexico than standing trial for murder. In the whole history of the Bureau, no SAC was ever tried for murder, either. Was he?"

"Of course not. What are you doing with that thing?"

I was making a production out of opening the milk carton with great care, and peeking into it like I was afraid something would jump out.

"I caught a baby rattler."

"What are you going to do with it?"

"Nothing. Just let it go."

I set the carton down on its side, the top opened enough so that the snake could get out. But it stayed inside, even when I tapped the carton with a long stick.

"Probably more scared of us than we are of him," I said, and smiled a Dr. Demento smile. "He'll come out after a while."

"Take that thing away from me."

"He won't bother you. He'll just go under the leaves or something. They don't crawl around till after dark."

Honig didn't say anything when I left, no doubt having figured out there was nothing in the carton. Eventually he learned different, because even off in the woods I could hear him hollering. After a while he gave up.

Now he'd have something new to think about all night, on top of how closely I seemed to fit the FBI academy's profiling work on serial killers who drifted around in pickup trucks. In fact I had designed a lot of what I had been doing to remind him of things they taught at the academy, things that wouldn't leave you with much hope if you were chained to a tree by a weird drifter in a pickup truck.

By morning Honig was cooperative up to a point. He was ready to do what he him-self had surely forced hundreds of suspects to do. He was ready to betray somebody else in hopes of helping himself.

14

"I can tell you who killed your friend," Honig said.

"Who?"

"Well, we haven't got a case against him that will stand up in court yet, but we're close."

"Only place it has to stand up is right here. With me."

"What if it did stand up? With you, I mean. Then you could let me go, couldn't you?"

"Sure, why not?" Only a moron would believe I'd do that, of course. Or somebody who thought I was a moron. I would be signing myself into jail for the rest of my life.

"Do I have your word on that?" Honig asked.

"Absolutely."

He nodded, but he didn't look too happy. What was the word of a serial killer worth? Still, a slim chance was better than none.

"Have you ever heard of a man named Hap Overholser?"

"Tell me about him," I said.

Honig didn't need to know that Overholser and I went way back, all the way to Cambridge. As Honig told me about how important Overholser was, I was remembering the tall man with his python-skin Wellington boots sticking out from under the table on the stage of the JFK School of Government's auditorium. Big-boned and rangy and still tough-looking, even twenty years or so past his days of playing in Tulane's defensive line. He had thickened up a little around the shoulders and waist, but a little extra weight wouldn't slow him down much. The NFL is full of lots fatter guys, and they still move like cats.

"Mr. Overholser spoke to me about it at least a half a dozen times," Honig was saying. "For years he's been negotiating to sell the entire Bear Claw Forest to the government for four hundred million, or else he'd clear-cut the whole thing. He was afraid that this new administration would use Rackleff's allegations of criminal activity to back out of the sale and stop the cut."

"How come he calls you with his problems?" I asked. "Are you Ann Landers?"

"Mr. Overholser has been helpful to us in past investigations," Honig said. He had been calling the man "mister" all along, which was interesting.

"He's an informant for you?"

"Not an actual one thirty-seven, no."

"What's a one thirty-seven?"

"What we call an informant, but he wasn't that. Mr. Overholser was what the Bureau classifies as an SAC contact."

"Meaning you don't have to pay him?"

"Certainly not."

"Kind of a volunteer snitch."

"It wasn't that sort of a relationship."

195

"What sort of a relationship was it?"

Overholser's corporations had thousands of employees all over the Pacific Northwest, Honig explained, including many security personnel. These thousands of employees saw things, they heard things, they were part of their communities. They could be useful in many ways. Actually, Honig was sounding a lot like Lamar Purcell, describing his network of pot farmers.

"Useful how?" I asked.

"Infiltrating white supremacy groups, survivalists, extremists generally. Keeping track of the movements of suspected eco-terrorists. Providing information on local drug traffickers."

"You're telling me you use Overholser's company cops to go places and do things that your guys maybe aren't supposed to do?"

"In some instances you could perhaps put it like that."

"For instance blowing up Robert Rackleff?"

"That would have been entirely his own initiative."

"You're telling me Robert was playing with bombs and blew himself up?"

That was the theory the FBI tried to peddle when a couple of environmentalists were car-bombed in California a few years ago. Back in the days of the Freedom Marchers, redneck sheriffs used to trot out the same line of crap every time the Klan bombed another civil rights worker. It wouldn't surprise me if Pontius Pilate reported back to Rome that Jesus nailed himself to that cross to get publicity for his goofy cult. Cops are cops.

"I didn't mean Rackleff's initiative," the special agent in charge explained. "I meant Mr. Overholser's initiative."

"Because Overholser knew better than to ask you to blow up Rackleff, is that it? He knew you would have told him where to get off?"

"Actually, that's more or less what happened, believe it or not. He hinted to me that a good way to get rid of Rackleff might be to do a Judi Bari on him. Judi Bari—"

"I know who Judi Bari is." She was the environmentalist who was disabled in the California bombing. It's still unsolved, although an antiabortion crazy wrote a letter taking credit for it. Bari had been active in the pro-choice movement, as well as in the Earth First! movement.

"Anyway," Honig went on, "I pretty much told Mr. Overholser where to get off when he started to make that sort of insinuation."

"Because the Bureau isn't in that kind of business?"

"Of course not."

"So then later somebody sure enough does do a Judi Bari on Rackleff and you call a staff meeting to get everybody's best thoughts and somebody suggests you might want to take a look at this Overholser guy?"

"More or less."

"You're so full of shit it's squirting out of your ears, Honig. You never had any meetings about any of this, except maybe when Rackleff filed a complaint about the skinhead letters."

"Maybe not a meeting with the full staff. I didn't—"

"Shut up. What were you doing coming out to see Max Wilhoite all alone? You're the head asshole in the Portland office. You're the special agent in charge. You haven't done any actual work in years. And suddenly here you are, running a big investigation personally."

"I wasn't the case agent."

"Who was?"

"A very capable agent named Doug Coulter. You said you overheard me talking to Robert Rackleff at the Belter residence. The young man with me was Agent Coulter."

"What was he, off sick the night you shot Wilhoite?"

"I didn't want to involve Special Agent Coulter."

"I bet you didn't. Probably he would have wondered why you pulled a gun out of your briefcase and murdered your own snitch."

"It was self-defense."

"Remember me, shithead? I was there."

"Wilhoite was violent and known to be armed."

"Give me a break, he was wearing sweatpants and no shirt. There's only one single way that you're ever going to get loose from that stump, and that's if you cut the bullshit completely. Now tell me who told Max Wilhoite to shoot up that house."

"Mr. Overholser did, indirectly."

"Directly, who did?"

"I truthfully don't know. I assume one of his security people did."

"They were just looking through the phone book and picked out Wilhoite's name? That how it was?"

"I suggested his name to Mr. Overholser."

"Why?"

"Because the Bureau had leverage on him. We had enough evidence to bring charges against him in the killing of the Nigerian any time we wanted to."

"So you were cooperating with Overholser's security people, through Overholser himself?"

"In a sense."

"So indirectly it wasn't Overholser who ordered Wilhoite to shoot up the house. Indirectly it was you."

"I suppose some people might think it was indirectly both of us."

"A court would say it was directly both of you. Why did you have him do it?"

"It was disruptive activity. We don't want to make life too easy for extremist groups such as Earth Everlasting."

This had a certain logic—weird FBI logic. Cointelpro wasn't dead just because they called it something else these days, or maybe didn't call it anything at all.

The Belters and Rackleff himself had told me all about its reborn version. Environmentalists and animal rights activists were two of its favorite targets. The Bureau, working directly or through go-betweens, would sow dissension by writing fake letters and planting fake rumors. In the old days, half the members of the American Communist Party were FBI plants. Now the stoolies were swarming into environmental groups. If the FBI spies couldn't find anything criminal going on, they'd been known to suggest illegal projects and even volunteer to provide equipment.

More than once, the Belters said, the Bureau set up its targets by sending phony letters to the papers. Hundreds of trees had been spiked in some wilderness area about to be logged, a letter might say. With this as the excuse, local and federal police would round up whatever activists they happened to feel like hassling. The cops would confiscate textbooks, students' notes, and personal papers, sometimes keeping them for years. Vehicles were seized. Environmentalists were forced to provide fingerprints and palm prints, and hair and handwriting samples. Few of them were ever indicted or even questioned by a grand jury.

So it wasn't impossible that Honig had conspired with Overholser to shoot up the Belters' house with Rackleff inside. But it was quite a stretch to believe that the Bureau would run the risk of murdering a highly visible environmental leader. I wouldn't have believed it for a minute, if I hadn't been right there when Honig shot Wilhoite down. Even now, I had trouble believing it.

The skinhead had been killed because he could ruin

Honig with what he knew. Honig probably did see it as self-defense. But Rackleff couldn't ruin him, and was certainly no more than a pain in the neck for the Bureau itself. Killing Rackleff was proactive, as the lawyers say, not reactive. Proactive measures would tend to be limited to safe and cowardly stuff from the shadows, like forged letters. Not risky stuff like car bombings.

On the other hand, I could see the FBI not warning somebody on its hate list that he was about to be killed. And I could see Honig, once he knew I suspected him of the bombing, wanting to drag Overholser down into the shit with him. Bureaucracy means never having to say you're sorry. No way would Honig ever blame himself for the fix he was in. He'd blame the other guy for getting him tied to a root wad and bitten-all-over lumps.

I gave Honig another push, though.

"You're a slow learner, Honig. You're still bullshitting me. You want to know what I'm thinking here? I'm thinking I made a mistake giving you water. Think we should speed things up? Cut off your water?"

I spat in his jug and set it within his reach.

"Enjoy yourself," I said. "That's your last water. You won't tell me the truth, fuck you."

"I am telling you the truth."

"Not till you tell me you killed Rackleff, you're not. You had a hard-on for Wilhoite, you killed him. You had a hard-on for Rackleff, you must have killed him, too. Got to be that way. Overholser doesn't know about bombs. You're the only one knows about bombs."

"I didn't. I swear it."

"Oh, yeah? Well, that's different. Cross your heart and hope to die?"

"Certainly."

"Say it, then."

"All right. Cross my heart and hope to die."

"Then die, you lying fuck."

Back in the woods, I thought about things. It was start-ing to look as if Rackleff had been killed by committee, almost. Certainly Wilhoite and Honig, at least, had been involved. And now maybe Overholser. Who else? People in Carswell? The whole damned forest products industry? Honig was still holding back, and if I pressed him much more he'd only tell me whatever I wanted to hear. There'd be no way to tell if it was true. But he had given me enough information so that now I had something useful to do next. I had thought of a way to make sure I got reliable information.

But I'd need help, and the only one in a position to help me was my fellow criminal, Lamar Purcell.

I stopped the pickup short of the chain across the log-ging road, and got out to check my various indicators. My twigs were unbroken. The dial on the padlock was set where I had left it. There was even a new indicator, a spider web stretched between one end of the chain and an overhanging branch. I unlocked the chain, let it fall to the ground, and drove on through. Then I went back to set everything back the way it had been except for the spider web. For that one, the spider was on his own.

I almost made it to the pickup, but not quite.

"Hold it," a loud voice said. I didn't quite jump, but I definitely jerked.

I couldn't see where the voice was coming from until a figure appeared out of the bushes. An old man stepped out into the road, aiming a takedown twelve-gauge shot-gun at me. It was a single-shot, which meant he was used to hitting what he aimed at. So I did just what he told me. I held it while we inspected each other.

He had jug ears and a turkey neck and an Adam's apple that made him look like he tried to swallow a doorstop. He was the kind of lean, dried-up man who looks old at sixty and won't look much older till the day he dies, thirty years later. He wore work boots and blue-gray cotton twill pants from JC Penney and a shirt to match. The shirt was buttoned to the neck. The cuffs were buttoned, too, but even though it was early summer the sleeves of long johns poked out of them.

"Hi," I said, smiling. "How are you doing?" What the hell, to have a friend, be one.

"Don't do no good talking," the old man said in a voice that was a little louder than it needed to be, and toneless. "I'm deaf as a goddamned post."

The old man walked around behind me, staying just far enough away so that I wouldn't have any chance of knocking his shotgun aside before he could shoot. I started to turn—it seemed to me that I hadn't really moved anything but my head—when something slammed into my ass so hard that I nearly pitched forward on the ground.

"I told you hold it," the old man said.

It hurt like hell. He must have rammed that barrel into me underhand, like a man slinging dirt with a shovel. If the thing had gone off, it would have emptied out my entire pelvic region. The old man plainly didn't care.

"Where's your wallet?" he said.

"In my jacket in the truck," I said, but of course he couldn't hear. I didn't want to risk a gesture, though, for fear of another jab from the shotgun.

"Just point to it," the old man said. "Slow."

I raised my hand, slow, and gestured with my thumb at the pickup behind us. I heard him get in and rummage around for a while. When he came back out he told me to turn around. I did, and saw that he was holding the card case that I carry instead of a wallet. He would have found a whole collection of credentials in it, all of them faked on my laser printer back in Cambridge. Most of them were in the Bartley T. Berger name, although some had other names, none of them my own. They identified me as a reporter for various papers and magazines, an investigator for various district attorneys and insurance companies, an assistant producer for Columbia Pictures, and quite a number of other things.

"You been around," he said. "Go over there to the back of the truck and stay put."

While I was staying put, he opened the door of the truck cap and got in, all the time holding the gun on me with one hand. With the other he rummaged through the junk I had in back. After a while he came up with one of the sets of handcuffs I had found in Honig's trunk. He climbed down and tossed the cuffs to me. He moved around to get behind me again and said, "Put them things on, mister."

I put them on. He was an old man and he was carrying an old gun, probably his first gun when he was a kid, and maybe his father's first gun before that. It hadn't gone off when he jabbed me before, which presumably meant his trigger finger had been outside the trigger guard. Theoretically the gun wouldn't fire no matter how many times he jabbed me, as long as he kept his finger off the trigger. In practice, though, the firing mechanism had to be badly worn in a gun that old. The next jab might easily blow me in half.

"Now get inside of that truck," he said. "In back."

I climbed aboard, while he closed in to watch.

"Now open up that toolbox. Any shit inside there,

throw it out to make room. Throw any of it my way and I'll shoot."

I cleaned out the toolbox with my cuffed hands, not leaving a thing inside. With this old man, I wanted to do exactly as I was told.

"Now climb in and pull that lid down on top of you."

The dark closed in on me. I felt the truck settle when he climbed aboard. There was a scraping noise as he forced the hasp over the staple. It was a little bit sprung, as I remembered perfectly. There was more metallic scraping, which presumably came from running something or other through the staple of the lock to secure it. The truck lurched again as he left it.

I was in near-perfect blackness. The box didn't widen toward one end the way a coffin does, so I didn't have enough room to lie with my shoulders flat. And it was a few inches shorter than I am, so that my knees were nearly touching the top. I got myself as comfortable as I could.

After a few minutes I heard what might have been a car in the distance, and then the noise faded away.

And then there was nothing else to do but think, so I thought.

Who was the old man? Certainly not a cop. Was he the landowner? Lamar Purcell had said the owner of the tract was a "cheap shit," too cheap to replant the clear-cut. The old man looked cheap, all right, but he didn't look like my idea of a landowner. On the other hand he looked exactly like my idea of an old guy who turns out to have a fortune squirreled away somewhere when he dies. Or he could be a watchman of some kind, sent out to check on the property. Or a hunter, since he had the gun. Or a trapper. Back home in upstate New York, winter was the time for trapping. But out here where there wasn't much of a winter? I just didn't know.

Was he going to leave me in my steel coffin to die? I didn't have much data to answer this one with, either. But if he meant to kill me, why didn't he just do it? Or did he want to make me suffer for days before I died? Why? What had I done to him?

It seemed more likely that he had locked me in the box for safekeeping till he turned me over to somebody else. The landowner? It seemed like extreme treatment for trespassing. The cops? Much more likely. There was no radio in the pickup, so for all I knew I might be all over the airwaves and TV, with the whole country looking for me.

The time passed as my thoughts chased one another uselessly around. How much time? It finally occurred to me that I didn't have to be in total darkness after all. I had my cheapo throwaway watch from Casio. I pressed the little button and read in the tiny glow that it was fifteen after three. I had been in my box slightly longer than a quarter of an hour. If it hadn't been for the evidence of the watch, I would have said the afternoon was mostly gone and sundown coming on.

I hurt where the old man had goosed me with his shotgun. I had two choices of position, left shoulder up and right shoulder down, or the other way around. Already the time I could stay in either one without having to shift was getting short. Pretty soon each would be uncomfortable as soon as I wormed myself into it, and then painful, and then agonizing.

I had eased a tiny cramp in one calf already. Sooner or later, one would come along that would be impossible to ease. I'd be lying there immobile, with a brick-hard knot of agony in my leg.

And I had to take a leak.

I tried reciting verse. Once I had set out, as a stunt, to learn all the poems of Gerard Manley Hopkins by heart. This was less of a job than it might have been, because Father Hopkins didn't write a whole lot. Still it was too much of a job for me to finish. I stalled out midway through "The Wreck of the Deutschland," but at least I had memorized all the shorter poems that I really liked.

So there I was, reciting: "I wake and feel the fell of dark, not day. What hours, O what black hours we have spent this night!" . . . "I see the lost are like this, and their scourge to be as I am mine, their sweating selves; but worse" . . . "But ah, but O thou terrible, why wouldst thou rude on me thy wring-world right foot rock?" . . . "Here! creep, wretch, under a comfort serves in a whirlwind: all life death does end and each day dies with sleep."

It began to occur to me that I might have done myself more good, under present circumstances, if I had memorized Rod McKuen.

I had to go something fierce.

I thought of a whole bunch of additional questions I should have asked Honig about his timber baron pal, Overholser.

I still had to go.

I thought about the awkward way that the things Honig had told me didn't fit together with what facts I knew about Rackleff's murder. There were pieces left over if Honig did it, if Overholser did it or had it done, if Wilhoite did it, if Lou Schecter did it. The pieces seemed to come from several totally different puzzles.

Which didn't help me a bit with my main, immediate problem. I considered the old story of the kid who died in the rowboat in the middle of the big lake with his best girl, because he was too embarrassed to let go over the side. Was it possible for a bladder actually to burst? Would it really kill you if it did?

More than an hour had passed since the old man had left. Of course he'd come back. Had to. Why stick somebody in a box and walk away, except to get instructions on what to do with him? Of course the instructions could be to leave him there. Or the old man could be a nut. Or he could have had a heart attack. Or just forgot. Sometimes old people just forget.

I checked my watch again—closing in on two hours now—and called Hopkins's nature poems up from the memory bank: "Why, raindrop-roundels looped together that lace the face of Penmaen Pool" ... "Degged with dew, dappled with dew are the groins of the braes that the brook treads through."

The hell with poetry.

I tried to think about Hope, and about Overholser, and about Honig and what to do with him if I ever got out of this box. But by now I could only think of one thing.

It had been nearly two hours, by the tiny glow of my Casio. By now I was huddled into as much of a fetal position as I could manage in the narrow box, squeezing tight every muscle in my pelvic girdle. I just couldn't hold it any more.

I let loose.

It felt wonderful, the way passing a stone must feel. Better than a load lifted from you, a boil burst, sweeter than that first gulp of air after too deep a dive. No feeling in the world so good as that final giving up. I just lay there happy in the moment as the warm wetness spread.

Time later for guilt and regrets and the warmth turning cold and clammy. Right now I was filled with contentment, back in babyhood.

Then I heard noise, the sound of an engine, the slam

of a door and then another, voices saying something I couldn't make out. The truck lurched as someone climbed aboard. The lock on my box squeaked, the hinges creaked.

I was dazzled for an instant by even the low light inside the truck, but then the face came clear.

"Goddamn it, Lamar," I said. "Couldn't you have come five minutes sooner?"

"ELLIOT NEVER FUCKED WITH LIP-READING," Lamar was explaining to me. "His niece told me they wanted to teach it to him at the V.A. hospital when they shipped him back from Korea, but he said he had already heard enough bullshit in the army to last him the rest of his life. Laura told me—Laura's the niece, grandniece, really—she told me he never had much to say for himself even before the mortar blew him up. So he didn't fuck with learning to sign, either. Elliot wants to say something, which isn't too often, he'll write it down for you. Same way if you've got something to say to him, you write it down. You don't have to worry about old Elliot talking. He wouldn't talk if he could."

I was just about done wiping the clammy piss off myself with the dry parts of my pants. "Actually, I've been doing a lot of worrying about old Elliot," I said, tossing the wet pants deep into the back of the truck. I pulled on a pair of dry sweats. "The thing is, he shoved a shotgun up my ass and then locked me into a toolbox."

Old Elliot stood by, unconcerned. Maybe he found it relaxing to be deaf. What, me worry? He wasn't carrying his shotgun now. Its barrel showed through the window of the old GMC ton-and-a-half he had driven Lamar out in.

"He thought you might have been a pot commando."

"Those Forest Service guys?"

"Yeah."

"He goes around putting Forest Service agents in toolboxes?"

"Well, he doesn't like them. I'll give you that."

"This isn't even national forest out here."

"Actually some of it is, to the northeast of that clear-cut I showed you guys. But Elliot doesn't give much of a shit who owns what. Far as he's concerned, it's all there for him to use."

"For pot?"

"Trapping, hunting, fishing. A little pot, but Elliot's got his disability check, so he doesn't need much for money. What he'll do, he'll put in a plant here and another plant there, over the next ridge. Not a chance of spotting single plants from the air. He'll be out in the woods for days tending them, just like running a trapline. And the way the old guy knows the country, they couldn't spot him if they had an electric collar on him."

"He couldn't make much money off a few plants like that, could he?"

"It's more like a hobby with him. Capture the Flag or something."

"He captured something all right."

"It was the handcuffs and all your different IDs that got him worried."

"He jabbed that gun up my ass before he saw any IDs."

"I'm not saying he's not a tough old fart. But I don't think he would have put you in the box if he didn't fig-ure cop."

210

"You can get in a lot of shit putting cops in boxes," I said. It was a thought that had occurred to me a lot lately.

"Well, they'd cut old Elliot a little more slack than usual," Lamar said. "He's the only Medal of Honor winner we've got."

"Medal of Honor, huh? That's heavy duty."

"From what I've heard, when the North Koreans blew him up it apparently didn't stop him."

My instinct had been not to try any of my tricks with the old man. My instinct had probably been right.

"So that's what old Elliot was doing out here," Lamar Purcell went on. "Making sure his woods were okay. What were you doing out here?"

"You're not going to believe this," I said.

And I told him.

"You better follow us back to Elliot's place," Lamar said when I was done. "We got a lot to talk about."

Elliot's place was in the hills a mile or so back of Agnes Beach. It was a bungalow with a small kitchen, a smaller bathroom, and a good-size room that he used as a dining room, living room, bedroom, and workshop all combined. Piles of soft-core skin magazines, mostly *Playboy*, *Oui*, and *Hustler*, leaned against the wall and against one another. There were hundreds and hundreds of them, probably going back in *Playboy*'s case to the early, pre-mansion period. A dozen or so all-time great centerfolds were tacked to the walls.

The old man wasn't much of a housekeeper, but he wasn't one of the Collier brothers, either. I suspected he took a hack at the place every six months or so, and right now we were three months into the cycle. Lamar and I sat at an old kitchen table with a chipped enamel top the color of pale mustard. Elliot sat down into an armchair covered with an army blanket. From how far he sank, the webbing had given away and the springs were sitting on the floor. He pulled an old pair of boots out from under his iron bunk and started in to grease them while Lamar and I talked.

"My original idea was to keep away from you completely," I told Lamar. "If things went bad, anybody that even had a sniff of what I was doing was going to be fucked."

"You got that right," Lamar said. "And now I got a lot more than a sniff."

"Elliot, too."

"Well, he doesn't know anything so far. But probably nobody would believe that. Sensible thing is for me to call the sheriff on you. Maybe you could take off and then I call the sheriff. Give you a little head start, anyway."

"I wouldn't blame you."

"Honig, man. Fucking Honig. You got Honig chained to a root wad. It's every boy's dream."

"You know Honig?"

"Better believe it. He's been sending these like assault waves of feebies against me for years. I hate that pompous fuck, although I got to admit he gave me one of my better ideas."

"What was that?"

"He set up a sting operation in Portland a few years back where you could buy equipment, Gro-lites, chemicals, all kinds of shit like that for growing and processing. Then he busted all his customers. Then damned if some fool didn't open another shop just like it and make piss-pots of money on account of everybody knew this new guy would never turn his customers in to the FBI. On account of everybody knew he worked for me. Honig knew, too, but he's never been able to prove it on me.

Drives him nuts. You really got fucking Honig tied to a tree? I love it."

"Tying him to a tree was the easy part. Letting him go is what's going to be hard."

"You planning to let him go?"

"Why not? I never let him see my face."

"Not planning to let him go in my backyard, are you?"

"I was going to take him for a long ride first."

"I hope you let him off in Alberta. I don't need that kind of shit anywhere near my nest."

"I wasn't going to let him off anywhere, not for a while anyway."

"Why not? He told you who did it, didn't he?"

"I don't know if he did or not. What's the story on those death threats? What's the story on shooting up the house? Why would this guy Overholser pull unnecessary shit like that?"

"To put the blame on somebody else."

"Why pick the skinheads?"

"Same reason Reagan liked to beat up on Libya. They're weak and everybody hates them."

"Okay, fine. But then the skinhead goes to trial. Is he just going to sit there and suck up thirty to life? Naturally not. He's going to say the FBI made me do it."

"He's not going to say squat. The FBI killed him to make sure."

"I just don't believe that, Lamar. That isn't the way the FBI does."

"Hey, you were there when it happened."

"Maybe Honig isn't the FBI this time. Maybe he's just Honig."

"Just Honig? Why would just Honig do it?"

"Exactly."

"So if you don't believe Honig, what's next?"

"Well, shit doesn't get any deeper than what I'm already in."

"Overholser, huh?"

"If I can figure out a way to get to him."

"From what I know about Overholser, you got a whole different problem. He's not a candy-ass like Honig, that you can just scare him into talking."

"I don't know. Maybe he doesn't like nature either."

"You're going to tie his ass to a tree, too?"

"If I can. Do him good to sit around in a clear-cut for a while."

"Is that where you were going when Elliot jumped you?"

"To tell the truth, I was going to find a phone and call you up."

"Just what I needed. The phone call from hell."

"I couldn't see any other way. I was getting tired of playing Gestapo with Honig. He's still lying to me, but I don't have any way to cross-check what he's saying except with Overholser. Only I can't just phone the guy and tell him to drop over. Maybe it'll take me weeks to catch him alone. Meanwhile, back at the ranch, that fucking Honig would die with nobody to look after him."

"Let me get this straight. You figured I would baby-sit the guy who runs the FBI in Oregon so you could go out and kidnap the richest guy in the state?"

"Actually I didn't think there was hardly any chance you'd do anything so stupid. I figured you'd tell me to shove it, and so then I'd have to let Honig go. Then I'd sit down and try to figure out some way to lean on Overholser."

"Very sensible plan. Only how about this one instead? Elliot baby-sits Honig while you chase down Overholser."

"Elliot? Why would he do something like that?"

"Because remember that Laura I told you about? His greatniece or grandniece, whatever the hell you call them? She was one of those smart local kids I paid for their college. And she's the only person in the world that old Elliot gives a shit for."

"That takes care of Elliot, then. How about you?"

"Bunch of different things. Payback on Honig for riding my ass all these years. And maybe you nail Overholser bad enough so he won't be able to cut down any more old growth to pay his junk bonds off."

"The guys that hold the junk bonds aren't exactly Mark Trail, either."

"No, but you do the best you can," Lamar said. "Besides, those are all bullshit reasons anyway."

"The real reason being what?"

"Rackleff. He was like the good part of you that you try to hide from people because you want to be cool, you know? He did it the other way around. He let the good part out and tried to hide the bad part. Naturally he got fucked."

"Naturally," I said.

"Anyway, Robert was a good guy, you know? I mean, you know, how many actually good guys are there? I mean, you don't want them getting blown up and shit like that ..."

He stopped, embarrassed like any other real American male who has just heard a small fart of altruism escaping from him in public.

"That's deep, huh?" Lamar said. "In fact it's getting up over my boots."

"Hey, don't worry about it," I said, throwing the poor guy a lifeline.

"One thing you've got to understand, though," Lamar

215

said. "I'll give you up to the cops in a New York minute if it ever comes down to where it's your ass or mine."

"Naturally," I said. "Why not?"

"So," said Lamar. "Where you going to start with this asshole Overholser?"

"I'll start by reading about him in the papers," I said. "Incidentally, what have the papers and TV been saying about Honig?"

"Only that it's still a big fucking mystery. Maybe Wilhoite was resisting arrest and got shot. Maybe Honig shot Wilhoite in self-defense, and then his Nazi buddies shot Honig and drove him out to the airport."

"Nobody's saying Honig murdered Wilhoite and ran away?"

"Nobody's saying that."

"Or that somebody kidnapped Honig?"

"Nobody's saying that, either."

"So maybe it worked, the way I set it up at the airport."

I tried to give Lamar money for Elliot and for Honig's food, but he wouldn't take it. And I asked him to put it in the instructions for Elliot to use the ski mask and not to leave fingerprints. He had been in the army, so his prints would be on file. Normally it's too much work to look for one set of anonymous fingerprints among the millions that the FBI has, but they'd make an exception for the kidnapping of a special agent in charge.

The nearest good library was in Portland, but I wanted to stay out of Portland. My first kidnapping had sneaked up on me, but I had been thinking this second one over for a while. The less time I spent hanging around the future scene of the crime, the better.

So I looked for the second nearest good library, which

turned out to be at Oregon State University. OSU was at
Corvallis, in the flat farmland of the Willamette Valley.

I ended up spending most of a day in the periodicals
section there. Harold P. Overholser thought highly of himself, as I knew from his performance at the JFK School,
and he didn't mind sharing his opinion with the world.
The national press had run plenty of stories about Hap
Overholser, and the Oregon press had run even more.

There were pictures of the undergraduate Overholser
posing for the publicity cameraman in his Tulane football
uniform, Overholser punching out a demonstrator at a
logging site sit-in, and Overholser waterskiing behind his
fancy speedboat. He still looked good twenty years after
graduation, looked like he could still anchor Tulane's defensive line.

Overholser testifying before Congress, and before Oregon legislators. Overholser with a born-again Christian
named James Watt, who was my very favorite Reaganaut
until he was driven from office for boasting that one of
his advisory boards included "a black, a woman, two
Jews, and a cripple." The *Washington Post* ran a poem
written especially for the occasion that went:

> One wonders what remains
> Inside Watt's head
> That he has had the tact
> To leave unsaid.

Maybe it was only a little poem, but what other secretary of the interior ever inspired any poem at all?

And there were pictures of Overholser with the second
of his three wives, a brunette the size of Tammy Bakker
but a lot better looking. In the story that went along with
one of these pictures, Overholser philosophized over his

divorce settlement with the brunette. "Ain't nothing in this world as expensive as free pussy," he told the interviewer. Probably he said classy things like that all the time to mainstream reporters who either didn't use the quotes or cleaned them up. But this time he had been talking to *PDXS*, an alternative weekly in Portland, and *PDXS* didn't give a shit what it said any more than Overholser did.

There were many pictures of Overholser with wife number three, who was six foot one and had legs like Cyd Charisse. She had been a personal trainer in Hollywood until she became moderately famous and moderately rich from an exercise video. Now she was immoderately rich, or at least her husband was.

Several pictures showed Overholser with his stainless-steel DeLorean DMC-12 with the gull wing doors. It wasn't the most expensive car a person could drive, but it would get more attention than a Rolls-Royce.

And there was a picture that took me back twenty-some years to Southeast Asia, a picture of Overholser with a booted foot resting on the wheel of his airplane. Like the DeLorean it wasn't quite the plane you would expect from a conspicuous consumer, but an eye-catcher all the same. It was a Porter Pilatus, a weird-looking aircraft that seemed to be all nose.

The stretched fuselage held an overpowered engine that let you take off from impossibly short runways. The Swiss developed the Porter for use in the mountains where a normal plane couldn't land. We used them in Laos to resupply the Meo guerrillas who fought the North Vietnamese for us. I logged hundreds of hours in Porters when I flew for Air America during the war, and hundreds more in Alaska before I got to drinking so much that nobody would hire me as a bush pilot anymore.

"Overholser drives his own car (very fast, friends say) and pilots his own plane (not so fast; it's a Swiss model specially modified to land on postage stamp wilderness strips)," the *New York Times Magazine* wrote.

"If there's no place to land where we're cutting," the financier says, "why, hell, I just tell the boys to bulldoze a few feet flat for me." Overholser is in constant motion around his far-flung empire, to an extent that is rare for even the most hands-on chief executives. Equipped with nothing but a PowerBook 180 laptop and an overnight bag, Overholser is likely to zoom in unaccompanied and unannounced and start asking questions anywhere from Eureka to Eugene, from Pocatello to Portland. His harried managers have learned that he wants answers not now but yesterday.

And so on. Overholser came across as a hard-charging, no-nonsense chief executive, which is how the business press spells bully. I looked at the full-page color photo of Overholser about to mount his airplane and thought that he would have looked right at home twenty-five years ago at our semisecret CIA base near the Plain of Jars in Laos. The sign on the hangar would have read Long Cheng instead of Dixie-Cascade, but his type was in long supply among the agency's contract employees. Like them, he looked the part. Like them, he was the part, too. The image was true.

Even the mountains in the background of the photo were appropriate. For some reason, the agency used to recruit a lot of former smoke jumpers for duty in Laos. Half the guys in the Sky Bar at Long Cheng sometimes seemed to be from Missoula. Overholser would have fit right in, pouring streams of San Miguel down the throats of the beer-drinking bears that lived in a cage below the windows. Those were the days, my friend . . .

Overholser had been a few years too young for them, though. By the time he got out of college the war had been Vietnamized, which is to say we were already surrendering in slow motion and the draft was essentially over. So all that was left for Hap Overholser was the continuation of war by other means.

The football hero got his start by marrying a Kappa Kappa Gamma whose father owned a chain of drugstores in Louisiana, Mississippi, and Arkansas. The father obligingly died two years after the wedding, and the Kappa obligingly went crazy, or maybe she did. Anyway, she was locked up in a rich folks' asylum and Overholser took over.

In partnership with a crooked Tennessee banker who knew how the game was played, Overholser used S & L funds and bank loans and junk bonds to expand into Alabama, eastern Texas, and the Florida Panhandle. By the time the Great Enabler entered the White House in 1980, Overholser was ready to binge big-time. After fattening himself up in several lesser corporate raids, he was able to swallow up Dixie-Cascade in a hostile takeover.

These things sound complicated on the business pages, but they really aren't. Basically what Overholser did was put a few dollars of his own money down to buy a shotgun on credit. He used the shotgun to force a rich girl to marry him. Next he mortgaged everything she had and stole the money for himself. And now he was making her meet the mortgage payments by peddling her ass on the strip.

To move from the example to the reality, Overholser was cutting down every American tree he could get his hands on and selling them to Japan, often illegally, so he could pay off the money he owed to his Fagins in New York. One Wall Street analyst called the process "cashing out the forests" and pointed out that some of the company's redwood stands had been bought from the federal government originally for as little as $2.50 an acre.

And he had drained Dixie-Cascade's pension fund for the same reason, to pay off the bonds he had loaded the company down with. And he busted his unions, which was no great trick once Reagan castrated the National Labor Relations Board. And he increased overtime and skimped on workplace safety until his tired loggers had the highest accident rate in the industry. Which was going some, since the forest products industry as a whole already had the worst safety record of any industry in the United States.

And he cut labor costs by automating his mills or moving them south, where men were cheaper than machines. He had closed four mills in Oregon and California already, and opened ten in Mexico. And he was shipping as much unprocessed timber to Japan as he could, along with the jobs that went with processing it in America.

And he blamed the whole mess on the spotted owl.

That argument didn't get very far the night I heard him make it in Cambridge, but it sounded good in ruined little towns like Carswell, Oregon.

The more I read, the more I looked forward to getting together with the hard-charging, no-nonsense chief executive.

As a little kid I spent a lot of time in laundromats, since we often didn't have a washing machine at home. I liked the Laundromat. It was the one public place where you didn't have to worry about the junker your pa drove or the clothes your ma got you at the Goodwill. Everybody else at the Laundromat was poor, too. Everybody kept chickens and maybe had a rabbit hutch out back. Everybody landscaped with rusted, busted pickups that had little bits of broken safety glass all over the ripped seats and the rotting floorboards. All the other kids in the Laundromat knew about pulling up the seat cushions when a car died to look for loose change. The Laundromat was the closest thing we had to a day care center and the closest thing our mothers had to a ladies club.

This one in southeast Portland had the same cozy feel to me as the one we used to go to back home in upstate New York. The machines had gotten bigger over the years, though. There was a bank of dryers as high as a man. My own little load would have been lost inside one of them, like satellites in orbit. So my socks and sweats were flopping around in one of the standard-size models.

I got a pocketful of quarters from the fat woman who made change, and went out to the pay phone on the wall outside the discount drugstore next door. Of course the phone book was gone, so I had to go back to the Laundromat and look up my number in the fat woman's book.

"Dixie-Cascade," the voice said once I had all my problems squared away. "How may I help you?"

"Mr. Overholser's office, please."

After a minute another woman's voice came on, and told me that Mr. Overholser was out of the city.

"When will he be back?"

"If you'll leave your name and the nature of your business, sir, someone will get back to you."

"Have any idea where he went?"

"I'm afraid we're not allowed to give out that information over the phone, sir."

So I gave up on the center of the line and decided to try an off-tackle slant. I put another quarter in and dialed again. When the Dixie-Cascade operator answered this time, I asked for Reginald Smith. It took her a moment to check.

"I don't have a Reginald Smith," she said. "Can you tell me what department he's in?"

"I don't know. I just have a message to call him back at this number."

"I could connect you with human resources. Perhaps he's no longer with the company." Human resources is psychobabble for personnel, these days. But personnel weren't the people I wanted to talk to.

"I could be wrong about the Reginald," I said. "I can't read my secretary's writing sometimes."

"Well, there's an Arnold Smith in external affairs. A Barbara Smith in purchasing, also a Harrison Smith.

There's a Smith in industrial security, too, James W. Smith. And of course Mr. Smith in plant operations."

"He sounds like the one." He was the only one who sounded like a big shot, anyway. "He's not Reginald, though?"

"Patrick. Patrick L."

"Well, it could be, with the handwriting she's got. Can I give it a try?"

In a few seconds a new woman's voice said, "Mr. Smith's office. May I help you?"

"Talk to Jim, please?"

"There's no Jim in this office."

"What office do I have?"

"This is Mr. Smith's office."

"Right. Is he in?"

"He's in a meeting right now. But his name isn't Jim."

"Isn't this the industrial security office?"

"This is the office of the vice president for plant operations."

"Excuse the call."

Now I had Smith's first name and title. But I wanted to give the woman who answered Overholser's phone a chance to forget my voice, so I went back inside the Laundromat and read *People* magazine for a while. Burt and Loni were having problems, which was too bad. Burt always struck me as the kind of guy you wouldn't mind having a beer with, so I wished him well. I wished Loni well, too. I wouldn't mind having a beer with her, either.

Although my laundry was probably dry already, I plugged a couple more quarters into the machine so the fat woman in the corner wouldn't think I was loitering. Back at the pay phone I dialed Dixie-Cascade and asked for Mr. Overholser again. A different voice answered, so my wait had been a waste of time.

"This is Steve in Mr. Smith's office?" I said. "Mr. Patrick Smith?" I made everything sound like a question because I hoped that way I would sound young. "Mr. Smith wanted to set up a time to see Mr. Overholser as soon as he gets back."

"Steve?" the woman said. She made it sound like a question because she never heard of any Steve in plant operations.

"Steve Stilwell. I just started in Mr. Smith's office last week. I'm kind of an intern or something? They just sent me over to plant operations to help out temporarily . . ."

"The earliest Mr. Overholser could possibly fit Mr. Smith in would be Friday morning."

"Oh, gosh. He doesn't get back to Portland till then, huh?"

"He gets in Thursday after the close of business."

"How much after? Maybe Mr. Smith would want to wait."

"After dark."

"Is he flying in?"

"Of course he's flying in. Why?"

"I meant his own plane, as opposed to commercial."

"He always flies his own plane on shorter trips. He's only coming from La Grande."

"I just thought maybe Mr. Smith might want to drive out, meet him at the hangar. . . . Well, maybe not. Probably a bad idea. Look, can I get back to you on this? I need to find out what Mr. Smith wants to do. Many thanks. Thanks a lot. Bye."

Next I called airports and was bounced from operator to operator and office to office until at last I had learned that Dixie-Cascade had two hangars: a big one at Portland international for its executive jets and a little one for Overholser's Porter Pilatus at Morgan Field, southwest of Portland.

This wasn't particularly convenient to the corporation's downtown office, but it looked on the map like a fast drive over relatively untraveled roads from Overholser's showplace hilltop home in the far suburbs. The *Oregonian*'s Sunday supplement had run a four-page color spread on the Overholsers at home in Eagle's Roost, as the owner called it. He told the reporter there had been a nesting pair of golden eagles on the twenty-two-acre property before construction scared them off. This sounded like bullshit. Vultures I would have believed.

Back inside the Laundromat, I watched my clothes going around. They had been dry for a good while, but I let them spin. I had paid my quarters, and I still had twenty minutes or so of loitering time. I started to wonder how far La Grande was, and so I went out to the pickup to find out. My book on radio detonation techniques was next to the road atlas, and I had something to check in that, too. So I brought them both in.

La Grande looked to be more than two hundred miles away as the crow flies. I could easily drive there before Overholser took off on Thursday, which was tomorrow. On the other hand, I didn't know what the layout of the local airport was, or even if that's where he'd be leaving from. The whole point of a short takeoff and landing aircraft like the Porter was that you hardly needed airports at all. Probably dozens of ranches near La Grande had tiny strips that were plenty long enough. A stretch of road or a field would do. The only place I knew for sure that he'd be was Morgan Field, at this end of his trip. So Morgan Field needed to be looked at.

But first I had another stop, which the radio detonation book had suggested. I unloaded the dryer and left the rest of my time for the next customer. The fat lady told me which Radio Shack in the yellow pages listing was more or less on my way out of Portland, and I headed for it. I bought a couple of walkie-talkies, a sack of batteries, and an inexpensive AM/FM tape deck. The total came to not much more than a hundred dollars.

Rush hour hadn't started, and I got through Portland with no trouble. I had found Morgan Field well before they closed up shop for the day. It was a trim-looking little fixed base operation, with everything freshly mowed, swept, or scrubbed. Hoses were neatly coiled, fuel drums were painted, the rocks that lined the walkway were whitewashed. An FBO can look like a junkyard and still be well run, but when an operation looks as good as this one you can totally relax. Your plane is in good hands.

There was a time up in Alaska that I had dreamed of saving my money and one day owning a place like this. But the reality was that I preferred drinking and fighting in saloons and running around after women. The further reality was that I would have been lousy at it anyway. Come on, Pete, look at those rocks. Call that white-washed? Do 'em again, and this time do 'em right.

So the hell with running a tight little FBO.

I pulled off onto the grass on the other side of the road and settled for watching one instead. Lots of people drive out to watch the planes landing at little airports, and no-body would be likely to pay much attention to me.

One plane was practicing touch-and-go's, where you touch down, gun the motor, and take right off without stopping. Then you climb back up into the pattern and do it all over again. The guy was pretty good. Another couple of planes were doing go-arounds, where you com-plete the landing, taxi back to the beginning of the run-way, and wait till there's no one coming in so you can take off again. One of the pilots was soloing, but his landings showed he still had a good deal to learn. The other student pilot had an instructor in the plane with him. The student was landing with the kind of wild, comical bounces and wing wobbles and tire squealings that aerial clowns do at air shows. Except the clowns do it on purpose.

The touch-and-go man gave it up first, while the light was still strong. By the time the other two taxied to their tie-downs the shadows were lengthening a little. Meanwhile a half-dozen other planes had entered the pattern, landed, and taxied off to wherever they parked. The flying school Cessnas were in a little cluster near the building; some privately owned planes were lined up along the runway for the night; some were berthed in a row of eight or ten hangars that backed up onto the highway. The fourth hangar down had Dixie-Cascade's logo on it, a green tree inside a green triangle. A brown stump would have been more accurate. In a day before the word twisters had taken total control of the world, Portland itself used to be called Stumptown.

I watched the pattern of activity as planes made their final landings and were buttoned up for the night. Students and pilots left, and a man went around to check that all the doors were locked in the one-story building that housed the FBO and its flying school. I drove off myself when the lights in the building started to go out, so when the operator came out he wouldn't see me hanging around in the dark. I didn't want him to register a strange pickup in his memory.

Instead I found a campground for the night and drove back to Morgan Field later to see if I could spot any guards or security patrols. The place was dark and de-

serted. In two hours I didn't see anyone, and so I went
back to my spot at the campground.

Next morning I left the campground around nine thirty,
a little later than most of the other people but not late
enough to attract any attention. I kept thinking of the Son
of Sam guy, caught because of a parking ticket he got
near the scene of one of his murders. I didn't want to
drive fast enough or slow enough to attract the cops. I
didn't want to loiter anyplace where I might catch anybody's eye. I didn't want anybody noticing either me or
my old pickup. I wanted to hang out all day someplace
where everybody else is hanging out, too. I wanted a mall.

I found one eighteen miles from the airfield, which was
plenty close enough. It was opening just as I got there,
but I waited in the truck for an hour until business picked
up. Some clerk or guard might let his eyes rest on an
early bird just long enough to remember, if he saw me
later in the day, that he had seen that guy somewhere
before. Normally this would be paranoid behavior, but
under the circumstances it seemed like good common
sense. I was brand-new at kidnapping. Berkowitz was
probably paranoid for his first few murders, too, and only
got that parking ticket after he loosened his tie and started
to feel at home, so to speak.

Flying's the same way. Those students out at Morgan
Field weren't very good yet, but they were safer than they
looked because they were scared shitless. So they didn't
get ambitious, did everything by the book, and stayed
alive. The most dangerous pilots are the ones who get
enough hours in to think they know everything and not
enough to know they don't.

This would be my first mall in Oregon, but I wasn't
excited. Crawl one mall, you've crawled 'em all. The an-

chor stores might be Nordstrom's or Macy's or Blooming-dale's or Filene's, but they've all got the same brands in them, displayed the same way and for pretty much the same price. A Waldenbooks or a Sharper Image or a Benetton or a Brookstone's or an Abercrombie & Fitch in Oregon is the same as one in Maine.

I had the same experience I usually have in malls. I wandered back and forth and up and down for hours, looking at all the things. And none of those thousands of things turned out to be anything I wanted to buy. I used to figure that this was just a defense mechanism developed because I had no money to buy with. But now I have a little money to spare, and I still don't buy.

I've never even bought a present for Hope, although there'd be no reason not to, now that her husband knows about us. She has never bought a present for me, either, in all these years. We've never talked about it, pro or con. We've just never done it. None of this is anything to be proud of. I'm not bragging and not regretting, I'm only reporting.

Books are the exception, but mostly what we've given each other has come from used bookstores. Still, I headed for the Barnes & Noble. Maybe they'd have something there that Hope would like. I didn't spot anything, though, so I wound up buying myself a book that Rackleff had talked about, called *Last Stand*. It was by a reporter named Richard Manning and it was about lawless logging operations like Overholser's. Maybe it would pump me up for tonight.

I read for a couple of hours, moving from bench to bench so as not to be conspicuous. By then it was time for lunch, and after that the cineplex opened. I watched Tommy Lee Jones walk away with the show in *The Fugitive*. Due to a good many years spent in places with poor

TV reception or none, I'm one of the few people my age in America who didn't know the plot of the movie in advance. But no matter who played the marshal in the TV series, Tommy Lee Jones blew his doors off.

After the movie I hung around some more until it was time to start checking on Overholser. I found a phone and dialed 1-800-WXBRIEF, which connects you to the FAA's network of flight service stations. WX stands for weather, which is what an FSS gives you briefings on. The stations are also where you file flight plans. There are no old, bold pilots, as the saying goes. Since Overholser was no kid anymore, maybe he was non-bold enough to file a flight plan.

"Hi," I said. "Look, I'm meeting a cousin of mine, supposed to fly into Morgan Field from La Grande? He's a little late and I wonder if you got anything on him?"

"Tail number?" asked the flight service guy.

"November six zero niner eight Quebec." I had seen the tail number in the magazine photo that showed Overholser posing with his foot up on the wheel of his plane, as if he had just shot it down.

"Nothing yet," he said after taking a minute to check his computer.

"Be all right if I check back with you after a while? Probably not a thing in the world wrong, but his wife's a little concerned."

"That's what we're here for."

"Well, I surely do thank you."

In Laos I flew with a guy from Louisiana, and sometimes we'd amuse ourselves by talking in each other's accent. He used to say I did it pretty well, and I know he did. At least he sounded to me just like a regular person. So I had done my Cajun imitation in talking to the flight service specialist, and I had also pitched my voice higher than normal. If the FAA taped incoming calls the way 911 did, I didn't want anything recognizable on there.

The third time I checked back it was seven o'clock and I was about to give up. I could always drive back to the airfield and hang around until Overholser got there—except I kept thinking of Dave Berkowitz. The less hanging around I did, the less time I'd be exposed to cops on patrol, kids looking for a place to neck, nosy neighbors, and so on. If I had an arrival time, I could be in and out fairly fast.

"Me again," I said to the flight service guy. I was getting pretty tight with him.

"Well, this time we got your boy," he said. "I've been keeping an eye out. He activated his flight plan right after takeoff from La Grande. Shows two hours and ten minutes en route, so he should be at Morgan right around 2100 hours."

The FSS man had said there was a little weather between here and eastern Oregon, although not enough to worry about. Probably that was why Overholser had bothered to file a flight plan, on the chance that he might have to navigate by instruments. But I could see the new moon as I drove to Morgan Field, although now and then it went behind patchy clouds. It was still too early for him to have arrived, so I drove till I came across a bowling alley, and parked with the other cars in the lot. By quarter till nine, I was back at the field, under some trees on the other side of the road.

Everything was dark at the field except for a night light outside the door of the operations building. The Dixie-Cascade hangar was a hundred yards or so down the line, well out of reach of the light. I walked over for a fast look. There were no windows, and I didn't want to go shining a flashlight around even if there were. The big hangar door was the kind that swung out and up and then slid back along the ceiling, activated by a remote control.

For the first time it occurred to me that Overholser might not have parked his car inside the hangar, the way most people would have. Someone might have driven him to the airport. If his wife or some flunky came to pick him up, all I would be able to do was watch from the shadows and try again another day. Still, nobody had showed up so far to pick up Overholser, so maybe nobody would. I went back to the pickup and waited.

A few minutes past the hour I thought I heard the sound of a plane, and, sure enough, then the runway lights went on. You trigger them automatically by clicking your radio to the field's UNICOM setting. He would have done it from a little ways out, which meant that I'd have time to drive the pickup, lights out, from where it was to a spot near the hangar. Overholser wouldn't be able to see much from the air as he landed except the lighted strip. I pulled in behind his hangar, cut the motor, and got out. I was already wearing dark sweats, and I pulled my ski mask over my face.

Overholser's plane was loud now, and I could see his lights as he approached the pattern. The plane itself was a darker shadow against the dark sky. I watched his landing critically, hoping he would botch it. But I couldn't have done better myself, and in fact had often done worse.

I watched from around the corner of the hangar as he taxied over. I knew he'd activate the hangar's huge door from the plane with his remote control, but I still jumped involuntarily as it started to rattle and clang up on its tracks. I stayed back, out of sight, as the plane drew near.

I risked peeking out again as he ran up the engine to turn around so he could back the plane in. For a moment the pilot would be facing away from the door that was now yawning open.

The moment was long enough for me to slip into the hangar, spot the silvery, stainless-steel DeLorean parked right inside, and duck down behind it. I stayed there without moving while Overholser made noises that were easy enough to interpret even though my head was down.

The engine died. The door of the plane slammed, and the door latch closed. Steps coming toward the hangar. A click as the overhead lights went on. Steps back out. A slight grunt as he lifted the tail assembly. Small, gritty sounds from the tires as he dragged the plane backward into the hangar.

Now he was all the way to the rear of the hangar, at an angle to spot me as soon as he glanced at the car. Which would probably be practically immediately, so what the hell.

I stood up wearing a ski mask, your basic terrorist nightmare when you're alone at night.

"Who the fuck are you?" Overholser said, not terrorized at all. He just sounded angry. If he was going to be mad instead of scared, I wanted him even madder.

I took out my keys and scratched the shiny fender of his exotic toy. Actually the brass key didn't make any mark on the stainless steel at all, as far as I could tell, but it was the thought that counted.

He was amazed beyond speech. Probably nobody had done anything like that to Harold P. Overholser ever, or at least since he had got his growth.

So I scraped the fender again, harder.

"Nobody does that to me!" he hollered, and charged, as if there were a quarterback somewhere behind me.

He was far enough away so that I still had plenty of time to put the keys back in my pocket and think about how to meet his charge, too. But I just stood there with my mind more or less idling.

The whole point of practicing a sport like wrestling for thousands and thousands of hours is to reach the stage where you no longer have to think. For most of my life I had been laying down and reinforcing those patterns of movement in my brain and my body. Move and countermove, counter to the countermove determining next move, and on through the double dance. I didn't have any conscious idea of what I was going to do until his left hand, moving at a certain speed, got a certain distance from my right. Then the autopilot took over.

I grabbed his left wrist with my right hand and caught the upper part of his arm with my other hand, turned my back on him, and pulled on the arm in a certain way that my body was smart enough to calibrate perfectly to his velocity and his mass but my brain knew only in crude outline and by the dumb name of flying mare.

In competition you can't do a flying mare as pretty as the one I did then, because you're supposed to drop to your knee on the mat so the shock to your opponent won't be too great. But that wasn't an issue here, first of all because there was no mat, only concrete. And second of all, fuck him.

His back smacked the floor like a sandbag dropped out a window and he lay there shocked senseless. I moved fast, like the Lilliputians must have with Gulliver, afraid he would wake up any minute. First the hands, cuffed, and then the shackles on his ankles. Then back to his belt. I pulled it free, ran it through the chain on his handcuffs, and then rebuckled it in the small of his back.

By then he was starting to stir. His eyes came into focus,

and he went for me. The belt and the cuffs caught him up short, and a prehuman sound came from him, the snarl of a trapped predator.

"Let's go, champ," I said, bending and grabbing him by the chain between his handcuffs. Mistake. His whole huge body jerked into twisting motion, like a shark trying to throw a gaff. Somehow my wrist got tangled in the chain and I was pulled on top of him and he tried to roll me under him. But of course that was my game, not his, and I got loose. Not before the chain had cut into my wrist, though. It hadn't started to hurt yet, but I knew it would, and Overholser kept writhing and rolling after me to kill me, never mind that he was effectively armless and legless.

My own prehuman impulse was to run, as if he were some monster snake that you beat and beat with a shovel but it won't die. My human impulse won out, though. I stood my ground and kicked him as hard as I could in the ribs. My hope was to break one or two of them. It would help calm him down.

"Get up, asshole," I said. "We're going camping."

He didn't roll after me anymore, and he wasn't making the noises anymore, but he didn't get up, either.

"Okay, fuck it," I said, and looked around for a rope. I didn't want to haul him with my hands. I was afraid he'd bite or butt or kick or spit. I found a heavy extension cord hanging on the wall, and while I was looking I spotted the door opener where it must have fallen out of his pocket.

He sure enough did try to kick, but after a couple of tries I managed to get the electrical cord between his shackled legs. I tied the two ends of it together and used the giant loop to drag him feet-first toward the door, him wriggling and fighting the line all the way. I cut the light and clicked the door shut. By now the automatic timer had shut off the runway lights, and you could see the large, dark shapes of the hangars but not much else.

All the way back to the pickup, Overholser kept twisting and flopping, hoping to find some purchase on the ground as I dragged him along. It was an impressive display of indomitable courage or pure meanness, probably both. But enough was enough. I had to get him up inside the truck and down into that toolbox.

I took a choke hold with my left arm, anchoring it with a grip just above my right elbow. Honig's canister of Mace was in my right hand. Overholser started to whip back and forth the instant I touched him. It was like trying to hold on to the head of a 240-pound rattlesnake, but he slowed down as his oxygen gave out. "Take it easy, tiger," I said when he weakened. "Here's what we're going to do. This that I've got here, it's Mace. I don't really know what it does if you squirt it right into a person's face close up."

I slackened up a bit, and he took a huge gulp of air before I tightened down on him. "We're both going to stand up just like we are," I said. "Then we're going to kind of wiggle into the truck together."

The tailgate was down and the toolbox was open.

"Inside there's a box and you're going to climb into it. If you give me the slightest little bit of shit about it, I'm going to choke you again. Only this time when you come up for air, I'm going to fill your fucking mouth with Mace. Then I'm going to hold your fucking eyes open and do the same thing. Nod if you follow me."

He couldn't nod, but I could feel him trying.

Honig had fitted in the box easily enough, even where his legs had to bend to accommodate the wheel well. I had fit in, but barely. Overholser's knees stuck up so high that at first it looked like it wasn't going to work at all. But by forcing them down and to the right I got the lid almost closed. By sitting on it, I got it down enough to work the hasp over the staple.

"First goddamned sound I hear from back here," I said, "I'll empty this Mace thing inside there. I don't really know what that'll do in a closed space, either."

17

IT WAS WAY PAST MIDNIGHT WHEN I REACHED
the hiding place I had made for the pickup
at the bottom of the clear-cut. I let Overholser loose for the night but not too loose.
He was outside the box but padlocked to it by his leg
shackles. I locked the rear door, made my bed alongside
the truck, and went to sleep in nanoseconds.

Next morning I woke up totally untroubled by that in-
definable sense of being watched. But when I opened my
eyes there was Elliot, sitting on a log with his shotgun
across his knees. His expression didn't change when he
saw I was awake. He just nodded and kept on sitting.

While I was rubbing my eyes and stretching and spitting and taking a leak in the bushes, I thought about the
old man. He might not know that I had Overholser in the
back of the truck, out of the box. Overholser had been
making noises, shifting around to get less uncomfortable,
but of course Elliot couldn't hear them. The less both Elliot and Overholser knew about each other, the better.

I put my forefinger to my lips and Elliot nodded. I
made a writing gesture, and he took a ballpoint and a
notebook out of his pocket. I wrote, "Many thanks for

keeping an eye on things. I'll take it from here." He nodded when I showed it to him. I tore the page out, put it in my own pocket, and gave him back his pen and notebook. He put them back in his shirt pocket, got up from his log, and walked off without nodding a fourth time. Elliot wasn't one to waste nods. The last I saw of him was when he disappeared around a bend in the logging road. He never looked back. Maybe that's life's big lesson, right there.

I shoved my sleeping bag and pads under the truck with the rest of the gear I had taken out of the back last night so Overholser wouldn't have anything to play with. I had taped his eyes, but I put the ski mask back on before I opened the door in case he had scraped the tape off somehow. He hadn't. He had worked his belt around so that he could undo the buckle, though, so now he would be able to use his cuffed hands to some extent. But his ankles were still padlocked to the toolbox.

"Here's the key," I said, tossing it to him. "Down by your feet. Turn yourself loose and climb down, take a leak. Whatever."

"I'll take you up on the whatever, coach," Overholser said. "How you fixed for paper?"

He had turned into a good old boy from the wild animal he had been back at the airport. What a difference a night makes, when you spend it chained up and blindfolded. I got a roll of paper for him and touched it to the back of his hand once he had felt his way down out of the truck. He might have been fast enough to grab me, although I generally used to win that game where you pull your hand out from under the other guy's and try to slap him. But Overholser didn't even try.

"Just walk straight ahead till I tell you to stop," I said. "Okay, that's good right there."

"You not going to watch, are you, coach?" he said with a friendly smile that didn't convince me. "I'm bashful."

I didn't answer, but of course I watched anyway. How many times do you get to watch the richest man in Oregon try to figure out how to manage with a pair of handcuffs and a roll of toilet paper?

Overholser was wearing one of those upscale tracksuits, the ones with fancy jackets and matching pants and zippers running halfway up the calf on the outside of the legs.

Instead of his snakeskin boots, he was wearing shoes that looked like running shoes except the uppers were of soft white leather. Actually the leather was getting closer to gray, after a night spent in the bed of the truck. His blue outfit with the white piping wasn't looking quite so snappy anymore, either.

"Grab hold of this," I said, handing him a plastic milk crate with various supplies in it.

"Where we going, coach?" he asked.

"I told you last night. Camping."

"Where at?"

"One of your clear-cuts." This wasn't so, but he had so many he probably wouldn't know the difference.

"You mind telling me what this is all about, coach?"

"I'm not coach, and I'm not buddy or pal or chief, either."

"What do I call you, then?"

"I'm the guy with the Mace. You want to call me something, try sir."

I knew this meant he wouldn't call me anything. I had never called officers "sir" myself. I got around it by calling them captain or lieutenant or whatever. And I was getting the uncomfortable feeling that Overholser and I were a lot alike, except that he took it out on the entire rest of the world and I tried to discriminate. Still, he had been acting all along just the same way I might have acted myself if the tables were turned. When he had thought he had a chance, he went for it as hard as he could. When he knew he didn't, he relaxed and waited. But if I let the scales tip even a hair, I knew he'd go right for my throat. No words. No flicker of warning. Just the throat.

I gave him the key so he could take the shackles off his ankles before we started up. But his eyes were still taped. I didn't want him to see the truck, or me, or the lay of the land on the way in. I stayed three or four paces behind him, telling him to go this way and that. He quickly learned to navigate blind, with a milk crate full of supplies in the crook of his arms.

His hands, of course, were cuffed. And he had a little bit of a limp, which I suspected was because his legs had cramped during the trip. Probably his ribs ached where I had kicked him, too, although he showed no sign of it. Still, I kept a safe distance between us, just in case, and kept my eyes strictly on him.

Too strictly.

My foot slipped on a log that was wet and pulpy under its moss, and I slipped, or half-slipped, really. Just down on one knee. No doubt I said a word or two appropriate to the occasion.

By the time my knee touched the ground, Overholser had dropped the milk crate, whirled, and closed the distance between us. I rolled to one side barely in time, and he tripped over the log going full tilt. Not many big men, blindfolded or not, would have had the reflexes to do what he did. He went into a loose forward tuck, and hit the ground rolling on the other side. But it didn't save him from smacking into the trunk of a tree a few yards downhill. He grunted when the air was driven from his lungs, and then lay still.

I was scared and impressed. I had already knocked Overholser senseless the night before, when we were on even terms. This time he was blindfolded and handcuffed, with the odds a thousand-to-one against getting his cuffed hands on me. And still he had been willing without an instant's hesitation to charge an ambiguous noise made by an enemy he couldn't see.

Overholser lay there without moving or speaking. After a few moments he heaved himself up to his knees. The tree had scraped his ear, and blood ran down his neck into his blue jacket.

"Through fucking around now?" I asked. "Let's get going."

Once we got near the spot in the wood line where I had hidden my tent, I fastened one end of the shackles to a thick root that crooked up out of the ground and back down into it. Nothing without a motor could have pulled that root loose. I clicked the other leg cuff over the big man's ankle. Then I put on the ski mask, grabbed the loaded milk crate and went out to get the clear-cut ready for my new prisoner.

I kept Honig's root wad between him and me as I approached. He must have heard me but he didn't call out, probably being used to getting no responses from old Elliot. Nor did I say anything. First I had arrangements to make with the milk crate and some of the groceries, and one of my new walkie-talkies. Once that was done, I went around the root wad to check on the FBI man.

"Been keeping all right, shithead?" I asked.

"All I've been getting to eat is Spam and bread," he said. "They come by during the night and every morning it shows up beside me. A can of Spam and a loaf of Wonder Bread."

"Looks like it worked. You're alive."

"We've got a lot to talk about," he said. "Sir."

"I already talked to you. Now I brought somebody else I can talk to."

"Who?" Honig said. He didn't look good. He knew who.

"He's a mean bastard," I said. "I hope he likes you."

"Oh, Jesus."

"Don't worry. I've got him tied up, too."

"If it's Overholser, there's something you've got to know about the man. He's a liar."

"I bet he is."

When I went back for Overholser, he had managed to work the duct tape loose from his eyes. I had expected him to, once I wasn't around to stop him. It didn't matter, now that I had the mask on. I unshackled him from the root.

"Let's move it," I said, gesturing with the Mace. "Over by your buddy."

Overholser set out in front of me. Some of the gray duct tape still stuck to the back of his head. He walked as if it hurt to move. My kick last night hadn't seemed to work, but maybe he had cracked a rib or two when he hit the tree.

We got close enough for Overholser to recognize Honig. I couldn't see the expression on the big man's face but Honig could. And Honig was making small involuntary motions that made him look like he was trying to run. Neither man was saying anything.

I took Overholser to a root wad that was more or less in line with Honig's, but about fifteen yards away.

"I'm finished fucking around with you," I said to the

big man. I told him what I wanted to do, and what would happen if he didn't. It involved the stun gun I had taken from the trunk of Honig's Grand Marquis.

He followed my instructions while I kept a safe distance. At the end he was standing up, cuffed to the giant root wad by the wrists and the ankles. I wasn't worried about whether it would hurt him to stand up, or how he was going to eat or drink or take care of nature's other little needs. Maybe I'd need to worry about it later, but I had an idea that maybe he wouldn't be with us that long.

I walked back to my camp in the woods, trying not to look as if I was in a hurry, even though I didn't want to waste a minute. Overholser would have jumped right down Honig's throat the minute he figured I was too far away to hear.

By the time I got to my little observation station, separated from the prisoners by nearly a hundred yards of clear-cut, he'd be free to shout if he wanted to. When Honig had been shouting for me back at the beginning, I could barely tell he was shouting, let alone what about.

I heard the FBI man's voice from my walkie-talkie even before I got to the wood line. By the time I was in the woods, the voice had separated out into words.

". . . not your simple schizophrenic. Your simple schizophrenic kills first and then he acts out. That's where you get your violations of the victim, your sexual mutilations of the corpse, all those types of typical schizophrenic perversions."

It was Honig's voice, sounding a little nervous but plunging on with the lecture. I had set the other walkie-talkie up on a stump where the two of them couldn't see it. The little machine was under the upturned milk crate. A folded tarp held in place with a stone was on the top of the crate, to keep the rain off. The weather had been mostly good so far, but there had been a couple of rainy nights while Elliot was keeping an eye on Honig. I pressed down the recording button on my Radio Shack tape deck. The spools started to record Honig's voice coming out of the walkie-talkie.

"This guy is different. This guy is what we call your classic organized killer, what the layman calls your psychopath. Fairly high intelligence, able to function normally in daily life, probably competent socially and sexually . . ."

I began to feel good about myself. In spite of the socially competent part, he seemed to be talking about me.

"With your organized killer, the crime scene is organized, by which we mean it shows signs of planning and premeditation. The place of captivity is prepared in advance, as was the case here. This guy is classic, completely classic."

"Classic asshole is what he is," Overholser said. I hadn't fooled him.

"But a dangerous one," Honig said. "Your organized kill is all about fear. The killer establishes control over his victim. He uses blindfolds, the way he did with both of us. Restraints. This guy is a master of restraint, I would say. Uses many different forms of restraint, which indicates long practice. The organized psychopath enjoys inflicting pain and suffering on his victims, which is this guy's pattern. Also he's emotionally flat, what we call without affect."

"He's affected you pretty good," Overholser said. "Considering he didn't really hurt you."

"That's because I know the profile," Honig said. "I know what this kind of organized killer is capable of."

"Hey, don't worry about it, coach. I understand why you gave him my name."

But Honig couldn't stop apologizing.

"There's a tape recording back at the academy, hours of just screams and begging," Honig continued. "It's a girl being tortured with pliers, a girl a couple of these organized killers had in the back of their van. These guys practically always use a van or a truck for their victims."

"I told you already don't worry about it," Overholser said. "It's history. What we got to worry about is here and now. First of all, I got to tell you something, Paul"— I hadn't been thinking of Honig as Paul, even though I knew it was his first name—"I think you been left out in the sun too long. This guy doesn't seem like some psycho killer to me. He seems pretty normal to me. He didn't just grab us off the street. We're not strangers."

"You know him?" Honig said.

"No, I don't know him. But he knows me, knows who I am anyway."

"I didn't mean he selected strangers, like the Zodiac Killer," the FBI man said. "I was talking personality profile."

"Fuck your profiles. You been out here a long time. If he got off on torturing you, he would have done it. This is about money."

"He's never mentioned ransom. All he talks about is Rackleff's death."

"So you told him I did it."

"No, I didn't."

"This ain't bullshit time, coach. This is get loose time. To get us loose, I've got to know exactly where we stand with this guy. Now he certainly didn't come after me because he saw my name in the paper, did he? He was asking you who killed Rackleff, and *then* he came after me."

"Well, from some of the things I inferred, he might have implied—"

"Come on, good buddy. Look, let's clear the decks here. I'm not mad at you. Some goddamn maniac in a ski mask has you tied up in the woods, what are you going to do? You tell him what he wants to know, is what you do. I'll go further, it's the only thing a smart man *could* do. If you hadn't done just what you did, I wouldn't have any use for you. Only a goddamned fool would have done any different, and I don't want any goddamned fools running my security operation."

"You mean if we get out of this . . ."

"You goddamned right. Day after you retire, you still go to work for Dixie-Cascade just like we agreed. I don't want somebody in that job that don't know anything but to wag his tail when I come in the room. I want a man with enough brains to think for himself. What you done with this maniac, I'll tell you what it says to me, Paul. It says you were in a spot where you needed help, so you figured out a way to get the maniac to bring you some help. And here I am. You took control of the situation. I'd have done exactly the same thing."

Believe this shit, Honig, I was thinking to myself, and I've got this genuine Rolex I'd like to sell you. It only looks like a Timex.

"Not many men would be big enough to say that," Honig said.

I didn't actually have a Timex, but maybe he'd take my Casio instead. Once Honig got out of these woods, he wasn't going to any job with Dixie-Cascade, or even to a retirement home in Ft. Myers. He was going to trial for the murder of Max Wilhoite. And Hap Overholser would be rooting for the district attorney's side.

"I do business," Overholser said. "I don't carry grudges. Grudges just fuck up your head, you understand what I'm saying?"

"Absolutely."

"Sure you do, man like you that's been around the block a few times. So let's sit down and talk business here. The papers said your car was found out at the airport with that Nazi asshole in the trunk. I figured it was you that shot the son of a bitch. Was it?"

Honig took him through the evening of the killing relatively truthfully, although I had forgotten about the heroic struggle he put up against me. And in the new version he had shot Wilhoite only in self-defense, after the Nazi launched an unprovoked attack. And Honig left out any mention of the supermarket check-cashing photo that was Wilhoite's alibi for the bombing. Which was an interesting omission.

"So you never saw this maniac's face at all," Overholser said at the end. "Not even in the gym."

"I hate to go back to profiling," Honig said. "But masks and blindfolds fit the profile."

"I can see blindfolds for the victim. But what's the point in a serial killer wearing a mask?"

"It adds to the victim's terror," the agent said. "Same reason headsmen used to wear them."

"Professor of mine back at Tulane said headsmen wore masks so friends of the dead guy wouldn't come after them later."

"Maybe that, too."

"Makes more sense to me that way," Overholser said.

"What way?"

Honig really wasn't too swift. He had probably succeeded in the bureaucracy the way a turtle succeeds, by staying safe inside his shell and biting anything that got near.

"Makes more sense that he's wearing a mask because he *doesn't* want to kill us. Otherwise, why would he give a shit if we saw his face?"

"I guess that's right," Honig said.

"In fact, if he really wanted to scare us, he'd take the damned mask off. So the question is how come he's got the damned mask *on?*"

"Exactly," said Honig. No flies on Honig.

"Only thing I can think of is that he figures one of us killed Rackleff, and once he finds out which one it was, he's going to let the other one go."

"What if he finds out it was both of us?"

"Then maybe he takes the mask off and we're in deep shit."

"What's the answer, then?"

"Only one answer, coach. We got to make him think neither of us did it. You better tell me exactly what you told him, so we can figure out the best way to go from here."

"I told him your security people got Wilhoite to shoot up the Belters' house. But I didn't say you had anything to do with the bombing."

"You didn't have to say it," Overholser said. "Once he made the connection between me and you and Wilhoite, that was enough."

"I'm sorry."

"Don't worry about it, coach. Now tell me something else. How do you figure this maniac ever got together with Wilhoite in the first place?"

"He had to know the death threats allegedly came from the Brotherbund. And it said in the papers that the leader of a skinhead group was being investigated in the bombing."

"Not what I meant, Paul. I meant him and Wilhoite somehow wound up working together. Couldn't have been an accident that Wilhoite gets you over to the gym and this guy happens to be waiting in the shower. What the hell did you go to the gym for, anyway?"

"It's complicated. He found out that I had possession of a certain picture that placed him far from the scene at the exact time of the bombing."

"What do you mean? Like a forged picture?"

"No, it was a real picture."

"You telling me the skinhead *didn't* kill Rackleff?"

"Well, not really."

"Who really did?"

"In a sense, I did."

"In what sense?"

"In the sense that I pushed the button."

"How did you have the button? Did you put the bomb in his truck, too?"

"Yes. I confiscated Rackleff's van weeks ago and installed the device. Then I parked it illegally so it would be towed away."

"Jesus H. Christ, man, I thought the skinhead was supposed to have done it! Didn't the damned skinhead do *anything?*"

"Wilhoite wasn't any rocket scientist. The only thing he was competent to do was stand there and be a lightning rod."

"Been a lot going on here that I didn't know about, coach, considering I'm paying for it."

"If there's one thing I've learned in my years with the Bureau, it's plausible deniability all the way up the line. I was protecting you by not telling you."

"Yeah, great. Now a maniac's got me tied to a tree."

Overholser kept calling me a maniac, but I doubt if he really meant it. He just felt better about being tied to a tree by a maniac than by some normal guy fifty pounds lighter than him.

"He was a factor nobody could have considered," Honig said. "We never even knew there was a bodyguard in the picture until that little episode with your people in Carswell."

"There wouldn't have been any bodyguard if there hadn't been those letters and the drive-by shooting. And now you tell me the son of a bitch was already riding around with the bomb under him. Why didn't you just blow him up right off the bat?"

"Because Wilhoite insisted on having what I convinced him would be an airtight alibi. The hearing before Judge Bullock was the first time we knew positively that Rackleff would be in a certain place at a certain time. So it was the first time we could arrange for Wilhoite to be somewhere else when the device was activated."

"Doesn't answer my question, coach. Fuck Wilhoite and his alibi, why didn't you just blow Rackleff up?"

This was my question, too. All along, this had been the big piece that didn't fit the puzzle. I leaned forward.

"Because of Garber."

"Garber?" Overholser said. "What the hell has Garber got to do with anything?"

I couldn't see, either. How could the new U.S. attorney in Portland be involved?

"Frederick C. Garber," Honig said. "That's it in a nutshell, right there."

"That's what in a nutshell?"

"Our real problem. You don't know the man like I do. He's undermining the whole concept of law enforcement in the state. I'd rather see a Communist in the job than a stinking, slimy, sanctimonious . . ."

The walkie-talkie went silent for a few seconds while Honig searched for the worst word he could think of.

". . . *liberal!*" he finally said, as if he were spitting out a wet cigarette butt he had swallowed by mistake.

"You better walk me through that, coach," Overholser said. "Naturally he'd be a liberal. We got one in the damned White House, too."

"Exactly. So Garber is going to be in the job for at least three more years, and maybe four more after that. He'll be crawling all over us, year after year after year. He's the one who decides what cases to prosecute and which ones to forget about. He's the one who thinks he's too good to take advice from the Bureau. He's the one who just loves to cuddle up with all the hippies and feminists and tree spikers. The baby killers and the dope peddlers and every other poor, poor, little abused criminal. You don't know, Mr. Overholser. You just can't imagine the damage this man is doing!"

"So you were going to stop him?"

"I was till Wilhoite died. Then the whole thing went down the tubes."

"What whole thing?"

"When I retired, I was going to leave our friend Mr. Garber with a little time bomb in his files. Wilhoite was the time bomb, but I didn't want Garber to see that he was. Garber had to think he could convict Wilhoite for Rackleff's murder."

"You got me confused here, coach, but go on."

"Let me give you a little bit of the history. I happen to have Wilhoite on tape confessing to stomping that Nigerian to death. Me, personally, not the office. He confessed to me. So I owned Wilhoite, and I was just getting started using his group to stir up trouble for the environmental terrorists.

"Then you and I had our talk about ways to deal with the Rackleff problem, and naturally I sounded out Max. But there's a limit to how hard I could squeeze him. I mean, you can't tell the guy he won't have to go up for life on one murder if he thinks he might go up for life on another one. So he demanded an ironclad guarantee that he would walk if I set him up on the bombing. Which gave me the idea for a plan to deal with both Rackleff and his tame U.S. attorney at the same time.

"I told Max he'd get the Nigerian confession back if he let himself be set up for bombing Rackleff. But we'd arrange it so he couldn't possibly be convicted. So first off I went to our dead storage files and pulled a few real nut letters so the language would sound authentic. Then I changed a few words as appropriate and retyped them and started to send them out. Sending death threats through the mail brought it under our jurisdiction as a federal offense. Only that goddamned Rackleff wouldn't make an official complaint about the letter. Finally I had to tell Wilhoite to shoot up the house, so Rackleff would take those letters seriously and bring them in, and we'd have a file to show Garber when the time came."

"A file?" Overholser said. "What was the point?"

"A file to show Garber. Something that would point to Max Wilhoite as Rackleff's killer. He didn't send the letters, of course, but they had his outfit's name on them and he couldn't prove they weren't from him. And then we'd go dig the bullets out of the house and match them up to Wilhoite's gun.

"I cooked up lots of other stuff, too. For instance I had Max buy various of the materials I needed for the bomb. I had him lay down a trail plain enough that my men would follow it on their own, without any involvement by me apart from normal supervision. Naturally all the evidence would be circumstantial, but it generally is in bomb cases.

"So at the trial everything's going along fine until all of a sudden the defense lawyer just happens to find out about a certain photo that the prosecution has in its files. Let's see Mr. Frederick C. Garber, Esquire, try to wriggle out of that one!"

"Tell me about this photo," Overholser said.

"Well, Wilhoite was standing by out in southeast Portland during the hearing, while I was parked down the block from the courthouse. The minute Rackleff came out, I called Wilhoite up on my cellular, the same phone I was about to set off the bomb with. Wilhoite went straight to this market nearby and cashed a check. They've got one of those machines that takes your picture. You see the beauty of it now?"

"I'm starting to."

Honig was so caught up in his own cleverness that he didn't notice the coldness in Overholser's voice.

"I would have been retired before the case against Wilhoite could come to trial," the FBI man went on. "But that picture would be in the prosecution's files where I slipped it, along with a receipt with Garber's initials on it."

"How were you going to get him to initial it?"

"Just forge his initials."

"How about handwriting experts?"

"That's ninety percent bullshit, particularly with stylized initials. Anybody can forge most initials well enough to fool the guy himself."

"All right, then what?"

"Then somebody tips the defense team that the prosecution is hiding exculpatory evidence consisting of a certain photo in the U.S. attorney's files. Then let's see the son of a bitch try to explain to Janet Reno why he lost a highly visible case by willfully concealing exculpatory evidence from the defense. And there you go. We're rid of Garber forever."

"Except that none of that's going to happen because Wilhoite's dead. Why is that, Paul?"

"I told you. He jumped me."

"Why were you over there, though?"

"He was worried because he found out at the grocery that I had picked up the check-cashing picture from them."

"Why did he jump you?"

"I really don't know. Maybe he thought I had the picture with me."

"Why I'm asking, Paul, is because I been thinking about that deniability thing you mentioned. What struck me is that you'd have pretty good deniability yourself if the Nazi was dead. So would I. I mean, the both of us couldn't have better deniability than that, old buddy. I'd admire somebody who was tough enough to go ahead and do what was necessary in a situation like that. I really would."

"Well, Wilhoite was coming apart, that's true," Honig said. "I was worried by his tone when he called me."

"I bet you were. So you went over there to kill him?"

"Well, it was a possibility. It was one of the options, I won't deny that."

There was a long pause with nothing but static coming over the walkie-talkie. I could hear the soft hiss of the tape turning in my recorder.

When Overholser spoke again, he wasn't the friendly

salesman anymore. He could drop the con, now that he had the information he wanted.

"You ignorant piss ant," he shouted. "You sorry goddamned fice dog. You puling, mewling, pitiful little sack of shit."

Silence again, then Honig crawling back, like a puppy that's just been kicked.

"What's wrong?" he said. "What did I do?"

"Listen to it. It wants to know what it did. I'll tell you what you did, dumb-ass. You dragged me into your fucking petty office politics without telling me and now I'm chained up to a goddamned root wad and not the chance of a fart in a whirlwind of ever getting loose."

"Office politics?" Honig said. He sounded genuinely shocked that his patriotism had been so totally misunderstood.

"You think I give a fuck if you got a hard-on for your boss?" Overholser shouted. "You think I give a fuck if he gets fired? Who did you think Clinton was going to send out to replace him? James Watt?"

"Well, but—"

"But, my ass. You wanted to fuck this guy and you wound up fucking me instead, fucking me on my own nickel. You could have just planted the bomb and blown the son of a bitch up and we'd all be home free. But no. You got some goofy little vendetta of your own going, don't you? So you drag some Nazi moron into your crazy Rube Goldberg scheme and pretty soon it all blows up in your face like anybody but another goddamned moron would have known it would."

"I'm sorry—"

"Shut the fuck up with your sorry. The only thing you said so far that makes the slightest sense is deniability. Quick as I get loose, I'll fucking deniability you with my

2 5 7

bare hands. You're the only thing that ties me to Rackleff and Wilhoite. You're dead meat, fucker."

Overholser kept on like that, tearing Honig a succession of new assholes while the special agent in charge whimpered apologetically. But I had all I needed, and the tape would still be running anyway, in case anything else interesting came out.

I started packing up my gear and carrying it down through the woods to the truck.

ALWAYS LEAVE A CLEAN CAMPSITE IS WHAT I say, most particularly when the least little bit of litter could cost me a life sentence in federal prison. So I was carefully policing up every bit of nonbiodegradable trash around my prisoners that I could find.

18

The FBI man was accompanying me with nonstop dialogue. Honig wanted to know why had I brought them here in the first place, why I was cleaning up now, what I was going to do with them once I was finished. He informed me at great length all over again of how important he was, and the FBI was, and America was, and Harold P. Overholser was. He wanted me to know about all the terrible things that were about to happen to me, unless I saw the light. He wanted me to know, however, that men as powerful as his own self and Mr. Overholser here could do a lot for me if only I'd give them the chance. And so on. And so forth.

Overholser had to listen to all this Bureaubabble, too. Being a class act, relatively speaking, he paid no more attention to it than I did. Now and then his mouth would twitch a little, though, as if he wanted to say something. Finally he did.

"Shut the fuck up," he said, "before I puke."

Honig didn't even say "Right," or "Sorry." He just shut up.

It took me half a dozen trips to get everything down the hill and stowed in the back of the truck. I left the walkie-talkies and the tape deck in operation as long as I could, to pick up anything interesting the two men might say while I was out of earshot. Finally, though, I slipped the hidden walkie-talkie into my pocket and went back to my observation station. I rewound the tape a little ways to see if they had said anything notable while I had been gone, but they hadn't. I packed my makeshift listening post up with one or two other leftover things, and carried a last load down to the truck. Then I went back uphill for my prisoners.

Honig was no problem. He knew he couldn't whip me or outrun me. Once I uncuffed him, he preceded me without objection down the mountain. Before we got to where he could see the pickup in its hiding place, I blindfolded him and gagged him with duct tape. I took his arm, led him to the truck, and handcuffed him to the front bumper for the moment.

Overholser was another matter. He must have played injured lots of times when he was a grid great, and a couple of cracked ribs weren't going to slow him down if I gave him a chance at me. So I got out Honig's canister of Mace again, and explained what would happen if he didn't follow my instructions on the proper sequence in which to unlock this, and then cuff this to that, and next unlock this, and so forth. In the end he was free from his root wad, but his legs were shackled and his hands were cuffed in front of him. Behind would have been safer, but he wouldn't fit into the toolbox that way.

At last I got both men squared away for the trip, Overholser jackknifed into the toolbox and Honig rolled up head to foot in my camouflage tarp. He looked like an oversize bedroll, which was the idea in case anybody should hear a noise and take a look inside the truck. If I picked self-service gas stations with nobody else at the pumps, I should be all right.

To keep any noise to a minimum, though, I had stuffed socks in their mouths, held in with a couple of wrappings of tape around the head. Honig had opened right up for me. So did Overholser, to my mild surprise. This didn't necessarily mean his spirit was broken, though. It meant Overholser had figured me out.

"Will you for Christ's sake relax," Overholser had said in the last few minutes of the tape—while I was carting gear down the mountain. "Why do you think we're still alive?"

"Maybe he's taking us somewhere else to kill us."

"You can be just as dead here as anywhere."

"Yeah, but—"

"Look, the only logical reason we're alive is that we're worth more to him that way. He stopped asking you questions about Rackleff once you gave him my name. Lost interest in you and came right after me, didn't he? But then he didn't bother to ask *me* any questions about Rackleff, did he? Why is that? Because all of a sudden somebody with money showed up in the picture, and who gives a shit about Rackleff anymore? This guy's no greenie. Maybe he was hired by the greenies, but now this guy's just in it for the bucks."

Now that they were in the truck, obviously about to go for a trip, Overholser would be even more convinced that he was right. Even the gag would be a good sign to him. If the point of the trip was to dump their bodies somewhere else, why bother with a gag? Why not make really sure that your passengers would be quiet?

Back in the cab, I unfolded my Oregon road map to find the best way east to the Clackamas River country. It was a long way from Lamar Purcell's backyard, for one thing. For another, Dixie-Cascade owned a huge tract there. I had examined aerial photos of it in the OSU library's map collection. The abandoned clear-cut I had picked out was twelve miles from the nearest paved highway, on logging roads. Even if Overholser and Honig didn't get lost after I turned them loose, I would be in Portland long before they could hike out to the main road.

Both men looked like hell when I had finally marched them up to the Dixie-Cascade clear-cut where I meant to leave them. By comparison, though, Overholser looked like Cary Grant in tails. His fancy tracksuit still looked expensive even if it was rumpled and filthy. He wore his hair just a little longer than a crew cut, so it didn't look uncombed. He had a few days stubble on his face, but no more than you see on the sullen, spoiled, stupid faces in the men's fashion ads. On Overholser, though, stubble wasn't a fashion statement. He didn't look like rough trade, he just looked rough.

Honig's stubble, on the other hand, was well on the way to becoming a grizzled beard, gummed up with grease and bits of food. It didn't look a bit rough. Neither did his ancient, baggy sweats from the Goodwill. His thinning hair was stuck with leaves and twigs. It was so stiff with dirt that it poked out in peaks from the sides of his head. His face was red and peeling from the sun and covered with insect bites. He had lost weight, which aged him ten years. He looked like something you'd find in the men's room of a bus station, passed out on the floor.

They stood there blindfolded in Dixie-Cascade's remote clear-cut, waiting for whatever was going to happen. Honig had given up asking questions, and Overholser had never lowered himself to start with.

I had led them up the trail with the length of cable from the gym. Honig was holding on to it in the middle and Overholser at the far end, so that he'd have to run over Honig to reach me. And the big man's legs were shackled. He could shuffle along after a fashion, but he couldn't run. They still held on to the cable, although I had dropped my end.

"We're here," I said. "You can let loose now." They dropped the cable. I picked it up and started to coil it. I wanted to leave a clean campsite this time, too.

They both had their hands cuffed behind them now. All by himself Honig might never have figured the problem out. But if Overholser didn't already know that you can maneuver cuffed hands over your feet, he'd figure it out soon enough. Then he'd have the use of his hands.

"Sooner or later you'll get the tape off your eyes," I said. "Look around and you'll find the keys."

I left the keys to the handcuffs and the shackles nearby, on top of one of Dixie-Cascade's millions of stumps.

Back in Portland, my first business was at the U.S. attorney's office on the tenth floor of the Pioneer Tower. The receptionist sat behind glass, like a bank teller. "Delivery for Mr. Frederick Garber," I said, and slid my brown envelope through the opening. Inside the envelope were the tapes and a block-printed note identifying the voices on them.

Back outside in the street, I found a phone and called

the law offices of Belter and Belter. Mr. Belter was in conference. Oh, I see. Yes, I'm sure he'll want to speak with
Mr. Garber. Just one moment, please.

"Fred," Bill Belter said after a minute. "What can I do
for you?"

"I'm calling about the pickup truck you advertised."

"Pickup truck? You've got the wrong number."

"The one I took for a trial run a couple of weeks ago."

"I don't even own . . ." He stopped. He had made the
connection. When he spoke again he no longer sounded
puzzled. He sounded cold.

"I'm afraid I don't know anything about any pickup
truck," he said. "Nor do I want to know anything. This
is a law office, not a used-car lot."

"Let me get this straight," I said. "You don't have a
pickup truck for sale, and you wouldn't even have any
use for one if somebody gave it to you?"

"No use whatsoever."

"Right. Excuse the call."

"Don't call again."

I couldn't blame him. He wouldn't want that pickup
back anymore than he'd want Typhoid Mary hanging
around. Or me.

I spent an hour driving to various strip malls, shopping
centers, supermarkets, and convenience stores. Item by
item, I left off everything at all distinctive that had been
in the truck. The walkie-talkies went in separate Dump-
sters, the tape deck I put in a paper bag, which I left in
a shopping cart outside a supermarket. The padlock, the
Ace bandage, the ski mask, the books on explosives, and
the length of cable went in various trash baskets. The
sleeping pads, the sleeping bag, and my assorted used
clothes went into the Salvation Army receptacle in a shopping center.

When the pickup was more or less clean and anonymous, I looked up junkyards in the yellow pages and found an area across the river where there was a cluster of them. I parked the pickup down the street from one yard and across the street from another and took the plates off.

Then I poured a gallon of water down the oil filler pipe and started her up. The gauge showed good oil pressure, but it was measuring water and not lubricant. I left the motor running, and got out, locking the doors with the key inside. I didn't wait to see how long it would take the motor to overheat and turn into a useless block of steel.

With the license plates under my shirt to be ditched along the way, I started hiking back toward the center of Portland. There I could catch a cab to the airport without attracting any attention.

Safely aboard a flight for Denver under the name of Joseph Anderson, I might have relaxed but didn't. I kept thinking about the call I made to Wanda Vollmer at Lordland before leaving Portland International.

"Could you give Hope another message?" I had said. "This time tell her I'm on my way back and I'll be in touch as soon as I get home."

"Sure, I'll pass it along."

"What did she say when you called her last time?"

"Her guy has another woman call her with a message that makes it sound like he's going underground, what's she supposed to say? She said, Terrific. I'm so happy for him."

"She was pissed, huh?"

"Of course she was pissed."

"Did she say that?"

"She didn't have to say it. I know what pissed sounds like."

I didn't know what it sounded like, not coming from Hope. Exasperated is as far as we ever got with each other, probably because we live apart most of the time.

But I still didn't see how I could have avoided hurting her and worrying her. Any link between us during the period after Rackleff's death—phone records, any paper trail at all—would tie her to the kidnapping. Nothing could be proven against her, probably, but that wasn't the point.

The point was she'd find herself in *People*. Her life would be stripped naked and then licked all over by a hundred million readers and listeners and viewers. Geraldo, Rush, Oprah, Phil, Jay, David. The *Star*, the *National Enquirer*. Maybe worst of all, the upmarket gossip sheets, too: *Vanity Fair, The New Yorker, Esquire, Vogue.*

It would look as if a respectable and highly placed official of the American Civil Liberties Union had hired a kidnapper, or at least recommended him. It would come out almost immediately that the prominent lady lawyer and the previously obscure kidnapper had been lovers for many years. The lawyer's husband, a wealthy Washington attorney rumored to be gay (his reputed longtime companion is a Midwestern congressman) ... And so on and so on until she died and even after. After a long and useful life, the headline on her obituary would be something like, "Kidnap Figure Dead at 92."

All in all, jail might be preferable to being on the cover of *People*. Not that it was necessarily an either/or proposition, of course. I, for instance, could expect both.

In Denver I changed planes and changed names. I planned on doing the same thing in Atlanta, but got there so late I had to wait till next morning for a flight to Boston. Eventually I managed to get to sleep in one of the plastic chairs.

When I woke up the sky was just starting to lighten. What had wakened me was the clang from a nearby *Atlanta Constitution* pay box, which a man with an electric cart had just loaded.

The headline read:

MULTIMILLIONAIRE FREED
AS MYSTERY KIDNAP ENDS
TOP FBI OFFICIAL
REMAINS MISSING

THE STORY STARTED OUT:

19

PORTLAND, Ore.—Multimillionaire financier and timber baron Harold P. Overholser, missing since Tuesday, walked out of the Cascade Mountains yesterday, the victim of an apparent kidnapping.

He told police a mystifying tale of being held captive in the rugged wilderness of Oregon with a top FBI official, who remains a captive.

The official, Paul Honig, is head of the FBI's office here. He has been the subject of a nationwide search since his abandoned car was found at Portland International Airport with the body of a slain neo-Nazi leader in the trunk.

It had taken Overholser longer than I figured to free himself and walk out, I learned as I read the rest of the story. No wonder, since he had apparently dawdled along the way to kill Honig.

A spokesman for the Clackamas County sheriff's office was the source for Overholser's account of events. According to that account I had taken Honig along with me, leaving Overholser behind. He managed to free himself and hike to the main road, where he flagged down one of his own logging trucks.

The rest of the story, apart from details of Overholser's kidnapping and captivity, was mostly a rehash of what had already run in the papers about his disappearance from the airfield, Honig's disappearance from Portland International, and Wilhoite's murder.

Naturally Overholser said he was mystified as to why he was kidnapped, but assumed a ransom demand would have come along sooner or later. He said Honig had been mystified, too.

Overholser might very well get away with Honig's murder, it occurred to me. There would be no particular reason to search the woods for a body. Soon the animals would find it, and there would be nothing left but scattered bones.

So I found a phone and got the number of the U.S. attorney's office in Portland from information. I dialed it. "Person-to-person for Mr. Frederick Garber," I said when the operator came on.

"They're three hours earlier out there," the operator said.

"It's okay. He works nights."

"You have reached the office of the United States attorney," a recording said. "Our regular office hours are nine to five, Monday through Friday. If you care to leave a message . . ."

"It's a machine, sir," the operator said. "Do you wish to leave your name and number?"

After the beep, I managed to say, "Look for your dead SAC along the trail Overholser walked out on," before the operator cut me off.

You almost never get the same operator twice in a row, so I was able to trick fresh operators into letting me leave four more brief messages on the machine. Altogether, they would tell Garber that Overholser had killed Special Agent in Charge Honig, just as he had threatened to do on the tapes already in the possession of the U.S. attorney's office.

Garber would know the messages on his answering machine were from the kidnapper, since no one else would be familiar with the tapes I had left off at his office. But in case the tapes ever wound up being played on TV, I had used my fake Cajun voice again.

I was in Boston's Logan Airport by late morning. The Boston papers had a few more details than the Atlanta paper, although only one item really interested me. Overholser was evidently now speculating to the police that his kidnapping might have been the work of environmental terrorists. So he was still keeping quiet about my interest in the Rackleff killing. He would have fun explaining why he had done that, once the U.S. attorney confronted him with the tapes with Honig saying repeatedly that my only interest in life seemed to be that very killing.

I was home in my Cambridge apartment in less than an hour, and looking unhappily at the telephone. At last I made myself dial Hope's direct line at the ACLU headquarters in Washington.

When she picked up, I said, "Assume we're not alone."

There was a second or two while she figured out what I meant. She knew who it was, of course.

"I'm assuming," she said.

"Can you get to an outside phone and call me at home?"

"I can."

That was it. Four words out of her, short and cold, and

she hung up. I hung up. I waited, cold too, but in a different way. Hers was furious; mine was afraid. I watched the phone, as if it were a snake that was going to bite me as soon as it got good and ready. I watched it for a very long time, although probably no more than five minutes in all. I actually jumped when it struck at last.

She started right in, before I even made it to hello.

"This is unacceptable behavior," she said. "You know that, don't you?"

"I know it. But at least you'll hear me out, won't you?"

"Of course I will. I'm not a child."

"I'll be down."

It's about 450 miles from Cambridge to Washington, nine hours if you're in no particular hurry. I wasn't even in that much of a hurry. I drifted along through the evening and the night in my low-mileage 1987 Subaru wagon. Low-mileage for me, anyway. It clicked over to a hundred thousand during the trip, and I was counting on the boys at MacKinnon Motors to keep it going for at least another hundred thousand. I hit most of the pit stops along the Mass. Pike, the New Jersey Turnpike and I-95, whether I needed to or not. Even with that I only managed to drag the trip out to eleven hours.

It was still dark when I got to the Potomac Boat Club, where Hope rowed every morning before going to work. I settled down to wait, going over and over what I would say to her and what she might say back to that, and what I could answer that with. But I don't play chess very well, and I wasn't any better at this game.

When Hope drove up, the first rower to show, it was still dark enough so that she had her running lights on. I got out as soon as I recognized her old Saab. Then she got out, tall and slim in the half-light but somehow not shapeless in spite of the loose sweatsuit she wore. Her office clothes were in the gym bag she carried. I forgot everything I had worked out to say.

"Jesus," I said instead. "I'm sorry."

"I hope so. First poor Robert is killed and I learn about it on the television and police want to talk to some mystery man. Bill Belter says he hasn't seen you since the court hearing, acts like he hardly knows you. Then a practically total stranger calls me up—"

"Wanda's no stranger."

"Well, she wasn't you, was she?"

Hope began crying. The only time I had seen her cry was years before, when she learned that one of her children had a growth in the colon that ultimately turned out to be benign.

I wanted to take her in my arms, but I didn't know if she wanted me to. I stood there.

"Oh, Tom, my heart fell out of me, just fell out of me, when I saw the picture of that FBI man's car on the news after Wanda called. The trunk was open, and the skinhead's body was covered up on a stretcher. What could I think, Tom? Did the FBI man kill you, too? Where were you? I called Bill Belter and this time I begged. He wouldn't say anything more than he did before. He sounded remote, almost hostile.

"It finally came to me that he was terrified of what he might be involved in. He must have thought you killed the skinhead and maybe you killed the missing FBI man, too. I knew you would never have shot anybody, but Belter didn't. Still, what was I supposed to think? If you hadn't killed them, were you dead yourself? And then nothing, nothing. For weeks, nothing. For God's sake, Tom. Was that fair?"

"No."

"Oh, my God, I was so worried. I was frantic. How could you? I thought we ..."

"I'm sorry, Hope. I'm so sorry." One of us—both of us?—made some little move, and she was in my arms, all firm and soft at once under the loose sweatsuit, and I knew after a while without words that it would be all right again. Bent some, maybe, but not broken. Her head was on my chest and she must have felt something strange in my breathing.

She pulled back and put her hand on my cheek and found it was wet. "Oh, Tom," she said. "Oh, Tom."

She was surprised and so was I. I hadn't cried since I was a little boy. I wouldn't give my father the satisfaction. The only way I could beat him was not to cry.

"I'm sorry," I said. "I didn't mean to ..."

"Don't say anything."

While we stood there holding each other and crying, a car came up and two other early-morning rowers got out. They looked at Hope and me, not knowing what to say, and wound up just nodding in embarrassment as they went past us.

We got in my car in case anyone else showed up.

"My God," I said, "I was so afraid I'd lose you. I still could."

"No, you couldn't."

"Not that way. Jail."

"Don't say that, Tom. We can talk about it, but not now."

So we let now just be now, with the two of us holding each other and not saying much of anything.

"You'll miss your workout," I murmured after a long time had passed.

"I guess I will."

"But you don't care, do you?"

"No, I guess I don't."

"Want to go out tonight?"

"Tonight I can't. We're having our annual budget meetings and we won't break up till late."

"Tomorrow?"

"Same thing tomorrow."

"Next day?"

"Do you mind staying that long?"

"I'd mind leaving."

On the third evening Hope and I were sitting in the dimly lit parlor of the Tabard, mostly paying attention to each other, when I spotted Overholser behind her. He was on the screen of the big television mounted up on one wall. He wore a gray suit with a white shirt and a blue tie and he was clean-shaven. But in one respect he hadn't changed. He was still handcuffed. Overholser was crossing a sidewalk from a car to the entrance of a building. A half-dozen agents or marshals in dark suits surrounded him, and journalists surrounded them.

"... recovered tissue sample from under the fingernails of the slain FBI official," the newscaster was saying.

"All *right!*" I said. "Way to go, Honig."

Hope turned to watch it with me. "What did Honig do?" she asked.

"The little brown-noser fought back," I said. "I expected him to just lie down and say thank you for killing me, sir. I needed that."

"... Overholser, the multimillionaire financier who heads the giant Dixie-Cascade forest products company, faces homicide charges in the death of Honig, whose body was found early yesterday in the mountainous area where the two men had been held captive. We have with us U.S. Attorney Frederick Garber."

"Pleasure to be here, Bill."

"Mr. Garber, there has been speculation over a so-called mystery man who is alleged to have kidnapped both Honig and Overholser. In view of today's events, can you comment on whether there in fact was such a man?"

"At the moment we are working on the assumption that a third man was present," Garber said. "An unknown individual delivered tapes to my office in Portland before the reappearance of Mr. Overholser. Our assumption is that this unknown individual was involved in the disappearance of Special Agent Honig and Mr. Overholser. We do not as yet know the circumstances of those disappearances nor the reason for them, although there is evidence of several further felonies on the tapes."

"What kind of felonies?"

"Extremely serious felonies that may involve both Mr. Honig and Mr. Overholser. Our investigations are continuing at this time."

"That's you he was talking about you," Hope said. "I recognized you right away. An unknown individual."

"Long as I stay unknown . . ."

"No prints on those tapes Garber has?"

"Those are the world's best-wiped cassettes."

"No camera in the lobby of the U.S. attorney's office?"

"I didn't see any. I wore a cap and sunglasses, anyway. Put a bandage on my chin."

"What's the point of a bandage?"

"Give people something like a bandage to look at, and that's all they remember."

"The old bandage trick, huh? Maybe you will stay unknown, then."

"I will unless the Belters turn me in."

"If that hasn't happened by now, I don't think it will," she said. "They let the time for that pass when the FBI was looking for the guy who ran away from the scene. How are they going to explain why they didn't come forward then? Why they didn't report the pickup stolen? Worst of all, what would you be likely to say if they turned you in? You'd have a certain tendency to drag them down with you as co-conspirators, wouldn't you?"

"I hope not, but I might."

"There you go. And the only other person who might cause a problem is your pal the marijuana dealer."

"Marijuana *banker*. Lamar Purcell."

"Well, he's in an even worse fix than the Belters. He's as guilty of kidnapping as you are and so's his friend, the old man."

"Maybe I'll keep on being an unknown individual, then."

"The Belters and Mr. Purcell certainly hope so, I'm sure. As much as you do."

"Nobody hopes so as much as I do."

"Oh, yes they do. Me."

The TV showed a Dixie-Cascade clear-cut. They all look a lot alike, the way bombed-out cities do. But the announcer identified this one as the tract where I had left the two men. Then came footage of Overholser in his football uniform, Overholser at the controls of his plane, Overholser testifying before a Congressional committee, Overholser posing with a thirty-six-inch chain saw. Then the pile of rocks that had covered Honig's body, and the standard shot of his body under a sheet, being loaded aboard an ambulance.

Now Overholser was going to be the one on the cover of *People*, but he was better adapted to it than we were. Overholser and the cover of *People* were like Brer Rabbit and the brier patch.

"You think Garber will get him for killing Honig?" I asked Hope.

"I don't know. He could say the fingernail scrapings came from an earlier scuffle of some kind. His lawyers might be able to create a reasonable doubt."

"How about the tapes?"

"Defense counsel will try to get them barred. Even if they fail, the threats to Honig could wind up sounding pretty ambiguous once the defense gets through with them. And they've got a mystery man who might have done it. It won't be that hard to create doubt in the jury's mind."

"How about the parts about Rackleff's murder?" I asked. Hope had listened to the copy of the tapes that I had dubbed for myself.

"I think he might skate on that one, too."

"Even so he's finished, Hope."

"How is he finished?"

"They won't let him sit by the money river anymore. You know about the money river?"

"I bet you'll tell me."

"In one of his books Vonnegut writes about this river where only a few people are allowed to go. But if you're one of them, all you have to do is dip your net in and pull money out. Overholser won't be one of them anymore."

"Why not? He's still got his companies."

"Not for long. Wall Street doesn't care if Overholser breaks every law on the books and steals every tree in the world. That makes him their kind of guy. They don't care if he swindles the bondholders or loots the pension fund. They don't even care if he's a white-collar murderer like the tobacco companies. But you're not supposed to kill people with your bare hands. It's embarrassing."

"He might well be found innocent."

"So was Lorena Bobbitt, but that doesn't mean she can get a date."

"Supposing they do call in loans and cut off his credit," Hope said. "What difference will it make? Dixie-Cascade will only wind up in the hands of somebody else no better than Overholser."

"True."

"So what's the point, ultimately?"

"Ultimately there is no point, I guess. It's the kind of thing you have to do when you find yourself in certain positions. Did I ever tell you about Jim Murphy?"

"I don't think so."

"He used to be what we called the Mad Bomber, in the embassy in Laos. He signed off for the ambassador on targets the air force wanted to bomb. They weren't supposed to bomb civilian targets, but there were a lot of bombs and not many military targets. So they'd bomb any goddamned thing. That's what they were there for, to bomb.

"Jim couldn't check every request, because sometimes there were hundreds of them a day. And he couldn't turn them all down, because they'd just give the job to somebody else."

"What did he do?"

"He picked as many requests out of the flood as he could every day and made the Seventh Air Force justify them. A lot of times they couldn't, and then he'd deny the request. Maybe he'd save a life or two, or a couple of huts. A water buffalo, maybe."

"A water buffalo?"

"They liked to bomb water buffalos. They put them down in their reports as pack animals."

"But he couldn't stop the bombing," Hope said.

"No, the bombing went on. But Jim would have a real good feeling about those water buffalos."

"As he should have," Hope said.

"Jim and Irene retired from the State Department a couple years ago. Went back to the family ranch in Oklahoma to raise ostriches. They keep asking me to visit, and one of these days I will."

"Would you really like to?"

"Damned right. Take along a case of Thai beer, tell war stories, check out the ostriches."

"Suppose they'd have room for two?" Hope said.

"Are you serious?"

"Come on, Bethany. You said we could go on a vacation."

"What about Olympic National Park?"

"I looked into it. Too much rain. No ostriches."